KILLING WITH KINDNESS

THE DAVIA GLENN SERIES
BOOK 2

LAURA E. AKERS

ISBN 979-8-9853221-6-3 ebook

ISBN 979-8-9853221-7-0 paperback

ISBN 979-8-9853221-8-7 hardback

ISBN 979-8-9853221-9-4 audiobook

PRAISE FOR DIOR OR DIE
DAVIA GLENN BOOK ONE

"OMMFG I'm in love with this book and I cannot wait to see what happens next!! Davia is interesting and her life is a colorful mess. Need more."

— AMAZON & GOODREADS REVIEW

"A Kick A$$ novel with a Kick A$$ heroine. Dior or Die is an extremely rich and imaginative adventure!"

— AMAZON REVIEW

"Davia Glenn is for Akers what Scot Harvath is for Brad Thor's series of novels—only with snappier dialogue and a better sense of humor."

— AMAZON AND GOODREADS REVIEW

KILLING WITH KINDNESS

By
Laura E. Akers

To all who stand against injustice

*If you wait by the river long enough, the bodies
of your enemies will float by.*
-Sun Tzu

I take like 500 selfies to get the one I want.
-Kylie Jenner

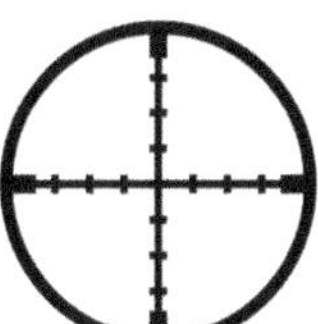

1

A heavy blanket covers the only door of a mud and brick hut containing the two hostages we plan to rescue. Pausing outside, we move seamlessly into position. We wait for James Warden, our team leader, to signal us to enter, engage the enemy, and hit our areas of responsibility. We wear tactical gear, helmets with night-vision goggles, and carry submachine guns.

Where's my weapon? I stare in disbelief at my empty hands. Frantic, I spin around and drop to my knees to search beneath a shrub.

My teammates enter the building, and Warden yells, "Come on, Davia."

Inside, Colonel Streeter stands above the bullet-ridden bodies of the hostages.

How did our commander get here? He never comes on missions.

"Have a seat," he orders. Tables appear out of nowhere, and we pull back chairs. Streeter points to a screen projecting photos of the hostages when they were alive. They're in their thirties with friendly, open faces. He says, "They were captives of ISIS-K and did humanitarian work."

An unwanted thought crosses my mind.

Seventy percent of hostage rescues fail.

Our training leaves no time for regret. Lifting the dead, we hustle back out and down a ravine toward a valley where we will airlift out. Warden and I are on point with Ned and Hodge carrying the hostages' bodies. K and Savant bring up the rear.

The familiar gray of a military helicopter speeds toward us, but a rocket-propelled grenade whizzes past with a thunderous hiss.

An explosion.

Smoke and fire engulf our extraction craft, and it plummets.

Hostiles surround us from the hills above, and ululations of victory accompany the bullets they fire at us from automatic weapons. My missing gun reappears in my hands, and we return fire. The relentless, noisy barrage from both sides is as familiar as music.

Our daily target practice pays off as our attackers fall.

We move to where the helicopter's twisted wreckage burns, eradicating enemy survivors as we go. At last, the only sounds are footfalls, ammunition clips jangling, and grunts as we work to extract the grim remains of the pilots from the wreckage.

"They're sending another bird, four mikes out," Warden's voice says in my earpiece.

Renewing our trek, I spot a group of militants in robes below us in a valley. Their leader is a woman dressed in an expensive red pantsuit and high heels paired with glistening gold earrings. She moves like she's on a catwalk, not an unpaved road.

Why is she wearing that outfit in Afghanistan?

"Warden, a group of hostiles is on a goat trail at 3 o'clock, and—"

An IED detonates.

The blast launches us skyward, and we crash to the ground. I lie dazed and disoriented, a haze of dust and smoke obscuring my view. Coughing, I force myself into a seated position. Warden is a few feet away, and I crawl to his side as dark liquid pours from his mouth.

"Warden, stay with me." I place my hands on his broad chest, and warm blood spills over them.

His eyes open, anger suffuses his face, and a feral growl emanates deep in his throat.

"Davia, what are you doing here? You're not a part of this unit anymore."

My brow knits in confusion.

"What do you mean? This team is my life."

The other men struggle to raise their contorted bodies.

They're gravely injured, and I need to get them help.

They turn hard eyes on me.

"Yes, Davia. Why are you here?" they chant.

"I don't understand."

The group reaches for me, unblinking. I scrabble backward and tear my palms open on the rocky path.

The scene vanishes as I bolt upright.

My hands clutch luxurious silken sheets. Bewildered, I don't recognize my surroundings for several seconds. Coming more awake, I realize I'm alone in bed in my 6500-square-foot home in exclusive Rancho Suprema, California.

I gulp deep lungfuls of air to calm my hammering pulse.

The dream twisted the facts, Davia. You got those hostages out alive, and no one was hurt or died.

Holding my queasy stomach, I throw back the covers and stumble to the bathroom, where I wet a washcloth to wipe my face and arms. The mirror reflects my colorless face and tangled mess of long, blonde hair. Pulling off my sweat-soaked t-shirt, I leave it on the counter and retrieve a clean replacement. After dressing, I run a wet brush through my disordered locks.

I'm alone to face the aftermath of my days as an operative and the guilt of taking a year's leave of absence from my team. If my convoluted flashback had occurred a few nights before, I would have sought comfort by waking Warden. He would have soothed me and nestled me against his solid body. Now, he's returned to Virginia and gone on a mission.

Still trying to make sense of the dream, I perch on the edge of the bed and rub at my eyes, willing myself to stop shaking.

My bedside clock reads two a.m.

Get it together.

Unable to sleep, I retreat to the backyard and throw myself down on a padded chair by the pool. Pulling my knees up and hugging them close, I wish Warden were still here. During his ten-day visit, he made sure every room of my home held fond memories of him.

"I can't believe we waited three years for this to become a reality," Warden said, rolling off me to catch his breath. He extended a muscular arm to pull me tight against him.

"World-record foreplay," I told him, prompting a deep chuckle.

Warden leaned over to kiss me, his green eyes dark with desire.

"I can think of a few more world records we should break," he said.

"I'm up for it if you are." I reached for him.

Missing Warden brings up pain almost as incapacitating as my nightmare, and I shake my head to return to the present.

My property sits on the crest of a hill with spectacular views. Tonight, clouds obscure the moon, and darkness shrouds the distant homes. All is quiet.

A series of short flashes light a window in a house across the valley.

I stiffen with shock and strain for a better view, but all is as dark and still as it was a moment before.

What did I see?

Playing back the images, I imagine calling 911.

Operator: 911. What's your emergency?

My name's Davia Glenn, and I want to report some light flashes at a house near mine.

Operator: Did you hear anything?

No.

Operator: Someone is probably watching TV or taking pictures.

Unless I disclose my secret past and how I can recognize suppressed gunfire, they'll conclude I'm a nutjob and scold me about wasting their time.

I'm not even one hundred percent sure what I saw.

Fighting off indecision, I rush to the bedroom closet to pull on clothes. Retrieving my .45 from the gun safe, I hurry to the garage, fire up my Maserati, and speed to the road opposite my house. Security lights on my property allow a quick read on my position, and I count driveways to find the correct address.

Do I miss a life of action so much I conjured an imaginary problem?

Heavy iron entry gates stand open, revealing a cobblestone drive with elegant pathway lights marking the edges.

Hesitating, I'm unsure what to do.

Take a peek. If everything is okay, I can leave.

As I turn into the drive, a car with no lights speeds straight at me from out of the darkness. I swerve. My headlights play through the cab and illuminate the driver's vague profile for an instant before a eucalyptus tree looms in my path.

Slamming on the brakes, I throw the car into park and jump out, gun in hand.

The vehicle screeches around a corner and is gone.

I crouch next to my car and listen. A slight breeze ruffles my hair, but chirping crickets are the only sound. Across an expansive lawn, flat stones decorate the one-story exterior of the unlit house.

The front door stands open.

That's not normal.

With my mobile set to private, I call 911 to report suspicious activity at the address displayed on one of the gate pillars and discon nect without giving my name. I set my internal clock to five minutes, planning to be gone before the police arrive.

Refusing to make myself a target by entering through the front, I run to the side of the residence. The backyard is fenced, but the gate I come to isn't locked. Ducking down, I open it in slow-mo and wait.

One-two-three.

Nothing happens.

I slip through and pause to scan my surroundings for any sudden movement. Making my way past the still waters of an L-shaped pool with teak furniture and standing umbrellas at its edges, I reach a door to the house. It opens with a slight click.

Now or never.

Staying low, I enter and dart through a laundry room and into a kitchen. Dim recessed lighting reflects on picture frames decorating a counter. The photos feature a family of four, a couple with two children.

If the family is fine, I hope I'm not mistaken for a burglar.

I pause to listen.

A grandfather clock ticks a steady beat, the sound magnified in the stillness.

Tiptoeing out of the kitchen, I slink across a sizable living room with cathedral ceilings, around a grand piano, and toward a hall. The home holds expensive furnishings, with artwork and mirrors hung in strategic places. Praying my shoes won't squeak on the hallway's polished wood floors, I sneak toward the side facing my house.

The first open door reveals a bedroom filled with stuffed animals, a young girl's domain. No one is in the pink-and-white canopied bed, but the covers are disturbed.

In the next bedroom, a college pennant hangs above a desk with a powered-on laptop. A chair lies on its back on the floor.

Ahead are two double doors, one open a crack.

Shadows hide me.

What am I doing here again?

A faint, agonized cry from the room breaks the silence.

How do I go in and not get shot?

I inch forward and give the door a slight push.

The scene widens.

An adult lies at the foot of a bed, surrounded by a dark pool of what is sure to be blood. Its familiar, coppery scent mixes with gunfire's lingering, acrid odor.

Without hesitating, I enter, sweeping my weapon to check every visible point. My back against a wall, I peer around corners to assess the closet and bathroom.

Whoever did this is gone.

The prone body is a woman wearing a nightgown soaked with blood. Did I hear her dying gasp? Three closely-grouped bullet wounds mark her upper torso, but I bend to check if she's alive. Her body is still warm, but there's no pulse. The hostage bodies of my dream merge with this dreadful scene as if an endless nightmare grips me.

Sirens wail in the distance, and I calculate if I can make it to my car, uncaring about CSI concerns.

As I rush to exit the room, a whimper from the opposite side of the bed stops me.

Damn it.

I can't check the sound's source and get clear.

Unwilling to leave someone who might need help, I raise my gun and walk around the bed's corner. A dark-haired young man shelters a female child on the floor, his bloody torso covering her still form. Putting fingers to his neck, I conclude he's dead. Lifting him aside with care, I murmur, "I'm sorry. So, so sorry."

The girl's shallow, stuttering breaths make me pull out my cell phone and redial 911.

"You'll need an ambulance at 2645 Camino del Sol. A little girl has been shot, and two others are dead."

"What's your name?" the operator asks.

I let out a long breath.

"This is Davia Glenn."

2

The child's bunny-print pajama top is stained red. After a quick assessment, I retrieve a hand towel from the bathroom and return to put pressure on a deep wound beneath her silver fall of hair. The girl's breathing grows more labored.

Sirens announce the arrival of law enforcement, and flashlight beams lance the darkness. It will be a triumph to make it out of this without being shot or arrested. Two male voices call "Clear!" at random points, and steady footsteps come down the hall. I place my weapon on the floor and push it under the bed. Leaving one hand on the injury, I raise the other.

"Sheriff's Department; put your hands up," a male voice commands, his figure filling the doorway.

"I've got one hand up."

"I need both where I can see them."

"Would you like this girl to bleed to death?"

Behind a flashlight's glare, the deputy points his gun at my head.

"I'm Davia Glenn. I called 911, and I'm a friend of Detective Montoya's. I'm not the culprit."

Another sheriff arrives. The first deputy keeps his eyes and gun on me but directs the other to bring in the paramedics once the house is clear. We hold our positions until the sweet music of wheels clatter toward us.

"Stand and keep your hands where I can see them," the deputy instructs, and I comply. "Now, back away from where you are, and come toward me. Stand over there, hands on the wall."

Two paramedics enter and split up to assess the bodies, and they concentrate their attention on the girl while the deputy pats me down.

"Let's walk now," he says. His weapon stays pointed at me, but he's so close I can take it away, hit him, and escape. I won't lecture him on the danger he's in from people like me.

When we're outside, I suck in the cool night air. The paramedics maneuver a stretcher down the front steps and hustle toward a waiting ambulance. They load their patient and drive away fast, sirens screaming.

The deputy places me in the back of a patrol car. He didn't handcuff me, and I consider this a positive outcome. Still, I'm behind a cage with locked doors and no way out. There is a way, but this isn't the time to prove anything.

The scene becomes a hive of activity. Sheriff's deputies, crime scene technicians, detectives, and others stand in groups, talking or gathering their gear. People are in and out of the residence. While they go about their jobs, I lock the bedroom images away with the other horrific scenes I witnessed during my three years as a covert agent. Still, questions linger.

Who were these people?

Will the little girl survive?

What can I do to ensure the young man didn't make a vain sacrifice?

There are no immediate answers, so I lean back and close my eyes.

I wake to someone tapping my shoulder.

"Ms. Glenn?"

I look into the hooded brown eyes of Detective Ricardo Montoya of San Diego Sheriff's Homicide. His black hair is messy, like he was asleep before getting the call, dressed in the dark, and rushed straight here.

He offers me his hand, and I get out.

"At least one of us got some rest." His tone is wry.

"Some friends and I have a motto to sleep when we can because we don't know what's next." I refer to my team, about which Montoya has no clue.

"I get it," Montoya says, and I'm sure he does. "How'd you become involved in this?"

I stick with the facts. Montoya takes notes, and I bet he underlines "recognized suppressed gunfire." His file on me will soon be so thick I'll merit a cabinet. The month before, we crossed paths at several crime scenes, and he's smart enough to discover more of my past if I'm not careful.

"Any idea who did this?" I say when I finish.

Will Montoya trust me?

"We have our suspects."

He doesn't.

"Where's the man of the house?"

Montoya doesn't respond.

Suspect #1.

"Have you had any news about the girl?"

"She's in intensive care, critical condition, but alive, thanks to you."

"I'm glad."

"Anything else you want to tell me?"

"My .45 is under the bed in the master."

"You can have it back after ballistics rules it out as the murder weapon."

Murder weapon? Terrific.

"Are you going to arrest me?"

"No, but you're not getting your gun back anytime soon. Will you come into the station and make an official statement?"

"Now?"

Montoya sighs, knowing I won't go. "Let me snap a photo of the bottom of your shoes."

I turn my tennis shoe-clad foot. "Size seven-and-a-half."

"Your fingerprints are on file from your concealed weapons permit, but give me a call if you remember anything else."

As we talk, our surroundings grow visible in the morning light, and birds begin to greet the day. Montoya pulls at his tie to loosen it.

"Will you update me on the girl's condition?"

"Of course." He closes his notebook. "I'm going back in now."

He walks toward the house and pauses to pull on protective booties.

I head home.

3

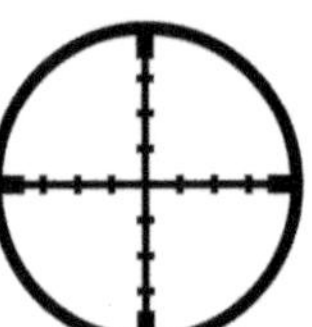

Six a.m. Will a scalding hot shower wash away the residual angst enough to relax me and make sleep a viable option?

After my shower, I put on a soft gray t-shirt Warden left. His lingering scent gives me some comfort, although his catastrophic injuries from the dream and my guilt at not being with my team still haunt me.

I'm drying my hair when my cell phone vibrates.

"Ready for me to visit?" It's Kyle Kavanagh, my parents' next-door neighbor in South Dakota and a former Delta Force operator. We met when I was eleven, and the course of our lives changed that day.

"Kyle." My voice isn't as welcoming as usual.

"What's wrong?"

"I spent part of last night and this morning at a nearby homicide scene."

"What happened?"

I tell him.

"And here you are, not two weeks from being targeted by Badger and his assassins. I think you should go back to work. It'd be less stressful."

I give a mirthless laugh. "I'm beginning to agree with you."

"At least you weren't the one shot at this time," Kyle says.

"I didn't expect a family to be murdered in this community."

"True. But now the million-dollar question, why did you get involved?"

"I'm not sure."

"Hmm. My guess is old habits. Still up for company?"

"Of course, I might need the backup."

Kyle snorts. "I can't wait to play your Rancho Suprema golf course. Do you own a car big enough to hold my clubs?"

Golf is Kyle's addiction despite losing his left leg below the knee during combat. An excellent prosthetic allows him to maintain an active lifestyle.

"I'll go buy one."

Kyle laughs, not realizing I'm not kidding. I scarcely believe I inherited a fortune from Aunt Lilah Latham, my mother's only sibling. I'm a reluctant heiress, tethered to a new and unwelcome life-style by the terms of her will.

Saying he'll text his flight info, we disconnect. I'm eating breakfast when my phone buzzes with another incoming call.

"Davia!" Sherilyn Silvers says. "I should've texted, but I'm so excited."

Sherilyn is my interior designer and new friend. Today, her high energy is in direct conflict with my worn state.

"What is it?"

"I'm going to make some upgrades to your home theater. I found a vintage popcorn machine and will have a new sound system installed to blast you right out of your chair; plus, I ordered these amazing recliner seats with drink holders—" Sherilyn continues to talk like she's stuck on fast forward.

Putting the phone on speaker, I wait.

"Davia? Davia? Are you still there?"

"Yes."

"What do you think?"

"Sounds great."

"Is something wrong?"

"I didn't sleep much."

"Oh, well, you never take care of yourself. One day, I'll find you passed out on the floor from either fatigue or starvation and have to call an ambulance. Since you persist in running yourself into the ground for reasons I never understand, you should give me a copy of your medical insurance card in case of future problems. Anyway, I'm having some things delivered tomorrow for the guest house. I found this divine little couch and recovered a chair in a fabric I painted, and the effect is *so* interesting. The color is super bright, which you'll *love,* but is difficult to match with throw rugs and artwork—"

I tune out until Sherilyn says, "Davia?"

"Yes?"

"Is Warden still there? You are one lucky girl. He could be Jacob Elordi's brother. I mean—"

"He left yesterday," I interrupt, not wanting to spiral back into a funk from missing him.

"I bet you're lonely. We can go to the Belly Up for some live music and drinks if you want. They blast their tunes crazy loud in there, so I, like, always bring earplugs. For most concerts, you stand in front of a stage unless you're lucky enough to get VIP seats, but scoring them requires some effort—"

"Thanks, but a guest's coming in from out of state, so I need to get ready."

"I'll be there in the morning, but I'm working in the guest house. José can let me in."

José Valenzuela Macías is my young groundskeeper who's proven to be a solid person in case of trouble.

"He can give you an extra set of keys to all the buildings and show you the security code so you have no problems with future access. Was there anything else?"

"Wait. Davia, this is embarrassing, but I want to ask you something."

"What?"

"Um, how well do you know Detective Montoya?"

I recall the chemistry I sensed between them when they met at the Ladies' League Gala last month.

"We crossed paths a few times." I don't go into details. "He's a sharp guy."

"He's hotter than Oscar Isaac, *and* he's got a brain? I might've hit the jackpot." She pauses. "But I'm not sure how to find him, except at a crime scene, and I don't think it would be cool to hang around those. Can you imagine? So, someone's dead and all, but I'm here to ask you out. *Beyond* awkward."

"I can text him your number. If he's interested, which I'm sure he is, he'll contact you."

"Really?"

"I promise," I assure her, and we say farewell.

Checking the time, I decide to go to the Suprema Market to fill my near-empty pantry in preparation for Kyle's visit. As I drive, I consider whether I should buy an SUV to tote Kyle's golf clubs.

I'm allowed to spend money on a mentor who's like a second father.

There are only a few cars in the parking lot, but as the automatic doors slide shut behind me, the shouts of men reverberate through the store.

"My display isn't big enough," a blond man yells at a red-faced store manager.

"No, *mine* isn't big enough," a dark-haired man asserts.

Were arguments between men always about size?

The displays in question are for rival soda companies.

"They're both the same," the manager protests, but the men continue their heated complaints.

A woman slides up next to me with her cart. "Those two need to grow up."

"Who are they?"

"They're Todd Hughes and Roger O'Neill, Huge Cola and ON Soda CEOs. Todd's the blond one. I witnessed them nearly come to blows over which soft drink was served at a reception."

"Why am I not surprised?"

"I'm Ava Gordon."

"Davia Glenn."

Ava's in her early thirties, her makeup expertly applied, and her designer clothes are subtle perfection. I'm in jeans, Chucks, and Warden's rumpled t-shirt.

"Have I met you?" She tucks her stylish dark-red hair behind her ears, revealing jumbo diamond earrings.

"I don't think so."

"I swear I've seen you somewhere."

I'm about to reply when Todd Hughes plucks a soda can from his display, shakes it, and pops the top. He unleashes an explosion of liquid at his rival.

You bastard!" Roger O'Neill wipes droplets from his face, picks up several cans from his display, and lobs them in retaliation. Todd ducks as the projectiles sail past him, hit the floor, and burst.

Why must I bear witness to another high society smackdown?

The manager steps between the men, holding them apart. Roger picks up another can and angles for the manager's head, but I close the distance and place his wrist in a painful hold.

"What are you doing?" Roger questions, struggling to get away. "Don't you know who I am?"

Perhaps Rancho Supreme residents should wear name tags?

I keep my voice flat. "I don't care."

"I'm Roger O'Neill, CEO of ON Soda."

"Then why are you acting like a preschooler?"

Ava and a group of new customers laugh.

"Let me go," he demands.

The manager is two rows over with the other self-important scion having a calm conversation, so I drop my hold.

Roger rubs his wrist. "I'll make sure you pay for hurting me."

"You do that."

He hesitates, then pushes past Ava and the other spectators. They step back as he rushes through the outer doors, and I expect the group to applaud, but most drift away.

Ava hands me a shopping basket. "You were brave."

"Not really."

"I swear I recognize you from somewhere," she persists.

"Were you at the Ladies' League Gala?"

"No, I was in Greece and missed it this year."

"I moved here recently, so perhaps you've mistaken me for someone else."

"Perhaps."

We go about shopping, and people whisper to each other when I pass.

Stop getting involved, Ms. Never Learns.

I obtain what I need fast, but disbelief makes me want to pause and consider why an exotic brand of olive oil is over $700, Matsutake mushrooms are $1,000 per pound, and Bluefin tuna is $5,000 per pound. If I spend time marveling over the myriad of expensive offerings, every shopping trip to this luxury market will last for weeks.

Ava is ahead of me at the checkout reading a magazine from a nearby display.

"Now I remember where I saw you," she says.

"Where?"

She turns the magazine toward me. "Here."

A popular entertainment publication's cover features a photo of me at the Fiftieth Annual Ladies' League Gala—being kissed by Adair Monroe, a British billionaire deemed one of the world's most eligible bachelors. The title reads, "Who's Adair's Mystery Girl?"

"Is this you?" Ava says.

My day keeps getting better and better.

I take the magazine and flip to the accompanying article whose headline blares, "Who Is Adair's Latest?" A photo of Adair and me smiling at the camera mid-dance lists our names below it. People wouldn't be wrong to think somebody photoshopped his flawless features, but he's all that and more. I recall Dennis from the *Suprema Gazette* snapping those shots, and hope I don't run into him anytime soon.

Ava reads the article over my shoulder. "That *is* you."

"Unfortunately."

"Being kissed by Adair Monroe is unfortunate? I thought he'd be an expert at kissing."

"He is." Adair's kisses could melt you into a puddle and make you want to stand forever in his arms. He seemed sincere in his affection at the time, but the likelihood of things working out with him, given my previous history, is improbable. He wouldn't last in my world, and I'm unsure I want to remain in his.

What am I going to do? I need to return the ultra-extravagant sapphire comb Adair lavished on me to wear to the gala, and now this. Coming out of my thoughts, I realize a group of women surround me, delivering questions of grasping interest.

"Are you Davia Glenn?"

"How serious is your relationship with Adair Monroe?"

"You left the gala with another man. Were you trying to make Adair jealous?"

"Stop crowding her," Ava says. "She's not going to talk about this."

The women hesitate but fall back and scatter.

"Thanks," I tell Ava.

"Everyone in this town thrusts their noses into other people's business. There are few secrets in Rancho Suprema."

Ava waits while the clerk tallies my bill.

"How long have you lived here?" I ask.

"Around eight years."

"Let's meet for lunch sometime. I owe you for driving the crowd away."

"I'd love that," she says. "You can never have enough sensible friends, especially here."

After an exchange of numbers, Ava gathers her groceries and departs.

Something always happens when I go to the Suprema Market, so I should start shopping elsewhere.

Outside, I bend to put the groceries in my trunk when a camera-carrying man steps close and takes my photo.

"Who are you?" I demand, moving toward him.

He backs away but continues clicking.

Paparazzi? Are you kidding me?

I decide to leave before I commit a crime.

As I get in the car, my phone sounds.

"Davia?"

"Hi, Mom."

"Well, I don't understand, but we've had numerous phone calls from reporters. They want to know if you're my daughter and wish to meet with your father and me to discuss your childhood. Kyle caught some guy on our land taking pictures. What's this about?"

Kyle would ensure no more photographers will be on their property, and no photos released anywhere.

"A man I met here kissed me at a gala, and he's famous. They think I'm his girlfriend."

"And are you?"

"No."

"What were you doing kissing him?"

"The situation is—" I search for a word other than complicated, the most overused word of my life. "—hard to explain."

"Davia, why are you kissing a man you don't know well?"

"We met under unique circumstances, and a connection formed between us."

"Tell me what happened."

Paparazzi appear behind me, leaning their cameras out of multiple car windows.

"Mom, I can't talk about this now."

"Why not?"

"I'm driving and need to pay attention to the road." I hook a hard right onto a side street and hit the gas.

"Those freeways scare me. Please be careful."

"I'll call you and Dad later."

"Okay, love you."

"Love you, too."

Disconnecting, I concentrate on putting some distance between the tailing paparazzi and me. Should I ask Adair to open his metaphorical black book and call some supermodel? I will pay for their dinner if he poses for a photo of him kissing her.

But that would entail speaking to Adair.

Choosing a circuitous route, I loop around the winding roads and back to my house, expecting more photographers to be staking out my entry gate, but no one is there.

My cell phone rings as I enter the house. Though the number is unlisted, it might be Warden, so I answer.

"Ms. Glenn? Detective Montoya."

"Oh, thank heavens."

"Is everything okay?"

"Life is interesting."

"Because of the cover of a certain magazine?" He sounds amused.

"Figures you already saw it."

"I make it my business to know what's happening with you."

Of course, he does. I bet San Diego Sherlock won't let go until he figures out my complete past.

"Yes, well, what did you want?"

"I'm calling to update you on the progress of Tilly Myles, the victim from this morning."

A memory of Tilly fighting to live hits me like a hard punch to the gut.

"How is she?"

"She's in intensive care, in a coma."

"Prognosis?"

"The doctors hope she'll recover but won't know for several days."

"Any leads on the shooter?"

"I'm not going to tell you."

I can't protest since I never tell Montoya anything, either.

"I want to ask you something," I say.

"What?"

"Do you recall meeting Sherilyn Silvers at the Ladies' League Gala?"

"The blonde in a pink evening gown?"

"Yes. She's a friend of mine and—"

"Would she mind if you gave me her number?" He sounds eager, unlike his usual controlled self.

"I'm sure she'll be delighted if you give her a call." I provide him with her contact. "A warning, though. She likes to talk a lot."

"I won't mind listening."

I want to tell him he might have a different opinion after he's been in her company longer than ten minutes, but I don't. Sherilyn may be a talker but possesses deeper qualities than her conversational skills.

"Please keep me posted on Tilly's condition."

"I will," Montoya promises.

Noon nears, and I can either make some lunch, take a nap, or go to my computer and run up the Myles family of Rancho Suprema.

I find my laptop.

4

Weary, I sink into a chair. Despite the grim scene this morning, the excitement, peril, and extremes were familiar territory.

Living on the edge isn't healthy, is it?

Aunt Lilah left a handwritten note provided to me by her lawyer, Mr. Morgenstern, after her death. She admonished me to examine the downside of my operative existence, which angered me when I first read it. After letting go of some of my initial outrage, I realized my penchant for living a risk-filled life, locking away disturbing memories, and maintaining an indifferent persona were some of my job's unsettling consequences. Would the negatives affect me long-term?

Powering on my laptop, I consider what I'm doing. The victims were once a family, alive with a happy future ahead. Was I right to be curious? I imagine them having dinner and sharing stories about their day. Mrs. Myles reminds Tilly to brush her teeth, and her brother reads her a bedtime story afterward. She protests she's old enough to read by herself but enjoys every second.

A heavy sadness fills me.

Who did this? Why? Will the person be found?

The computer's screen lights up and displays a photo of Warden. He's posed shirtless in black swim trunks with a Pacific Ocean backdrop. His close-cropped, dark hair is wet from a swim, and the well-defined chest muscles and rock-hard abs of his six-three frame glisten. His emerald eyes hold a devilish gleam, and a half-smile edges his full lips.

Memories of the three years we spent together on our covert team scroll past. From the start, we tried to best each other at fighting, shooting, running, or anything else. Now I recognize our ongoing competition was a substitute for the relentless vortex of forbidden attraction pulling us toward each other. How many times had our hands brushed as we reached for the same weapon? How often had we caught each other's eye and turned away, pretending it was a concern for a teammate, nothing more? When we finally gave in to our mutual attraction, it was better than anything I had imagined.

The day I took his photo at the beach, children almost bowled us over in excitement to go into the water while surfers studied the swells before paddling out. Seagulls whirled above us in the blue, cloudless sky, and shorebirds hunted in the surf for food. The ocean was chillier than expected when we waded in, giving us a jolt. We stood waist-deep in the water, arms around each other, and Warden bent to plant a quick kiss on my forehead.

The thumping noise of the rotors on a military helicopter drew our attention when it flew past farther out over the ocean.

"Glad we're not on it." Warden trailed his hand along the six-inch scar on my left thigh caused by a bullet when our last mission went wrong. But for his quick thinking, I might have died. It was the last time we were together in a helicopter, and we watched the aircraft until it disappeared from view.

"How's the team doing without me there?" I fought to keep the pain from my voice.

Warden put his hands against my temples and smoothed back my hair. "Do you want me to answer?"

Did I? I nodded, and he pulled me against him, resting his chin on my head.

"We aren't the same anymore, Dav. At first, it was like sitting at a table with one leg too short. We were out of balance when you left but had to go on. The job doesn't stop for anyone, as you know."

I closed my eyes to stay present and ignored the turmoil inside me. Warden ran his hand up and down my back as the tide continued its inexorable in-and-out journey. The push-pull of the waves brought forward a distant memory.

My dad found me slumped on the couch, despondent at not making the high school track team. He sat next to me and put an arm around my shoulders, smelling of sweat and dust from his day in the fields.

"Davia, life contains ups and downs. Thinking you're a failure because you didn't achieve a goal isn't the answer. It would be like believing a tide swept away all the prosperity in your life, never to return."

"That sounds awful, Dad."

"But what does the tide do?"

I looked up at him. "It comes back?"

He hugged me tighter. "It always comes back, kiddo. Sometimes when something you wanted doesn't happen, the tide returns with better opportunities."

I trained to make the covert ops paramilitary team from an early age. My work was swept away with a shot, and Colonel William Streeter, our commander, discovering Warden and me fraternizing against regulations.

When the tide returned with the inheritance, was it good or bad?

Before Warden left, I disclosed Aunt Lilah's will condition requiring me to date a man with a net worth of a million dollars or more every quarter.

"Have you been on a date other than with the Brit I met at the gala?"

"Adair and I never dated. I did go out once with a multi-billionaire CEO, but it was a complete disaster."

He smiled. "I'm sure you'll be in for more of the same. I won't worry."

"No?"

"No. Let me demonstrate what you'll miss if you dump me for one of these moneybags." He kissed me gently before ramping up the passion. We soon forgot all about our conversation.

Now my fingers trace my lips, recalling his kiss and what occurred afterward.

Forcing myself to ignore the endless emptiness caused by Warden's absence, I type "Myles Rancho Suprema" in the search bar. The first article is from the *Suprema Gazette* and came out last month. Eric Myles had been accepted to the University of Southern California with a full scholarship because he was a star lacrosse player. A photo shows a young man with dark, curly hair and an engaging smile, confidence radiating from him. He gave his life to save his little sister.

He was only eighteen years old.

I work to replace my grim memories with an image of Eric when he was alive and full of promise.

The article lists his parents as Stephanie and Markus Myles. I type in their names and hit search. After sifting through a few items mentioning the couple attending various social functions, I find an image of Stephanie with Eric at a lacrosse meet. He's a head taller than his mom, and she wears a baseball cap over her blonde, shoulder-length hair. She's a proud parent, beaming up at her son.

As I click through more search results, a headline stops me.

"Stock Prices Plummet as Maxim Myles Investigated for Bribery."

I hit the link to a business magazine article from the previous month.

Maxim Myles Inc. responded to reports the Securities and Exchange Commission and Department of Justice are investigating alleged bribes made to a Saudi Arabian royal on behalf of the company. Founder Frederic Maxim, age fifty-two, has an estimated personal fortune of 400 million U.S. dollars and denies accusations he or co-founder Markus Myles, age forty-six, bribed anyone to receive preferential defense contracts. Saudi Arabia awarded Maxim Myles Inc. $8 billion in contracts in the past five years.

Maxim and Myles live in Rancho Suprema, California, one of the most exclusive zip codes in the United States. Myles sponsored a celebrity golf tournament earlier this year to benefit Cystic Fibrosis research, donating one million dollars for a prize. He's an expert in negotiations and meets with high-powered leaders who want to obtain advanced defense equipment for the remotest countries.

Maxim stated the company maintains a rigorous anti-corruption compliance program and is cooperating with the investigation. "Our experience and background should clarify this is an overreaction on the part of the SEC and DOJ," Maxim said. "The allegations have no merit, as any further inquiry will show."

Since the news broke, stock in Maxim Myles Inc. decreased by almost 25%.

Would this make a person kill their own family? Was Markus Myles on a business trip or running like hell from what he'd done?

A photo accompanying the article shows Frederick Maxim and Markus Myles in front of their headquarters. Markus has brown hair and mild eyes, whereas Frederick is a tall, sharp-featured man with a distinctive shock of thick, silver hair.

I yawn, fatigued from my research and lack of sleep. It won't help to ponder whether Markus Myles was the killer, a job I intend to leave to Detective Montoya. Powering off my laptop, I stretch and consider a nap. When I start toward the bedroom, my cell phone sounds again, and I curse before answering.

"Beatrice Gibbs here. I'm calling to remind you about our board meeting this afternoon at one-thirty. We'll vote on your nomination for Vice President, so I suggest you attend."

Beatrice is the president of the Ladies' League, a local non-profit organization. The only thing we have in common is our dislike of each other, which began when we first met. A position on their board fulfills another of Aunt Lilah's will conditions, but I wish I found a group blessed with better leadership.

I force out my thanks and disconnect.

Marching to the closet, I search through the various garment bags containing the unworn outfits I bought at Bryce's Boutique when I moved here. I'm not going to wear a skirt, dress, or anything ladylike today. I select an Armani pantsuit in navy blue, pair it with an ivory silk tank, and dig around for a pair of Christian Louboutin flats. I put on Aunt Lilah's two-carat diamond earrings to lend me some upper-crust credibility. When I finish fixing my hair and makeup, I have fifteen minutes to eat lunch and drive to the Ladies' League building.

Hurrying to the kitchen, I power down some yogurt, retouch my lip gloss, and check the security cameras. My home has two entrances due to my safety concerns when I moved here and was on a terrorist's hit list. Now the bad guys in my life carry cameras and are parked outside the gate to the lower driveway. Two men slump in their cars, large lenses resting on open windows. I check the upper gate, and no one is there. My official address is on the lower street, and the upper drive provides an escape route. Smiling, I get my keys and leave.

THE LADIES' League meets in a Spanish-style building near downtown Rancho Suprema. Flowers in the lush gardens give off a sweet perfume, and water trickles softly from a tiered fountain. I want to sit on a bench in the sun and not go inside, but I would feel the same if there was a lightning storm. My innate shyness and lack of experience with the country-club set make me want to leave.

Forcing myself forward, Francis Downs greets me near the double door entry, golden-red hair framing her face. She chaired the auction committee for the annual gala, and I worked with her.

"Hi, Francis. How are you?"

"I'm so glad the gala is over," she states as we walk toward the board room.

"I completely agree."

"I saw your photo with Adair Monroe, though, " she says. "You make such a lovely couple."

"We're not a couple."

"You're not?"

"People are making our kiss out to be way more than it was."

"If the press linked me with someone, incorrect or not, I wouldn't be unhappy if it was Adair Monroe."

He is what most women dream of: rich, attractive, and super sweet. But my Prince Charming wears camouflage and tactical gear.

We arrive at the meeting room. Printed agendas, pens, and water bottles sit at tables. Five people visit with each other but go dead silent when Francis and I enter, their faces fixed with inquisitive expressions. I want to announce, "I'm not dating Adair Monroe, so mind your own business," but sit in the nearest chair and hope I won't fall asleep. Francis goes to a side table to pour herself some coffee, which I don't drink, and the group resumes talking.

Beatrice Gibbs sweeps in, and people settle into their seats. She's in her mid-sixties, and I'm sure she's related to the Antichrist. Her expression is a mixture of loathing, amusement, and curiosity. She's seen the Adair photo. I consider bringing it up under new business to discuss and dismiss the topic.

A man with a deep tan sits to my right. "I'm Henry Adams." He holds out his hand with a practiced smile.

"I'm Davia Glenn. What's your board position?"

"I'm in charge of the grounds."

"You do a great job. The gardens are stunning."

"Oh, I don't do the work. I supervise the gardeners."

Of course.

"Let's come to order," Beatrice says. "First order of business is the nomination of Vice Presidential candidate Davia Glenn."

After a nomination, second, and a unanimous vote, I'm elected.

"Davia? Please stand," Beatrice orders. "Raise your right hand. Do you solemnly swear to uphold the laws of the Ladies' League and perform your duties as Vice President to the best of your abilities?"

"I do."

"Let's welcome our new Vice President," Beatrice says, and everyone claps a few times.

Aunt Lilah wins again.

"The next order of business will be Old Business, namely the success of our annual gala," Beatrice says.

A woman in charge of renting out the facility begins a lengthy report detailing the number of attendees and other boring data. Next, a dour man named Fred gives the financial statement, only becoming enthused when discussing a discrepancy in the accounts. He speaks at the speed of a tortoise trapped in quicksand, making the fact the club earned over $350,000 at the annual gala sound as exciting as learning you have five cavities. Various board members give mind-numbing details about membership drives and the club newsletter while I fight the urge to stab myself in the neck with a pen.

Next is New Business. A local Girl Scout troop requested to use the facility for their monthly meeting, and a school for the blind needs new braille machines. I raise my hand to vote in favor of the Girl Scouts and the braille machines, but I'm the lone aye vote. The final item is establishing a scholarship in the name of deceased board member Willie Weston. The scholarship is enthusiastically supported and well-funded. If the guys on my team were here, our Texan medic Hodge might say, "You own more than you can say grace over, but you're all as crazy as bullbats."

Appalled at the skewed placement of priorities by the board, I fix my eyes on a point over Beatrice's shoulder and stop listening. I'm surprised to hear my name.

"You will, won't you, Davia?" Francis says.

"I'm sorry, but I didn't—"

"You'll model in our fashion show to benefit literacy, won't you?" Francis pleads.

Model? Me?

"She will," Beatrice states this like a foregone conclusion.

The woman who reported on membership smiles at me. "She's our new celebrity."

"I'm not—"

Beatrice cuts me off. "You and other community member models will be driven by limousine to Los Angeles for a fitting with Kincaid Foxx. Our show will be the West Coast Premiere of his new Fall collection."

The board members whisper to each other in a babbling rush while I speculate about who Kincaid Foxx is and where his clothes land on the fashion scale. I recall photos in women's magazines where models were clad in stuff from horror movies and appeared to either be on heroin or severely constipated. How am I supposed to do this?

The meeting adjourns as I try to find a way out of the obligation. Francis approaches me with a woman who might have been a *Vogue* cover model thirty years ago, all bones and angles, her platinum hair in a tapered cut.

"This is Sophie La Chance, coordinator of our fashion show."

"Charmed," she says.

"Beatrice is mistaken. I'm not going to model in a fashion show."

"But you must," Francis says.

"I don't have any reason to."

"Oh, but you do, Ms. Glenn," says Sophie.

"What would that be?"

"You'll double our attendance."

"I'm not dating Adair Monroe, okay? I'm involved with someone else and—"

"We know," Sophie interrupts. "And the other man is *so* dashing. Your love triangle is on everyone's lips."

"Oh my—I am *not* modeling in a fashion show." I start to leave, but Francis takes my arm. It's like a gnat trying to stop a runaway train, but I remain.

"Davia, we need you. Think of the money you'll raise for our literacy project," Francis implores.

"I'll donate." Teaching people to read is an important cause, but I refuse to be on display so people can speculate about my love life.

Beatrice's haughty voice interrupts. "Modeling is a requirement of staying on our board."

I call what I'm sure is her bluff. "Show me the rule book."

"I'll go find one." Francis hurries in the direction of the office. When she's gone, we have a contest of who can look down their nose better at whom: me, Sophie, or Beatrice.

When Frances returns, she carries an open booklet which she thrusts at me. "Here it is." Her finger points to Rule No. 12: *All new board members must model in the annual charity fashion show to introduce themselves to the community.*

I must stay on the board or lose my inheritance. *Did I care?* Ten months remain on my leave, and I promised my parents to try living in Rancho Suprema until then.

"This rule is a bit antiquated," I say.

Sophie and Beatrice are indignant. "The club's founders wrote it."

"Does it apply to men, too?"

Henry Adams is nearby and says, "Yes, and the experience wasn't bad."

"Fine." I'm too tired to continue my protest and hand the booklet back to Francis. "What day is the fitting in L.A.? I have out-of-state company arriving."

"This Friday. Come to the club at eight a.m. A limo will transport the models to be fitted, taken to lunch, and returned by five," Beatrice says.

Friday was two days away, and the trip wasted a Friday. Or any other day of the week.

"I'll be glad to assist you in learning how to work the catwalk," Sophie says.

"How kind of you, but I have a coach." Bryce, owner of Bryce's Boutique, would be the perfect instructor. I prefer to make a fool of myself in front of him than anyone from this crowd.

Now, no one speaks. The topic is exhausted, and we can't come up with pleasantries.

"I'm off," Beatrice says, and both Francis and Sophie chime their agreement. I let them go ahead of me, hanging back to pretend interest in a painting. Once they're far enough away, I consider banging my head on the wall.

Beatrice waits for me near the front doors so she can lock up the building.

"Have a pleasant day." She sounds like she means it, which should have alerted me.

I move past her and outside— right into a crowd of paparazzi.

5

The photographers only get pictures of my scowling face hidden by oversized sunglasses, but I want them to have a photo of me knocking Beatrice into next week. Power walking to my car, I drive away to a soundtrack of clicking cameras.

Is this story never going to die?

Punching it, I speed out of town and hit the freeway to Laguna Beach, a community located on the ocean about an hour north of Rancho Suprema. Boutiques, art galleries, and charming cottage-style homes make up the quaint community. Parking near a surf shop, I buy casual clothes and flip-flops, change, and throw my now-rumpled suit in the trunk.

Next, I wait for a table at The Cliff, an outdoor patio restaurant with a stunning ocean view. The sound of surf and seagulls calms me, and no one recognizes me, which doesn't hurt either. Hungry, I order the signature crab dip and a plate of fish tacos.

As I eat, I consider my reasons for fleeing Rancho Suprema. Why did I find the Adair situation so untenable? Were the paparazzi more troublesome than fighting terrorists? Anonymity cloaked my operative job, so the unwanted attention presents a new challenge.

The memory of Adair lying in a hospital bed after getting in the way of an assassin pursuing me reinforces my belief that life with a regular man isn't in the cards. Even if I didn't have Warden, my past would be a forbidden topic, and deception the foundation of any relationship. Since a terrorist leaked my team's identities, anyone associated with me might become collateral damage.

After lunch, I make my way to a bench near the beach, and video call my mom.

"Sorry it took me so long to call back," I say when she answers. She has high cheekbones and wide-set eyes, a younger version of my glamorous aunt.

"I understand. Tell me more about this fellow you kissed."

Who wants to talk to their parents about their love life?

"His name is Adair Monroe, and he's a British billionaire."

"Is he nice?"

"Yes, but I like a guy I worked with in Virginia."

"Who is he?" Mom's voice is keen with interest.

"His name's James Warden."

"What does he do?"

"He's a, um, consultant."

"What type of consulting?"

"He solves international issues."

"Sounds like he's capable."

"He is."

"I'd like to meet him sometime," Mom says.

Was I ready to be at a "meet the parents" level with Warden?

"His job doesn't give him much time off," I say, but I can tell Mom's not buying my statement.

She decides not to press and says, "Davia, before I forget, I want to visit Lilah's apartment in New York. I worry about what's there and the state of the residence."

Aunt Lilah owned a penthouse on the Upper West Side of New York City and probably haunted the place, screeching at anyone who didn't live up to her standards.

"Mr. Morgenstern sent in a cleaning crew to clear out the kitchen items and trash."

"That's good, but I want to sort through Lilah's personal effects for photos I might like to save." She tells me the school where she works as a nurse will be on break soon, and she will fly to New York then.

"You'll be better at sorting through photos and memorabilia than me. I'll tell Mr. Morgenstern to arrange for you to have the keys. I told you I have everything from her safe, the jewelry, bank documents, and the like, right?"

"Yes. If I find anything else we might want, I'll photograph and text it to you. How's everything else been?"

I tell Mom about the Ladies' League board position and fashion show but omit the murders, not wanting my parents to worry.

After the call, I dawdle in the town's boutiques and art galleries. A framed print in the back of a consignment shop appeals to me. The image is of a duck sitting in a lawn chair holding a drink, head tilted to regard the three bullet holes in the wall behind it. The title is *"Sitting Duck."*

This sums up my life.

"The print is from the late 1970s by an artist named Michael Bedard," the clerk tells me as he wraps the piece. "Universal made a cartoon series based on his art."

When I put the print in my car's trunk, the lack of sleep catches up with me, and I decide to head back. On the drive, my subconscious sends me an alert.

Kyle Kavanagh's coming tomorrow.

With all the distractions, I didn't shop for an SUV. Range Rovers are one of the most common vehicles in Rancho Suprema, so I decide to buy one, marveling at my ability to purchase almost anything I want. Besides my gratitude toward Kyle, blending in is a positive with the paparazzi on my tail.

I pull into a Land Rover dealership, and a fit man in a polo shirt monogrammed with the company logo opens the showroom door.

"I'm Don Cross. What are you in the market for?"

Every vehicle in the place appears the same to uneducated me.

"What's your best model?"

"Our SVAutobiography Dynamic, and we have it parked right out front. Let me get the key."

In minutes we're back outside and down the steps.

"We're fortunate to have this one in stock. This model has a 550 horsepower supercharged V8 engine with all the bells and whistles."

The car is black. *Perfect.*

Don turns on the radio; the music quality is superior, and owning a fast car with stellar sound lifts my spirits.

"And here's the *pièce de résistance!*" Don opens a back-passenger door with a flourish and hits a button. Two champagne glasses rise from between the seats, and another button activates a compartment to chill a bottle of champagne.

When would I serve champagne from the back of an SUV? With my current life trajectory, I couldn't rule it out.

"Here's another unique feature," Don says and causes the lighting in the vehicle to scroll through ten colors. "Something for every mood."

Why isn't there a black option?

Don tells me a rechargeable flashlight is $260, but he'll throw it in for free. The total package is about $250,000, so he should. I don't haggle, and he's beyond accommodating, promising to deliver the vehicle to my address by this evening.

After I sneak home through my upper drive, I check my cameras, and the paparazzi have gone.

Perhaps tomorrow will be better after all.

6

The airport is packed, but Kyle Kavanagh is easy to pick out. He comes toward me with only a slight hitch in his gait from his prosthetic leg. He wears his brown-red hair trimmed like he's still on active duty and is fit from a daily exercise regimen.

"Davia, I mean, I think you're Davia." His blue eyes twinkle as he pulls a long tendril of my hair extensions with affection.

I hug him, overwhelmed with emotion. After staying in his warm embrace longer than necessary, I step back. "Ready for some golf?"

"Sure am."

We wait for his baggage with our backs to a wall, eyes split between people and luggage watching, but the only danger I detect are parents with out-of-control kids. We catch up on South Dakota happenings, which doesn't take long.

"Your parents don't appear anxious to visit," he says.

"California's not their thing."

"The crew of farmhands you sent us sure helped. Your mom spent more time volunteering at the free health clinic, and your dad took off to some farm equipment show in Georgia."

"I think they're avoiding me. Mom's heading for New York instead of here."

"I'm supposed to report back about rubbing elbows with the hoity-toity people of your new town."

"Do me a favor and lie. I want them to come out sooner than never."

Kyle's luggage and golf clubs eject from the carousel, and we load them on a handcart we have ready.

"I'll meet you at the curb." I rush up the escalator and across a bridge to the lot, pay the parking machine, and spend a second remembering I'm driving the Range Rover, not the Maserati. Trying to find where I parked, my attention's drawn to a tall man, his bald head gleaming in the sun. He boards a bus bound for one of the off-site car rental places.

Was that Craig Kilburn?

When I check again, the shuttle has pulled into the stream of vehicles leaving the airport. Craig Kilburn, a veteran operative, took my place on my team when I decided to accept the inheritance. Before his reassignment, he worked alone, going into areas that made the fiercest men hesitate. I write it off as a doppelgänger coincidence. Kilburn would be gone with my former team since Warden is on a mission.

"Hungry?" I ask Kyle once we're loaded and heading out of the airport.

"Famished. The free pretzels on my flight didn't cut it."

"I told you to let me fly you in first class."

"I should've taken you up on your offer, had some decent chow, and gotten a preview of the types of people who live in places like Rancho Suprema."

"You were right not to, except for the food."

A bay-front with rows of anchored sailboats and a retired battle-cruiser, the *USS Midway*, frames the skyline of downtown San Diego. Sunshine reflects off the water while joggers and cyclists speed past.

We stop at El Indio, a Mexican restaurant established in 1940, and stand in a long line to order, but the food is worth the wait. Tearing a fresh flour tortilla, I scoop some *pollo asada* and beans on it, take a mouthful, and sigh.

Kyle takes a bite of a rolled taco with guacamole. "This is scrumptious, much different from the Mexican food I'm used to."

"We're close to the border, so we enjoy the benefits."

After lunch, we head to Rancho Suprema. Kyle stops talking, scrutinizing the roads. I head for the lower entrance and pray the paparazzi are gone.

When we get close, Kyle says, "I can have a friendly chat with them."

"Thanks, but the coast is clear."

When I pull into the garage, Kyle gets out and stands at its entrance. "Some spread you got here." He takes in the panorama of citrus trees, the barn, and the arena. I unlock the rear gate, pop it open, and join him.

"It was the most defensible place available," I say.

"If you have to see them coming, you have a beautiful view."

The sound of helicopters draws our attention. Two craft circle the Myles' home, and numerous people and vehicles crowd the street in front of the property.

Kyle points. "What's going on?"

"That's where the murders happened."

"You weren't kidding when you said it was close."

"I forget tragedies can become a media circus. No wonder the paparazzi aren't following me anymore."

We watch for several minutes, then heft his luggage inside.

"My decorator isn't finished with the guest house yet," I say as we enter the kitchen.

"There are words in that sentence to give you grief about, but I won't," Kyle says as he takes in the home's immense grandeur, a wondrous expression on his face.

"This is like something out of one of those luxury home shows I scroll past when channel surfing."

"Living like this is absurd. The house is six times the size of my childhood home, not including the guest house. There are five bedrooms, a theater, a gym, and a pool. My bathroom has a built-in sauna, and the two closets in my bedroom could house a family of five."

"Did you need all of this space?"

"Of course not, but I chose one of the smallest estates in the community."

Kyle takes me by the shoulders. "I prefer you deal with this existence while you recover from your injury than lurk around in Virginia and push yourself too hard."

"You're right, although I don't like living here and doing nothing of importance."

I situate Kyle in one of the bedrooms farthest from mine and then show him around.

When we finish, I say, "Anything you want to do?"

"Take a shower since I have air travel grime all over me, and then have a nap."

"I understand. I'll run to the Association offices to set up your golf privileges."

"I hope it won't be too much trouble."

"It won't be," I lie. Nothing in this place is simple, but all the inconveniences fall under first-world problems.

Sticking with the Rover, I drive to the Rancho Suprema Association building. The parking lot is empty, and I grow optimistic. The brunette receptionist wears a button-up blue Oxford shirt and khakis.

"Hi, I'm Davia Glenn, and I want to obtain a golf membership."

"I'm Victoria. What's your association membership number?"

"No clue."

"Give me your address, and I'll check."

A muted flat screen in the waiting room shows aerial footage of the Myles property before the scene shifts to an anchor speaking earnestly into the camera with photos of the Myles family projected beside him. Text of what he says scrolls beneath.

"Here," Victoria says, and I turn back to receive a slip of paper. "You'll need it when you sign up at the golf club."

"You mean I can't sign up here?"

"No. Ask for Dylan Davis, director of membership."

Figures.

Victoria nods at the TV. "I'm shocked a double murder happened in our community. I met the Myles eight or nine years ago when they moved here."

"What were they like?"

"Stephanie Myles wanted to mingle and meet people, and she was proud of her son. She told me he did well in school and athletics."

"Only her son?"

"Stephanie was pregnant with their first biological child then. Eric was from one of Stephanie's previous relationships, but Markus adopted him. I got the idea she came from a poor background and struggled as a single parent before she met him. Anyway, I explained the activities our community offers, and I think Stephanie became a member of the tennis club and the Ladies' League."

The Ladies' League? Had she and Markus attended the gala? Had we ever crossed paths?

Victoria gestures to the TV where Frederick Maxim stands before a bank of microphones, making a statement to the press. "I'm going to turn on the sound."

The backdrop for the press conference is the corporate headquarters for Maxim Myles. Frederick stares straight into the cameras. "I want to thank the Sheriff's Department for their diligent work to solve the tragic murders of Stephanie and Eric Myles. We're thrilled Tilly is recovering, with Stephanie's brother and his wife at her side. Next, I want to address speculation Markus had anything to do with this tragedy and if the investigation of our company and our subsequent stock losses are a motive. Defense contractors must maintain their companies with scrupulous integrity, yet allegations of bribery by jealous competitors are common. Markus and I are confident this will resolve in our favor, and our market price will increase above what it was before these events. Accusations of Markus murdering his family are preposterous."

The moment he pauses, the press begins to call out questions.

"Where is Markus Myles?"

"If he's innocent, why hasn't he come forward?"

"I lost everything because of you and Markus," a bulky man in a suit roars, charging straight for Maxim. Before Frederick's bodyguards react, he bowls through them like a linebacker and hurls the stunned CEO off the makeshift stage and to the ground. The man smashes his fist into Frederick's face several times, and Victoria gasps, a hand flying to her mouth.

When the attacker is pulled off and marched away by bodyguards, Frederick rises and puts a hand to his bleeding mouth. Other security swarms around him in a protective cocoon, shoving back anyone who attempts to draw near. More people shout at Frederick about needing answers regarding the investigation and their investments, but he turns his back on them and goes inside the building.

"I'm shocked," Victoria says as she mutes the TV. "Emotions are running high because of the DOJ investigation, but I never thought it would make anyone violent. I recognize the man who attacked him, John Freeman, and he's usually mild-mannered."

"Why is the investigation causing so much upset?"

"Many residents invested with them because Frederick Maxim and Markus Myles live here, and now they want answers. Why haven't they located Mr. Myles, though? I mean, his wife and son died."

"I think everyone's curious, but perhaps he's concerned about his safety."

"Wouldn't he contact the authorities?"

I shrug. "I can't say. I appreciate your help."

"You're welcome." Victoria gives a quick shake of her head. "I need to get my mind off the murders."

"I understand."

More than you ever will.

I'm almost out the door when Victoria says, "Tell Mr. Monroe hello for me."

"Sure." I slam on my sunglasses and depart. How long will this misconception continue?

The golf club's only a few minutes away, and I park near the front, another black Range Rover in a long line of black Range Rovers.

Perhaps members planned an off-road adventure across the greens.

Young men help off-load golf gear from trunks in an assembly-line process. I approach an employee, and he points me toward Dylan Davis's office. Inside, I pass a golf shop and a room with a view of the greens before making my way down a hall to a door with Mr. Davis's name. The door's not closed, so I knock on the frame.

Dylan Davis is seated behind his desk and has thin brown hair and chubby cheeks. "May I help you?"

"I'm interested in joining the golf club, and Victoria at the Association directed me to you."

"Come in and have a seat." He stands to shake my hand and tell me his name. I introduce myself and sit in a chair before his desk. He goes back around and pulls up a screen on his computer.

"May I have your address?"

I tell him, and he types it in.

"You have full membership privileges," he says.

"Doesn't everyone who owns property here?"

"No. Some of the townhouses near downtown don't. Old rules prevent certain properties from being part of Rancho Suprema's Golf Club. People get upset when they find out they can't join."

"I can't imagine."

"We have an eighteen-hole golf course, double-ended driving range, two practice putting greens, and a two-acre short game practice area. We also host an annual championship tournament that receives international press coverage." When I don't say anything, he hurries on. "I'm sure you'll enjoy playing here. What's your handicap?"

"I don't play golf. I have a friend staying with me who does, so I want a membership so he can play."

"How generous of you. The membership fee is $80,000, plus monthly dues and greens fees."

But for Kyle's happiness, I would have left.

"We have some skillful instructors should you wish to learn," Dylan continues.

"No thanks." I don't add my usual line about having enough frustration in my life without golf. Lately, I do.

We finish the application and sort the payment. He hands me a pamphlet containing membership rules, including a dress code of a collared shirt and dress pants or skirt.

"Can items in the shop be charged to my account? My friend might need some things."

"Of course, Ms. Glenn. Give your guest your golf club member number. Here's your membership card and a folder of information."

We conclude our business, and Dylan walks with me to the front of the building. He fills me in on the golf club's history and tells me about some celebrities who founded it. "We still have quite a few notable members," he says. "Ah, here's one now."

Framed in the sunlight of the double doors is Adair Monroe.

7

"Davia?" He's in a dark blue golf shirt and checked pants. A navy ball cap covers his sandy brown hair, making the aquamarine of his eyes pronounced.

"Hello, Adair." My tone is polite, but my pulse quickens at seeing his broad shoulders and six-foot, lean body. I force myself away from the memories of him holding me against it.

"You two know each other? Perhaps Mr. Monroe can teach you to play golf," Dylan says.

"Please don't call me Mr. Monroe. It makes me sound ancient." Adair's British accent adds to his charm.

"Ms. Glenn just became a member," Dylan says.

"Yes, I have a friend in town who likes to play golf."

Adair stiffens. "The man I met at the gala?"

He means Warden.

"No. A long-time family friend," I clarify, hoping Dylan doesn't note the sudden tension.

"I should get back to work." The manager radiates relief to be going.

Adair and I don't move or speak. I'm not one to break silences, so I wait. Finally, Adair caves. "How have you been?"

Pursued by paparazzi thanks to our now-notorious magazine cover.

"Fine. You?"

"I just got back from London. I enjoyed visiting my mum and sister but spent the rest of the time stuck in endless meetings."

We are two people avoiding everything we need to discuss.

"I didn't know you golfed," I say.

"I learned because business people like to play together, and being outside is better than being in a boardroom."

"Makes sense." Unlike this conversation, which is going nowhere fast.

Adair moves closer, and I catch a whiff of his cologne, a mix of spices as enticing as his perfect features. It brings back memories of him cradling me into his chest, and my brain short circuits. I can't come up with anything else to say, so I gaze at his sharp jawline, ignoring his lips and how sweet they felt when he kissed me.

"Davia, we need to talk. Can I take you to dinner this Friday?"

"Uh, I'm going to be in LA for a fitting. We should be back by five, barring traffic."

"We?" His chilly tone returns.

"I have to model at a Ladies' League fashion show for literacy, so I'm going with other community members."

Adair smiles. "I'll make sure to attend."

"The organizers will love it." More people might buy tickets if both subjects of this allegedly torrid romance are there.

"Would a late dinner work? How about eight?"

"Allowing for traffic issues, eight should be fine."

Adair pulls his cell from a pocket. "Tell me your address. I'll pick you up."

"How about I pick you up?" I want to be able to lose any lingering photographers.

Adair gives me a long look. "You're on."

"I should let you go about your day." I start for the door, but he follows me out.

"Where'd you park?"

I indicate the line of black SUVs. "Somewhere over there."

"See you Friday." Adair squeezes and releases my hand, and I swallow my disappointment. What did I expect? The last time we were together, I left with Warden and threw myself into my burgeoning romance with him.

"I'll text you if I'm running late," I say.

"Righto." He joins his waiting caddy.

Once I'm in the car, suppressed emotion makes my hands shake. Where are my battlefield nerves of steel? I admonish myself that Adair isn't a deadly weapon, or is he?

On the drive back, I loop through the downtown area. Should I pop into Bryce's Boutique and buy a new outfit to help my confidence for my upcoming engagement with Adair? Perhaps a suit of armor? It didn't matter if the garments in my closet from my previous shopping trip to Bryce's store were unworn. He'll help me choose the right ensemble since I'm still not a pro at camouflaging myself as a society girl.

FRAGRANT JASMINE on a trellis covers the path leading to a cottage housing Bryce's Boutique. Bryce is behind the counter when I open the door, flipping through a magazine. Most days, he prowls around his space like a caged panther on Red Bull, choosing the perfect items for the most demanding customers. The instant I'm inside, the magazine slams shut, and he's right in front of me.

"*Bonjour.*" He's in his twenties, pale and thin, with dark hair. He wears a black scarf with white polka dots around his neck in the casual but elegant way the French tend to dress.

"Where is everyone?"

He thrusts out his lower lip. "Not here. I've straightened everything until I've gone mad."

"So, business is slow?"

"I had a dozen women this morning, but this is a lull."

I bet a customer left two seconds ago.

"What do you need?"

"I'm meeting Adair Monroe for dinner—"

"Adair?" Bryce interrupts, excitement spreading across his face. He takes my hand and drags me to the counter, where he snatches the tabloid with my infamous picture from where it leans against the cash register. He shoves it toward me. "This is true?"

I hesitate. " It's compli—confusing."

Bryce makes a face. "What's confusing? Kissing a heartthrob is *not* confusing. And he sent you an expensive piece of jewelry to wear at the gala. These are the actions of a man who's serious about you."

"I'm dating someone else."

"Someone other than Adair Monroe? Who is he? Harry Styles? Timothée Chalamet?"

"No. He's someone I used to work with."

"Work with? *Work* with? Some average man versus Adair Monroe? Have you lost your mind?" Bryce's eyebrows are raised so high they almost touch the ceiling.

"For one thing, James Warden is not average," I say.

Not average in any way, lucky me.

"Wait. Is he the hunk of perfection I glimpsed at the gala?"

"Yes."

Bryce crosses his arms. "Then why are you in here buying something new to wear on a date with Adair?"

"I need to return the comb and set a few things straight."

Bryce sniffs.

"You can wear what you have on now." He points at my white jeans and baby blue silk button-up blouse.

"Yes, but—"

"Fine," Bryce interrupts, apparently done judging my personal life. "Where are you going?"

"I'm not sure. I'm picking Adair up at his place."

"You're picking *him* up?"

"Geez, what century are you in, Bryce? Women can—"

"I've dressed enough of the women Adair has dated to know they would never consider suggesting it. No wonder he finds you so interesting."

Bryce's brown eyes leave mine to search his shop. The latest and most expensive clothes, shoes, and accessories fill every space. He zips away and is back before I can blink.

"Dressing room one." He hands me a pair of black pants, a black sleeveless top, a Gucci belt, and a cashmere camel-colored coat. "I'll be back with the shoes."

I go in, strip, and put everything on. The pants have slits up the front to mid-shin, and the coat is lightweight and chic.

"Here," Bryce dangles some leopard print loafers over the door. I take them, put them on, and come out.

"I also have a pair of pumps if you prefer," he says.

The fashion show dives back into my thoughts like a knife to the brain.

"Speaking of heels, I'm required to model at the Ladies' League Fashion Show because I'm now on their board. Will you help me learn how to navigate a catwalk?"

"What will you be wearing?"

"We're going to LA on Friday for a fitting with some designer I'm unfamiliar with."

"Who?"

"Kincaid Foxx."

Bryce wrinkles his nose. "Him? His clothes are, how you say, bizarre?"

"Isn't that how most fashion is?"

"It depends. Some designers like Yves St. Laurent, Armani, or Chanel have a certain style. Others push the boundaries, like Kincaid Foxx."

"Fantastic."

After changing, Bryce rings my total cost.

"Come back when you learn what you'll be wearing. Be sure and take a photo of the outfit with your phone."

"You mean I can't take the clothes with me?"

Bryce puts my new items in a bag. "No. You'll try them on there and put them on again in a dressing room with the other models on the day of the fashion show."

"This is a nightmare."

"Don't worry. I'll have you working the runway like Gigi Hadid."

Who?

"Huh, if you say so. How's Ramon?"

Ramon is Bryce's partner and the owner of Salon Divine.

"He's busy as ever. Be sure and have those extensions checked soon. You don't want to start losing strands."

Nothing like wasting more time in a beauty salon. "Will do."

Two women enter as I exit, sparing Bryce any dreaded downtime. I make my way to where I parked in a back lot, trying not to reminisce about this being where I first met Adair.

Adair. A dare. Even his name sends a challenge.

A non-descript dark sedan backs out of a spot, and I catch a glimpse of the driver before the car accelerates away.

Craig Kilburn.

8

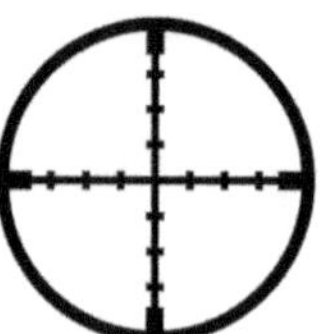

Running for the Rover, I throw my purse and bag of new clothes on the passenger seat, start it up, and do a fast reverse. The downtown area contains numerous intersections, but his car isn't on the cross streets.

Where did he go?

Would Kilburn be at a hotel? The only one in town is the Suprema Resort and Spa. Further away is Hacienda Verde, a more secluded lodging. Which would he pick? Both are ultra-expensive and the last places anyone would expect him to stay, which is a tactic. I decide to check them both, starting with the closest one.

Pulling into the Suprema Resort, I put down my window to talk to the valet.

"Are you checking in?" he inquires.

"No. I'm supposed to meet a friend here and wondered if he's arrived yet. He's driving a dark sedan and is about six-four and bald."

"I just parked his car."

Why in the world is Craig Kilburn in Rancho Suprema? Collecting the ticket, I head toward the lobby. I hope his visit has nothing to do with me, but I have a weapon in case.

I WAS on my team for less than a year when I first encountered Craig Kilburn. We were at a base in Iraq, back from a mission, waiting for transport. His size and intensity drew my attention. He spoke to a group of soldiers, who listened to one of his stories. One of the troops asked him a question, and Kilburn deployed a knife and pressed the sharp blade against the guy's throat. Instead of coming to their colleague's aid, the other men backed away.

"What the hell?" I said to Warden. "Who is that?"

He shook his head, lips pressed together. "Craig Kilburn, a wetwork guy."

Wetwork was slang for an assassin and a euphemism for spilling blood.

"Aren't you going to intervene?"

"No."

"Why not?"

"Most men in his line of work would do their jobs for free. They live on a different moral plane than us, and I don't want to be on his radar."

"But the man he's threatening is on our side," I persisted, taken aback that my lionhearted leader wouldn't do anything.

Warden picked up his gear. "They'll sort it out."

Ned came to stand beside me as Kilburn put his knife away, laughing. The soldier's face remained ghostly, despite the assassin's now-relaxed expression.

"Kilburn goes from zero to you're dead in nothing flat," Ned said. "Out of all the whack jobs we have working in that field, he's the most effective but also the most unpredictable. Be careful around him."

"No need to tell me twice."

ENTERING the lobby and registration area, I check for Kilburn. Cushy seats inhabit the wood-beamed ceiling room, and an arched door leads to one of the restaurants where a trim hostess waits to seat patrons.

"Hi, I'm supposed to meet a friend." I give her Kilburn's description.

"He's not here yet. Did you have a reservation?" She scans her book.

"No."

"He might be on the patio. They have separate seating."

"I'll check." I thank her and go back outside. Diners enjoy the warm weather and excellent cuisine at tables under umbrellas.

He's not there.

Unsure what to do, I decide on a quick perimeter search. A path leads me past a discreet sign reading "Suprema Spa: A Holistic Experience." Rounding a corner, I find myself in a courtyard with covered cabanas and lounge chairs surrounding a fountain. Scanning them, I spot a familiar face and do my best to stop my mouth from falling open.

The formidable assassin wears a puffy white robe with a towel around his bald head—and he's getting a pedicure.

THE ENCOUNTER LASTS LESS than a second, and I plunge straight ahead on the path, not wanting a manicurist to listen in on our conversation. *Did he recognize me?* I appear much different than when I was with my team. Returning to the hotel lounge through the back gardens, I find the number to the spa and call it on a house phone.

"Hi, my dad's getting a pedicure right now." I use a whiney voice. "When will he be done? He promised to take me shopping."

"Do you mean Mr. Banks? Tall, bald?"

Mr. Banks? "Yes."

"He's almost finished with his pedicure, sweetie, but he also booked a massage. Expect him about two hours from now."

After disconnecting, I debate whether I should wait. I decide to have lunch on the patio, taking a seat with a view of the exit from the spa. Will Kilburn return in this direction or collapse in his room for a nap?

Soon, I munch on Angus beef sliders topped with crispy onion strings and Swiss cheese, plus a side salad to make me feel virtuous. Due to my still-healing leg injury, my old routine of running five miles first thing in the morning is history, so I decreased my calories. As I pick up my iced tea, a man slips into the seat next to me.

"Well, well," Kilburn says. "I thought that was you."

Few people can get the drop on me, and I fight a jolt of unease.

"You were a beauty before, but this is beyond words." He touches my long tresses and steals an onion string off my burger.

"What are you doing here?" I say as he tosses it into his mouth.

"Vacationing, like you, I imagine. I rescheduled my massage when I caught sight of you and thought we should catch up."

I guess Warden didn't give him the details of my new life. "I don't believe you."

"Which part, the vacation or the massage?"

Before I can answer, a diffident waiter brings Kilburn a menu and leaves to fetch the draft beer he orders.

"The whole thing."

He leans forward, inches from my face. Scars mark his bald skull and hands, and his eyes are devoid of emotion.

"You were always a smart one," he says close to my ear, then leans back in his chair.

I exhale.

The waiter returns with Kilburn's drink, and he orders a Reuben. We fill the time until his lunch arrives by enjoying the view of downtown framed by manicured lawns and mature trees. I let him dig in when his sandwich comes. After a busser clears our plates, we have our drinks refreshed. Now, we wait. We both know the subject, so the contest is about who will go first.

"You live here, don't you?" Kilburn says at last.

"What makes you think so?"

"The suntan Warden returned with from his mini-break and his cat-ate-the-canary grin. Also, your new long hair. You wouldn't give an opponent something to hold unless you were trying to fit in."

I don't confirm his statement because he's right. "My team is gone, and you were my filler. What brings you here?"

He takes a sip of his beer. "I'm trying to find a guy I used to work with."

Vague is an operative's standard self-expression, so I'm not surprised. "What's his name?"

Kilburn hesitates.

"It's not Mr. Banks, is it?"

"Found me out already? I'm going to have to keep a better eye on you."

The prospect doesn't make me happy. I don't want to be on guard due to this loose, lethal cannon.

"I might know him."

"He's all over the news."

I sit up. "Do you mean Markus Myles?"

"I said you were smart."

"Was he in our line of work?"

"Yes, in a way. He wasn't as directly involved in the up-close and personal things as we are. More a spook."

A spy.

"What type? A James Bond or a paper pusher?"

"More the latter, but a blend. He got released into the wild on occasion."

"Do you think he did it?"

"Do you?"

We're back on familiar ground, neither of us disclosing anything.

"What's your plan? Wait for him to book a massage?"

"Nah. I'm listening to the local gossip and attempting to figure out where he went or who took him."

"Took him? Do you think this is a kidnapping or a revenge job?"

"Dunno yet, but I did learn his wife was a spa regular and a lousy tipper."

The waiter brings the check, and Kilburn puts a hand on it. "My treat, you can buy next time."

Next time? I will not be a regular lunch buddy with a guy who keeps me mentally scrolling through self-defense techniques. "Sure. Thanks."

"Before you go, give me your number. I might need assistance."

"Why?"

"If I have to maneuver through the local social scene, I wouldn't know where to begin."

"I'm not much better."

"You have a head start. Come on. I won't give it to anyone."

"Fine." We trade numbers, and I stand.

Kilburn lets me around him, and I'm a few steps away when he says, "Tell me when you're ready to talk about the crime scene."

I force myself to continue, a fool for buying his line about lounging around the spa to obtain intelligence. Despite his unorthodox ways, or because of them, Craig Kilburn always gets answers, and I have some he wants.

9

"How'd it go?" Kyle's at the kitchen table eating a sandwich.

"Mixed. Did you have a nap?"

"Yes, a long one, and I raided your kitchen. Want me to fix you anything?"

"Thanks, but I ate. Say, did you ever meet a guy named Craig Kilburn?"

Kyle's sandwich is partway to his mouth. He sets it back down. "What brings him up?"

"Do you know him?"

"No, but I heard stories from my friends in the mix."

Though Kyle's been out for nearly twenty years, many of his colleagues are still on active duty.

"What kind of stories?" I go to the fridge, pour myself a glass of water, and join Kyle at the table.

He studies me. "Why are you asking me about him?"

"Remember the murder case I got wrapped up in?"

"Of course."

"Kilburn's here in town searching for the missing head of household, Markus Myles. He said Myles was a spy."

"A spy? Why does he care? He's a wetwork guy."

"You think he tells me anything?"

"Being scant on giving details is our M.O." He finishes his sandwich, thoughtful. After washing it down with the cold Guinness I made sure to have in the fridge, he leans back in his chair.

"One of my friends told me about a time Kilburn got dropped into some hellhole to meet an informant who was dead by the time he got there. Only one plane flew in and out each week, the place crawled with hostiles, and he had to hide out in a home abandoned by some European national who bailed out of the country after things went south. He raided the guy's pantry and lived on cold canned food, but found and befriended an Albanian who stayed to keep an eye on things. They shared cigars on the guy's patio each night, watched bombs drop, and listened to gunfire. My friend said Kilburn considered it a pleasant memory."

"I'm not surprised. You hear anything else?"

"Not a lot. I took scraps and formed them into an impression. He's eliminated a lot of HVTs through the years, and some of the elite teams failed to get them. I don't have details, but that's how it goes."

HVTs are high-value targets.

"Being in Kilburn's proximity at lunch was enough for me."

"Yeah, doesn't sound like he's the sort of guy you want to team up with on much of anything. I prefer predictability."

"Speaking of that, I have your golf pass."

"I'd argue golf and predictability don't go together, but thank you. I studied the course and can't wait to try it."

I hand Kyle the membership folder and relay everything the golf club manager told me.

"Now I think about it; I have a friend who might like to play with you. He's from here, the realtor who sold me this house. Bob Brooks is a super guy in his sixties who walks with a cane."

"So, we're both equally handicapped."

"Ha. If you want, I'll call him."

"Sure. A conversation is more important than the competition at my playing stage."

Bob is delighted with the idea of getting out of the house and onto the golf course. "Alexandra will be glad for some alone time, I'm sure. I don't have any new listings, so I'm home too much for her."

"I doubt it." I met Bob's wife, and they have a close relationship.

"What would you like to do now?" I ask Kyle after giving him Bob's information.

Kyle takes his plate to the sink. "Absolutely nothing. After all the farm work, I'm ready for a break. Some people like to do the tourist thing and hit every attraction, but for me, the attraction is laying by your pool and resting today."

I toss his empty bottle in the recycle bin and have him follow me to the pool house. Sherilyn stacked a pile of blue and white striped beach towels in a closet, and I get him one and make sure there's more beer in the mini-fridge.

"I might grow used to living like this." Kyle fetches another Guinness and twists off the cap.

"Well, you saw how spacious the house is. If you move in, we'll never run into each other."

"True. Are you happy living here?"

I pause. "I'm not sure yet. The rush from going to the murder scene made me miss the team and our missions. After thinking about it, I decided living on the edge isn't always healthy."

Kyle lays a beach towel on one of the poolside lounge chairs. "When I got hurt, it was agony not being with the guys. It nearly killed me, missing my brothers and not being part of the action, as you know."

He means that literally. The memory of the shotgun he pointed under his chin and my young self frozen with fear is still vivid.

"What did you do to adjust?"

"I guess it came down to appreciating I was alive and enjoying the next chapter. And my neighbors." He gives me an affectionate hug.

Water spills over the pool's disappearing edge, and I gaze across the valley at the vans, camera crews, and crowd of people still outside the murder scene. Markus Myles's whereabouts are of interest to the world, not simply Craig Kilburn.

"I need to change into my trunks and figure out how to stop this Irish skin from burning," Kyle says.

"You're not going for a swim?"

"I think I'll decorate the edge."

We move one of the umbrellas to shade his chair, and he goes back inside to change.

WHILE I DO a final check to ensure Kyle will have everything he needs, I recall the barbecue we held in the same area during Warden's visit. Sherilyn and José brought side dishes, chips, and guacamole while I grilled marinated chicken and carne asada on a built-in gas grill. The weather was warm, and we splashed around in the pool before dinner.

"I haven't enjoyed a pool party since high school," Warden said, toweling himself off before we ate.

"High school is such an odd time, isn't it?" Sherilyn said. "I bet you were captain of the football team and head of the jocks?"

Warden set down his towel and picked up a plate to fill with food. "You're dead wrong. If we're going off stereotypes, were you a cheerleader, like Davia?"

"I wasn't a cheerleader, were you?" I said to Sherilyn as we put down our plates at the shaded table where we planned to eat.

"Oh, hell no," she said. "I was student body president and a member of the honor society. I was way too studious."

José sat across from us.

What about you, José?" I asked.

"I did cross-country running and wrestling, so it was the jock crowd for me," José said. "But I got crowned homecoming king since I was popular with most kids in my class."

"Homecoming king? Did you get a crown?" I teased.

"Of course." José gave us a mischievous smile. "The ladies liked me to model it for them."

It wasn't hard to understand why José was selected. Not yet

twenty-five, his thick, dark hair, and handsome features were enhanced by his engaging personality.

"That brings us back to you, Warden. Are you going to share?" I said when he joined us.

"Well, until my senior year, I was only five-foot-four."

"No!" everyone gasped in unison.

"I'm not kidding," Warden said. "Then the 'late bloomer' stuff kicked in, and I bounced to my current height in one year. Growing pains weren't fun."

"What about your brothers? Did that happen to them, too? " I said.

"I'm the third out of four, but they were all around six feet by high school. Now, I'm the tallest in the family."

"I find you being a shrimp difficult to fathom," Sherilyn said. "What was it like before your growth spurt? Were you one of those nerdy kids who scuttled through the halls and got picked on?"

Warden smiled. "There were quite a few challenges, for sure. Being with my brothers, I already had some insight into dodging and ducking, plus arguing my way out of problems. At first, I ran when I saw trouble coming, and I was quick. I think I excelled at running in college because of my earlier skirmishes. In my later high school years, I used humor to defuse situations. It didn't hurt that two of my brothers were still at the same school and were protective, but I made my way."

"What about you, *jefa*?" José said to me, using the Spanish term for a female boss.

"I was a bookworm and a band geek, but I wanted to do sports. The PE teacher was angry I wouldn't quit the band, so when I auditioned for the track team, she said I was too slow, despite me beating her star runner."

"No fair." Sherilyn gave me a supportive squeeze on my shoulder.

"It was small-town politics, I think. It provided me time to do other things, so it was probably best."

"You play an instrument?" Warden said. "Which one?"

"Trombone. My dad had one from his elementary school days.

Money was tight, so he said the trombone was my only option if I wanted to learn an instrument."

"Were you an accomplished musician?" Sherilyn said.

"Yes, but all the other trombone players were boys. When I carried the case around campus, the non-feminine instrument was like wearing an invisibility cloak."

"Oh, come on. I'm sure guys clamored after you in high school," Sherilyn said.

"Not at all, but my nickname in band was Hot Lips, which referred to my playing skills and nothing else."

Warden took my hand and leaned close. "I'll have to check if you can live up to your nickname later."

"You two." Sherilyn rolled her eyes at us

Later that night in bed, Warden made good on his promise to check the accuracy of my band nickname. My breath catches at the memory of straddling his magnificent body and beginning kisses at his face before moving lower.

Letting out a long breath, I force my mind away from the memory, and go back inside.

I'M TIDYING the kitchen when the intercom for the gate buzzes. Checking the monitor, two men wait in a plain-wrap car.

Feds.

I hit the speaker button. "Yes?"

"We're here to take the statement of Ms. Davia Glenn regarding the Myles case. Is she available?"

Perhaps this visit is a surprise because Detective Montoya wanted to share the pain of Famous-But-Incompetent raining on his parade.

I hit the buzzer to open the gate, hustle to my closet to retrieve my ankle holster, and slam on some Ray-Bans with polarized lenses. I exit through the courtyard gate as the car pulls up. The men haul themselves out, a matching set of clean-cut bureaucrats in Men's

Warehouse suits. I say, "ID, please," before they're too comfortable. They exchange a glance, then do the pull and flip.

"I need your supervisor's name and phone," I say while examining their IDs, then call their boss and hit her with enough questions to test anyone's patience before relenting.

"What do you want?" I say to Agents Fider and Penn. Or Frick and Frack. Whatever.

"We want to ask you some questions about the Myles murders. We understand you were first on the scene."

"Not first. The killer or killers were there before I was."

And yes, I would be that way.

"Is there somewhere to sit and talk?" Agent Fider says.

"No. Why are the Feds involved?"

Another look passes between them.

"The information is classified," says Agent Penn, who comes around from the passenger side and props himself against the front of the car, audio recorder out. Fider takes a small notepad from his pocket.

"Ms. Glenn, what made you go to the Myles property on April sixth?" Fider's pen is poised.

"I gave my statement to Detective Montoya at Sheriff's Homicide. Wouldn't it save time to read it?"

Fider's jaw clenches. "Tell us again."

I recite what happened, and the words "suppressed gunfire" don't have the same effect on them as Montoya. The FBI has access to most of my unclassified history and a better idea of who they're speaking with than I hope Montoya ever will.

"Where's Markus Myles?" Fider's stillness gives away that this is his most important question.

"You would have a better idea than me."

Penn huffs. "We know you went to the residence because you're—"

"A citizen who saw something suspicious," I interrupt. "Why are you so sure I know where Markus Myles is?"

Fider flips his notepad closed with an angry snap. "We can't comment."

Before either can move, I say, "I heard Markus Myles was a spook."

The men freeze and confirm Kilburn's statement.

"Where'd you hear that?" Penn says.

"I can't remember. Sorry."

They don't believe me, but they also can't make me talk. After waiting for a few beats, the men give up.

"We'll be back if we need more," Agent Penn says.

They leave.

10

A gleaming stretch limousine idles outside the Ladies' League for the trip to the Kincaid Foxx showroom in Los Angeles. Four women stand nearby, but Beatrice and Sophie are the only ones I recognize. The other two are close to my age, late twenties, and wear mini-dresses in bright colors with platform sandals. They lean in close for group photos on their various phones.

Another woman comes to stand beside me.

"Hi, Davia." It's Ava Gordon, the woman I met at the Suprema Market.

"Ava, are you going to be modeling?"

"Yes." She makes a face. "I dodged it for years, but this is my penance for missing the gala. I learned you would model, so I became more enthused about the whole enterprise."

"I'm glad you're here and not dressed to the nines." We're both in jeans, t-shirts, and tennis shoes.

"You inspired me."

Beatrice waves at us, and we follow the others into the limo. The luxurious interior is spacious enough to seat ten people, but Ava and I are stuck with the seats facing backward, of course. After introductions, I learn Brittany Guinn and Kennedy Connors round out the group. They have thin frames, goldfish lips, and immovable foreheads, their calves muscled from years at spin class. Sophie doesn't remove her black sunglasses, an Aunt Lilah habit.

Beatrice retrieves a bottle from a fridge in the wet bar. "Who's ready for some wine?"

I decline. If I begin drinking now, I won't be responsible for my words or actions.

While the others hold out glasses, Ava says, "Why are you modeling?"

"I'm a newly elected vice president of the Ladies' League, and a rule requires I model to introduce myself to the community."

"I think you should be drinking."

"Why aren't you?"

"I'm relying on my inner fortitude for now."

Soothing music begins to play as the limo pulls out. The drive to L.A. is two hours without traffic. *When is there no traffic?*

"Where are you from originally?" I ask Ava.

"I was about to ask you the same question," she says.

"I beat you to it, so you go first."

"The East Coast, I worked on Wall Street and smartly invested before moving to Rancho Suprema.

"Why here?"

"Climbing the social ladder of New York got to me. I needed to escape their artificial scene and have some space. The networking there cost me a fortune, what with all the clothes, personal trainers, stylists—"

"What's a stylist?"

"Someone who advises you on the latest fashion trends, hair, and makeup. They select outfits for you to try on and save you time."

Sounds like Bryce.

"My aunt lived in New York and enjoyed the jet set life, but we never talked much about it," I say. "Actually, she talked about it a lot, but I didn't listen."

"What was her name?"

"Lilah Latham."

"You're kidding."

"No. Why?"

"She was one of the real movers and shakers."

"Yes, she was." *And a control freak from hell.*

"You didn't have a close relationship?"

"We were too dissimilar. Did you know her?"

"We moved in the same circles but didn't talk much. Lilah had a reputation for running everything to her liking, and if she snubbed you, your society days were over. To compete, I spent over $200,000 yearly on tickets, $150,000 or more on the stylist, and more for a publicist."

"Forgive my ignorance, but what does a publicist do?"

"They get press coverage for you."

I think of the current paparazzi situation. "I want press like a hole in the head."

"If the right magazines or social media accounts feature your photo or an article about you, you're invited to better gatherings."

"Sounds dreadful." I can't imagine caring about any of this.

"Now you're on a magazine cover; I'm sure people will swamp you with invitations."

"I hope not."

"No? I guess high society's not for everyone. I throw parties here to inject excitement into my otherwise quiet life, and the only pressure is to model at this little fashion show. But enough about me. Where did you grow up?"

I share some information about my South Dakota childhood and recite my standard employment cover of being a personal assistant to a CEO. I tell her about the inheritance but not the conditions. Ava would likely understand as she knew Aunt Lilah, but I find it too mortifying to discuss.

Ava snaps her fingers and says, "I recall a time when your aunt talked about you."

"She did?"

"I was at some function where attendees touted their children's accomplishments, and she said, 'My niece is fearless, and I'm proud of her.' Or did she mean someone else?"

"I'm her only niece. Aunt Lilah might have said that for appearances."

"I got the impression she meant it. She said ever since you were a little girl, you set goals and achieved them, not caring what anyone thought, even her. Everyone laughed nervously, given her status."

Was it truth or social platitudes? Underneath her judgmental persona, had my aunt admired me?

Beatrice diverts my thoughts. "What does everyone think about the Myles murders?"

"I'm sick of the constant news reports," Brittany complains. "Whenever I turn on the TV or look at social media, someone is talking about the 'Rancho Suprema Massacre.' The reporters always mention how wealthy everyone here is, as if being rich caused the murders."

"Honey, everyone loves a story mixing money and murder," Sophie says. "The Menendez brothers killed their parents in Beverly Hills, and because those boys were handsome, the murders were headlines. Robert Durst killed his best friend, some poor man in Texas, and his wife. Durst's family owns sixteen million square feet of real estate in New York and Philadelphia, so his crimes got swept under the carpet for decades until a documentary brought it all out. And let's not forget OJ Simpson."

"And many more," Beatrice adds.

"I can't believe the murders happened in Rancho," Brittany says.

"Yes," echoes Kennedy. "Have they located Markus Myles?"

The other women shake their heads.

"I wonder where he is and if he's still alive," Beatrice says.

There are murmurings at this statement, some shuddering at the notion he might also be dead.

"If someone's holding him as a hostage, he must carry kidnapping and ransom insurance," Sophie states with a wave of her hand.

Ava doesn't say anything, and I'm glad. Murder is a sensational topic to some, but it's a grim reality to me. I remind myself to contact

Montoya to check on Tilly's condition. I can't imagine having to tell her that her mother and brother are dead and her dad is missing.

"Stephanie Myles taught a bonsai class for us and headed up the annual flower show last year," Beatrice says. "Her children came along to help bring in her supplies, and her son was well-spoken and polite. She mentioned she planned to have more children soon. Motherhood was her forte."

So far, all I know about Stephanie Myles is she prided herself on motherhood, wanted a bigger family, played tennis, was involved with the Ladies League, and might not tip people enough. These tidbits didn't give me much insight into her personality and background or why someone would shoot her. If someone died, were they reduced to broad-stroke labels?

"Ava, you're quiet. Did you know them?" Beatrice says.

"Not well."

"And Davia, you just moved here, so I assume you don't have anything to add," Beatrice states.

I weld my lips together and shake my head.

"Davia," Sophie says. "You must schedule a time to practice your runway walk with me."

And, just like that, the deaths of two people and the critical injury of another are shunted aside.

"Why?" I question.

"What do you mean, why?" Sophie challenges. "Do you want to be a complete failure?"

Fake politeness, fake politeness.

"I have an instructor, but thank you."

"Who?" Sophie is imperious.

"Their identity is my little secret."

"*Ooo,*" Brittany and Kennedy speak in unison, leaning forward. "Will you share with us?"

"I promised not to tell, and I keep my promises."

They sit back, disappointed, then ask Beatrice for more wine.

THE LIMO GLIDES to a halt outside Kincaid Foxx's showroom, and the women step out in a mass of wobbly limbs and giggles. Ava and I wait until they totter off, then exit and stretch. An assistant inside the store flings the front door open.

"Welcome to Kincaid Foxx! Come in," she invites, and the women enter, clutching each other's arms.

"Are you ready?" I say to Ava.

"As I can be."

We enter an open space filled with racks of garments, sewing machines, and mannequins. The walls hold sketches pinned with fabric samples, and the group moves forward with excitement to examine the designs. A man enters, talking to a brunette who taps on a tablet. When he notices us, he says, "I'm Kincaid Foxx."

Kincaid is in his forties and sports a light shadow on his square jaw that doesn't detract from his rugged good looks. The other ladies swoon a bit, murmuring their pleasure at being in his company.

"This is my assistant, Bronwyn. She'll take your measurements, then bring you to my fitting room to try on what I select for you from my upcoming collection." His voice is cultured, with an undercurrent of complete boredom. I like him.

As each woman is measured, I move around the room, checking out the designs, most of which appall me. Bronwyn approaches with a tape and inputs my measurements into her screen. "I'll bring you to Mr. Foxx soon," she promises, then leads Beatrice away. I sit on a chaise lounge near a wall, and Ava joins me.

"If they take you in first, try to leave me something easy to wear," I tell her.

"I doubt we have a choice if past fashion shows are any indication."

When my turn arrives, I follow Bronwyn down a hall as if it leads to the electric chair. "This is Miss Glenn," she introduces and leaves me alone with Kincaid Foxx.

"I understand you'll be the most important person at the fashion show," he says.

"That isn't correct, I—"

"If you're dating Adair Monroe, it is."

I want to tell him I'm not, then think of tonight's dinner engagement. I refuse to consider it a date, but rather a friendly meeting to return the comb—a *friendly meeting.*

Kincaid walks around me a few times, and I clear my face of emotion like a drill instructor inspects me. He swipes through different designs on his tablet. "I have a garment in mind."

"Can you show me what it looks like?"

"I can't."

"Because?"

He touches his brow. "The idea is still up here."

What's inside his head? Did I want to know?

"We have your shoe size on file. I'll send heels along with the outfit. Wear your hair down, and I'll figure out a style to enhance the dress."

"A dress? Will it be long or short?"

"Hmm, not sure yet, but I think long."

"I have a scar on my thigh if it makes any difference." I indicate my left upper leg, where the significant surgical scar is a broad white line.

"I think it won't show but will add to your mystique if it does."

"Mystique?"

"Yes, and I will have you in five-inch heels."

FML

"You aren't very excited about this," Kincaid says.

"I'm not, but it isn't because of you or your clothes."

"I'll try not to take it personally."

I forgive him for the sarcasm. Ava told me Kincaid's clothing line nets him over five hundred million annually. Society women modeling his designs for other rich people won't add or subtract much from his net worth.

"Don't wear any makeup the day of the show. My people will be there to do it for you."

Bronwyn sweeps in and returns me to the group. Everyone's eyes sparkle and their voices are high and excited as they discuss whatever they get to wear. Ava joins me as we file out of the building toward the limo.

"I'm happy with my outfit," she says. "You?"

"The design is still in Kincaid's mind. What's yours like?"

"The piece is difficult to describe, slouchy gym-type pants with a bright green flowing jacket-cape top. Did he give you a hint about yours?"

"He plans on a short or long dress requiring five-inch heels."

"Yikes. The runway can be slick."

"*What*?"

"Several guest models have fallen in the past."

My head sinks to my chest.

Ava loops her arm through mine and pats my forearm. "Don't worry."

Why do worst-case scenarios run through my mind?

THE LIMO STOPS, and the chauffeur opens our door. "The Waldorf-Astoria, Beverly Hills," she announces.

Vases of fresh flowers fill the elegant lobby. The staff welcomes us, prosperous patrons ignore us, and we make our way to the elevators. Beatrice says we have a reserved table at a rooftop restaurant. We emerge on the twelfth floor to spectacular views of mansions, the Hollywood sign, mountains, and skyscrapers. Sea foam green cushioned chairs, and granite tables with oversized canvas umbrellas dot the patio.

Our hostess seats us at a table close to the roof's edge, and I'm next to Brittany and Kennedy. They leap up to pose for photos, leaning close together with the view in the background. They pucker their lips and throw up their fingers in a V, perhaps an influencer gang sign. I pick up the menu and decide on a lobster burger costing over thirty dollars.

Brittany sinks into the chair beside me, thumbs flying as she types on her phone. "Why aren't you posting to Insta? The photo backdrop here is perfect."

"Oh, uh, not my thing," I tell her.

"You at least post to TikTok, don't you?"

"I'm not on social media."

Her hand flies to her chest. "Why not? You could be an influencer, like Kennedy and me."

Influencers of what? World policy for the witless?

"I like my privacy."

"Then you shouldn't have kissed Adair Monroe. We want you to come on our podcast to discuss what it's like to get your hands on that hottie."

Internal screaming.

Before I can decline, Kennedy drags her away to ask a server to video them performing dance moves near the railing. Southern California's sunny skies favor us, so I relax. More wait staff arrive carrying plates of appetizers to share.

"We have spiced chicken samosas with cilantro yogurt for dipping sauce and guacamole mixed with pistachios served with warm tortilla chips." They set down several trays. I'm hungrier than expected, piling enough food on my plate to scandalize Brittany and Kennedy.

"You sure eat a lot," Kennedy says to me. "Do you, you know?" She makes a motion of sticking her finger down her throat.

"No."

"You must work out constantly to stay, like, so trim." She speaks with an uptalk at the end of her words, so every sentence sounds like a question.

"I don't."

Seated between Beatrice and Sophie, Ava has turned to alcohol. She catches my eye and raises her martini glass, and I lift my iced tea.

"Oh my god, oh my god, *oh my god!*" Brittany grasps my forearm so hard her long, polished pink nails bite. She focuses on a man in a white chef's uniform talking with a hostess.

"Who is he?" I cover Brittany's hand with mine and pry off her fingers.

"Chef Rafael Sebastian. He owns restaurants worldwide, but his primary establishment is in New York. His food takes my breath away."

How? You don't eat.

He comes to our table, takes Ava's hand, and bows to kiss it. Brittany and Kennedy snap photo after photo with their phones held low like naughty children. They rush the chef to coo their admiration and pose for pictures and videos with him. He says something to them, and they squeal with delight.

Once Chef Rafael can free himself, he says, "Since my friend Ava Gordon is dining with us today, my signature dessert will be on the house. Please enjoy your lunch."

Waitpersons appear with our orders. The influencer duo takes photos of meals they won't touch, then speak into their phones for whatever videos they're doing. I tune out their voices and concentrate on my food, which is divine.

"Are you going to eat that?" I point to Kennedy's Caesar salad with no added protein.

"No, but I did dip my fork in the dressing."

"I don't mind."

She hands me her plate.

"Do you want mine, too?" Brittany lifts her baby kale salad.

"You should take it to go."

"I'll give it to my housekeeper. I always do." She returns to her phone.

Ava converses with Beatrice and Sophie during lunch and appears to enjoy herself.

Will I ever be able to engage in meaningless, social conversation and like it?

Servers clear the table and emerge with plates of chocolate cake and vanilla ice cream. I take a bite, and a chocolate volcano erupts in my mouth. Ava takes her phone out to photograph her slice, and I realize I might need to start miming these habits to fit in. But *why*?

Beatrice charges the substantial bill to the Ladies' League. I imagine the club's accountant scowling over the expenditure and dissecting the cost at the next board meeting.

We make our way to the ladies' room, then back to the limo, where the chauffeur opens a rear door. It's three p.m., and, barring any accidents, we might be back by 5:30. Champagne replaces the wine, but my meeting with Adair is next, so I decline an offered glass, settle into my seat, and ready myself for what lies ahead.

11

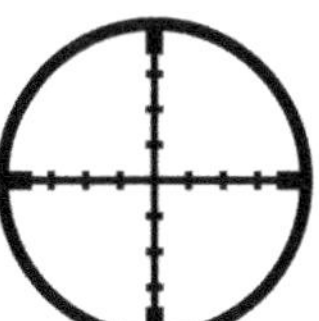

Τhe gates to Adair's thirty-plus acre estate stand open. The sun has set, and discreet spotlights highlight Jacaranda trees in full purple bloom lining the long drive.

As I park beneath the portico, Adair bounds out his front door. He's in dark jeans and a pale blue t-shirt paired with a casual navy bomber jacket, but he could wear almost anything on his rangy frame. When I open the door, he leans into the car and takes my left hand.

"Hello, Beautiful." He pulls me forward, bending to brush his lips over mine. My hand involuntarily squeezes his, and he smiles against my mouth.

"Where are we going?" I ask as I stand.

"It's a surprise. I have dinner all planned out." Adair glances at his heavy gold wristwatch, which likely cost as much as a condo. "We're going to be late."

He doesn't release my hand, and we pass a grand fountain at the front of his English-style mansion that's only slightly smaller than Buckingham Palace. A stone path beside the residence leads to a sleek black helicopter. A man I recognize stands beside it.

"Hello, Jason," I greet.

"Hello, Ms. Glenn." His face is glacial.

Jason McCall is Adair's right-hand man and former MI6, a real-life 007. The last time we met, I was sure he would try to kill me to protect Adair from my operative past and its complications. I still wonder.

"Ready, Mr. Monroe?" he says as Adair claps him on the shoulder with affection.

Adair opens the craft's door and helps me up the stairs. The interior is opulent, unlike my recent past military conveyances. We buckle in and pull on headsets, the polished wood of the seat dividers and moldings gleaming in the soft light.

"Have you ever been in a helicopter?" Adair says.

Have I ever flown one? Jumped from one? Survived a crash of one?

"A few times."

Soon, we're off, and I wish to trade places with Jason, one of the pilots, to test the chopper's limits. Lights stretch below us, and I choose to let go, not calculate our destination. The Coronado Bridge, which spans the bay between downtown San Diego and Coronado Island, comes into view. Near it is a superyacht longer than a football field.

Adair retakes my hand. "We're about to land on a boat. Don't be nervous."

I want to laugh at his characterization of this mega yacht as a boat but say, "I'll be fine."

The landing is smooth, and Adair exits first, reaching back to assist me. "Would you like to dine indoors or out?"

"Outside, I need air after a day in a limo."

We descend stairs to where two men in white jackets and dark trousers wait. Adair greets them by name and indicates we'll be dining outside. They light candles on either side of a vase of flowers at an intimate table set for two, pour wine into glasses, and depart. I don't want to speculate how many times—no, how many women—have enjoyed the same treatment.

"I'm glad we can have dinner together," Adair says once we're seated. "You told me we didn't know each other well when we attended the gala, and now we'll have more time to talk."

"Yes, but I want to return this before I forget." I unzip my bag and hand him a small box containing the silver and sapphire comb.

Adair's mouth sets in a line. "You sure know how to interrupt the mood of a romantic evening."

"I appreciate your thoughtful gift," I rush to say. "But I can't accept it."

The comb cost over $200,000. To Adair, it's chump change; to me, it's too much. Should I have waited until later or brought it up right away? I didn't know.

Finally, he takes the box and slips it into his jacket pocket.

"Did you settle on the bloke I met at the gala? He said he was your boyfriend."

Warden. We haven't said the L word yet, and he's okay with me dating other men so I can comply with the will. What a mess.

"In a perfect world, if we saw each other more often, that would be correct."

A warm breeze comes up from the bay, blowing Adair's hair across his forehead, and he smooths it back. "What keeps you apart?"

"His job's in Virginia."

And he travels to some of the most treacherous places in the world, where I should be beside him, not here in designer clothes having dinner with you.

"If you were my girlfriend—"

"But I'm not," I interrupt.

Adair studies me as he drinks his wine, then says, "Yet."

The firmness of his statement startles me. Is he a wolf masked beneath an affable front?

I don't know Adair at all.

Before I respond, the staff appears with an appetizer followed by an elegant gourmet meal. One of the servers holds a bottle of Chardonnay. "More wine, miss?"

I agree, although I'm unsure if drinking more is a terrific idea. The boat sways softly, and cars cross the bridge above us. Smaller boats cruise past, some for scenic tours and others with fishers who cast their lines.

"Do you like it?" Adair motions to the meal.

"Yes."

"I'm glad. I convinced a Michelin star chef to step away from restaurants."

"You did? I thought your staff would do the hiring."

"They do for the most part, but I was in Paris and went to the kitchen after an exceptional meal to persuade the chef to work for me."

I think about how many people he must employ, from business to personal, and an omission occurs to me. "Why don't you have a bodyguard yet?" We explored this topic several times, and Jason also nagged him about needing protection.

"Why don't you?"

"You're ducking the question," I say. "Mine's an easy answer. I'm not famous."

And I'm better than any bodyguard.

"My time's rarely my own, and sharing my personal space with minders would imprison me more. We vet my staff."

"What about threats from outside your people, like superfan stalkers or criminals who might kidnap you for a hefty ransom?"

"So far, no one's caused problems."

He's been in more danger hanging around me than ever in his privileged life, or at least the part he's shown me.

"Have you ever—" *learned to defend yourself*? "Um, tell me about your life."

He sets down his utensils, and I notice his long fingers and manicured nails, symbolic of his prosperous existence.

"You want to ask whether I drift through my life with a careless attitude."

"I would never frame it like that, but I worry about you."

Adair's focus turns inward. "I've been through rough patches and hard times, like anyone."

"Such as?" Will he answer, or is there something he doesn't want to discuss in his past, like me?

Adair takes a moment, weighing. "I don't tell many people, but if we're going to have any type of future together, I want to."

A future together?

Before I can question this, he says, "My Mum was a ballet dancer and caught my dad's eye when she performed at Manchester's Palace Theater. He was there as extra security because Princess Diana was attending a charity event for Leukemia Aid or something. He was much older and a former MI6 agent, but they married after a whirlwind romance and had me and my sister, Adalyn, who is three years younger than me."

"Your dad was MI6? What was he like?"

Adair pauses, a shadow clouding his face. "Dad was dishy and capable but often a raging drunk. One night after too many pints, he threw Ada against a wall. She was two and a half."

I put a hand to my mouth, stunned.

"Mum tried to get past him to help, but dad hit her, and she fell. I threw myself at his legs but was still too little to make any difference. He kicked me out of the way and left. Mum called an ambulance, and we went to the hospital with Ada while Dad went on a bender. Later that night, he drove his car head-on into another, and he and the other driver died."

"Oh, no, Adair. I can't imagine. Was your sister okay?"

He clears his throat. "No. The impact damaged her brain. She can't speak and uses a wheelchair because the injury left the right side of her body paralyzed."

"Where is she?"

"In a care facility in England. She's made some progress with therapy but won't be able to live a normal life."

"I don't know what to say."

Adair lets out a long breath, eyes downcast. "What's odd about the whole thing is losing Dad was also devastating. Despite his tirades, he was a lot of fun. He took me with him everywhere. We would kick a football around and go hiking. Once, we rented a campervan to travel as a family and enjoyed a memorable trip to Gulliver's Kingdom, an amusement park. Since not all my childhood was bad, the conflicting memories wreaked havoc on me."

"I bet. What happened after that?"

"My early childhood became a bit Dickensian. Mum struggled to provide for us by teaching dance, but bouncing between my sister in care and me at school ran her ragged. One day, Roger McCall, a former colleague of dad's, came by. He's Jason's father and was the best man at my parent's wedding, but he had been out of the country. When Roger saw our state, he brought us food often because Mum wouldn't take his money. Roger dragged a teenage Jason along on one of his visits. I was about seven and followed Jason everywhere, much to his annoyance."

"It can't be fun for him to call you Mr. Monroe."

"He told me every time he says 'Mr. Monroe,' what he's thinking is 'bloody tosser' or, as you Yanks say, 'supreme asshole.'"

"I believe you."

What does Jason think when he calls me Ms. Glenn?

"Sorry to whinge about my past, but I didn't want you to think I was born with a silver spoon."

"I appreciate you sharing, as I'm sure the story is difficult to discuss. Bryce told me you let abused women shop at his place and paid the bill. At the time, I thought it was for a tax write-off. Apologies for my cynicism."

"Until you get to know someone, you can pin labels on them that aren't necessarily true."

The wait staff interrupts our conversation to clear our plates. "Would you like dessert now, sir?"

Adair looks at me.

"I'm full. How about you give me a tour?"

We leave the table and step through a door leading to a room filled with luxurious seats and modern tables.

"This ship can hold up to thirty-six guests, and most rooms have fold-out balconies so people can enjoy some private time outside."

"Have you had that many guests onboard?"

"Yes, and it was barmy."

"In what way?"

"Trying to make everyone happy. Most people aren't as laid-back as you."

"More evidence you don't know me."

"You're right. Race you to the next level." He shoots me a playful smile and bolts up the stairs. Taken by surprise, I run after him but can't catch up. When I get to the landing where he waits, he does a victory dance.

"You cheated," I accuse, not wanting to admit I find his antics charming.

"I like to win," he says.

"Evidence I don't know you either."

Adair shows me around the level, which contains an opulent cinema room, a luxury spa, a steam room, and one with ice-covered stone walls.

"What's this?"

"A snow room. It stimulates blood circulation plus helps you burn off fat."

When he finishes the tour and is preoccupied with turning off the snow room's lights, I charge toward the next flight of stairs.

"Oh no you don't." Adair chases after me.

When he draws level, I push him toward the wall banister to throw him off his stride, but he doesn't falter. We reach the landing at the same time, and Adair pulls me to him and spins me around. We're now in his private domain, out of breath and laughing. He places his hands on either side of my face and gives me a quick kiss. When he raises his head, he wags a finger at me. "You cheated, or you wouldn't have won."

My pulse pounds more from his kiss than the race, and I work to steady myself. "I like to win, too."

"I plan to outmaneuver you next time," he promises.

There can't be a next time.

The words never leave my lips.

"Come on." Adair takes my hand, and we pass a gym, study, and spa and exit through glass doors to a covered seating area near the yacht's stern. A hot tub the size of a swimming pool, padded chairs, and tables fill the deck.

"Don't worry, I won't ask if you want to take a dip, so I get to see you starkers," he teases.

But I might ask you. If I were your girl, Warden didn't exist, and I could be open about who I am.

Adair hits a button on an intercom, instructs his staff to bring dessert, and they arrive with crème brulée. When we finish eating, I say, "I should sit in the snow room to lose some of the weight I gained from our meal."

Adair pats his flat stomach. "We both should."

I sip hot tea, and he consumes coffee. He's seated within inches of me, his long legs stretched out, an arm behind his head.

"How's your mom?" I met her at the Ladies' League gala.

Adair sits forward. "She asked after you and sends her regards. She's in Africa, working at an orphanage I fund. There have been many orphans due to AIDS, Ebola, and war."

"Parts of Africa are unstable," I say.

"Have you ever been?"

"No." During my last mission there, one of Badger's people shot me.

Lie after lie. When will it end?

"Do you like living in Rancho?" Adair asks.

"Do you?"

He faces me. "I wouldn't usually be here now. I have a lot of hands-on business in the EU because I expanded my offices, but I decided to come back to find you."

"Why?" Hadn't my leaving the gala with Warden sent him a clear message? "You can have your pick of almost anyone."

"I can, but ever since you came into my life, I can't stop thinking about you."

"Adair—"

"I get it. You like the brute who came to the gala, but—" He reaches out and takes my hand. He laces our fingers, running his thumb against my inside web in a soft caress.

I raise my eyes. "But what?"

"He can't give you what I can."

Displeasure floods me, and I pull my hand away and rise. "I don't want your money."

Adair cocks his head, half-smiling. "Did I say anything about giving you my money? I like my money."

"Money's the only thing you have more of than Warden."

Adair stands. "You're wrong."

"What do you mean?"

"I considered this a lot before returning to find you. It's a wanker move to come for a woman dating another guy and something I've never done."

"Then why are you back?"

"When we first met, I learned you're a keen observer of people, but so am I. One of the unfortunate side benefits of having a dodgy childhood is I grew proficient at gauging people and situations for survival. You became a different woman when you stood beside that guy at the gala. There was no emotion on your face, and you were locked down, unlike when we danced that night."

I can't tell him about my work relationship with Warden and the ordeal we faced right before Adair met him at the gala.

"Adair, I like you, but I—"

"Davia, I want you, not for a fling but for as long as we can stay together. Before you get the wrong idea, this isn't some small-minded competition to win you away. I'm a man you can be open with, someone who won't think any less of you if you don't always keep yourself together."

My traitorous heart flutters at his words. Or is my reaction caused by how he looks at me, so earnest and enticing?

Adair leans to kiss me, but I step out of reach. I need time to figure out why I hesitate to tell him he's not an option. "I'll think about what you said, but I should go home. My parent's neighbor is visiting."

He doesn't fight my withdrawal, but he wears a knowing look. "How'd the fitting go?"

"It didn't. Kincaid Foxx can't decide what I should wear."

"I can't wait for your runway debut."

"You'll enjoy the show more than I will, trust me."

Before we leave, I ask to use the bathroom. I pass an opulent sunken tub and spacious marble shower with three multi-setting shower heads. An inset fixture in its ceiling would create a waterfall spray. What would it be like to use it with Adair?

Stop. Just stop.

Adair is propped against the door frame to the landing when I return and straightens. "Ready to go?"

"Yes. Thank you so much for this evening. Tonight's been—" I search for the right word. "Perfect."

"I wanted it to be, Luv."

He brings me close, claiming my mouth and parting my lips with his tongue. He tastes like a mixture of coffee and sugar, bitter and sweet. I want to take him by the hand to his solid king-sized bed, push him onto it, and unbuckle his belt. I want kiss him until the world disappears. I want to find out why I'm unable to walk away from him.

Would I be happy with what he offers? Or would my past tear us apart?

I pull back, but he doesn't let go and trails kisses from my jaw down my neck.

"I can't do this." I force the words out.

As desire radiates between us, he rests his cheek against my hair, and I relax into his arms for longer than I should. I'm conscious there's much more than his hard chest pressing against me, but if I give in to my attraction for him, then what?

"I need to go." My voice doesn't hold conviction.

"I need you to stay," Adair whispers, tightening his arms. "But I understand."

He skims his lips over mine, then takes my hand to walk with me down the stairs and return to the waiting helicopter.

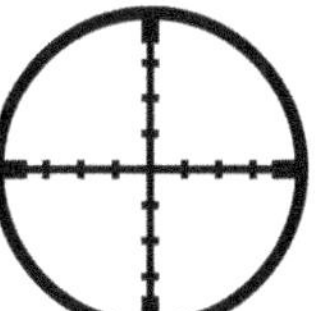

12

Back at Adair's estate, Jason skewers me with a glare of disapproval as we exit the craft. At my car, Adair says, "I hope tonight gave you reasons to believe I'm better for you than that chap back east. I don't give up easily."

Neither Warden nor Adair ever calls the other by name, using distancing language to show their disdain. That fellow. That Brit. That guy.

I start to respond, but he says, "Don't say anything now. Think about it."

The whole drive home, I mutter recriminations despite Adair's honest words.

What was I thinking? Why did I let him kiss me? Is there an Adair Anonymous meeting I can attend to rid myself of this addiction?

A crowd of people will attend the fashion show, and I'll make sure I'm never alone with him again.

Midnight nears as I navigate my driveway and hit the garage door remote. The headlights swing toward the opening and illuminate a figure standing in the way. I slam on the brakes.

Kilburn.

My gun is in the center console, but his hands are up in a

placating gesture. Do I trust him? He backs away so I can pull in. Once parked, I jump out with my gun, not caring if he's offended. He doesn't lower his hands, but I don't let down my guard.

"What are you doing here?" I demand.

"I came for our crime scene talk."

"At this time of night?"

"You weren't home, but I decided to stick around—comprehensive security system, by the way. One of your tripwires almost got me. Almost." A corner of his mouth quirks with amusement.

"How long have you been here?"

"Not long, but I did have to tie up your resident guard dog when he came at me with a shovel."

"José? You tied up José?"

"Better than killing him."

"Where is he?"

"In his quarters in a comfy chair, I knew if I got rough with him, it would piss you off."

"I'm pissed anyway. I can't believe you're here at this hour and assaulted José. Let's go." I wave my gun toward my property manager's living quarters in the barn and make Kilburn walk in front of me, staying far enough back he can't turn and disarm me.

We reach José's home entry, and I have Kilburn open the door.

"*Yaa!*" José's arms are bound to a chair, but he launches himself at Kilburn. The men slam into the cement of the barn floor as José shouts curse words in Spanish into the assassin's face.

"It's okay, José." I pull him upright. "I know him."

"*Él está loco!*" José exclaims.

"*Sí*, he is crazy," I agree as I untie him. Kilburn gets to his feet, unperturbed. He apologizes to José in Spanish, but my protective employee is unconvinced. He leaps up once he's free, balling his hands into fists. I touch José's back and apologize. He shakes off my hand, goes into his residence, and slams the door. Considering how unpredictable his life has become, I hope he won't quit working here.

"You realize showing up to talk at this hour's not normal, right? Text me next time," I tell Kilburn, who doesn't apologize.

We return to the garage and enter the house, where Kyle sits at the kitchen table—my .22 in his hand.

"I sensed an issue outside," he says.

"Kilburn crashed the gate."

"Are you okay?" Kyle's eyes and the gun muzzle stay trained on Kilburn.

I nod, but Kyle doesn't lower the gun.

Kilburn pulls a chair out from the opposite side of the table and sits, relaxed.

"I never thought you'd hire a bodyguard, Bombshell," he says. "You must be getting soft."

"I am." It might make him sloppy if he thinks he can take advantage of me. "So, what exactly is it you want?"

"Tell me what you saw at the scene."

I relate the story of what I observed from my backyard, then stop. "Your turn."

Irritation plays across Kilburn's face before his passive expression returns. "I need details."

"Why are you here?" I demand.

"I told you already."

"You don't strike me as the altruistic type, so I'm not giving any other information unless you tell me what your goal is."

Kilburn ignores my request. "Three to the chest for mom, two in the back for the son, and a head wound for the little girl. Am I correct?"

"Yes. If you already—"

"And the only person you saw was the guy in the car?"

"Since I only caught a glimpse, I'm unsure if it was a man or a woman."

"Interesting, very interesting." Kilburn imitates Arte Johnson from Laugh-In, a TV show from the Sixties, something my dad made me watch with him on DVD years ago.

"Why are you here?" I ask again.

"Long story, but I owe Markus one."

"Are we done now?" I don't want a lengthy tale to delay his

departure.

Kilburn doesn't take his eyes off Kyle, and his expression hardens. "You must be paying this guy well. He's taking his job way too seriously."

"He's not. Now, are you leaving?" *Or will I have to make you?* My coat is too snug to fight in, but I still hold my gun. Even with the two of us, I'm unsure about our odds.

Kilburn shifts his weight, and I try not to jump, but his face returns to a pleasant expression. "Give me your conclusions about the scene."

"About what specifically?"

"The shooter or shooters."

I think about the position of the bodies.

"He had them in one room. He shoots the wife first, tight grouping. Professional." Why shoot her first? I imagine Tilly screaming and her brother Eric moving to protect her.

"What are you thinking?" Kilburn says.

"Whoever did it either got interrupted or wasn't prepared for what happened. A pro, they'd all be dead."

"In their beds," Kilburn says. "But someone collected the brass, which puts us back to a pro."

"Yes," I agree, recalling there were no spent casings. "I need to think about it more, but the hour's late, and you need to leave."

"You can put that down now, cowboy." Kilburn directs this to Kyle, who doesn't move the barrel a hair.

We exit the way we came in, and Kilburn strides down the drive, raising a hand to acknowledge his departure. I close the garage, lock each door I pass through, and reset the security system.

"What a charmer," Kyle says. The gun rests on the table.

"Hitmen don't have a sense of humor. Thanks for the backup."

"Welcome. Glad I guessed your gun safe code."

We share a smile; Kyle and I have the same codes for all our gun storage.

I exhale. "It's been a long day."

"I think more for you than for me. I played a pleasant round with

Bob, and we ate dinner at the clubhouse. He's going to show me around the area tomorrow." Kyle gets up with a yawn. "Do you want to talk about what happened?"

"I think I need some time to process it."

We head to our rooms.

When I get in bed, I pop in my headphones to listen to relaxing music and release some of the tension caused by Kilburn's impromptu visit. My phone vibrates with a text from Adair.

Thanks for tonight. Up for a game?

I hesitate before I answer. *Game?*

Adair: *Let's learn more about each other with some questions. I'll go first with a real soul searcher. What's your favorite color?*

I can't help but smile as I type. *Black. You?*

Adair: *The blue of your eyes after we've had a proper snog.*

Memories of Adair's scorching kisses makes me crave more.

Damn him.

Me: *Goodnight.*

Adair: *Maybe you'll see me in your dreams.* (kiss emoji)

I lie back and use all my willpower to avoid fantasies about his touch, his promises, and where this could lead.

13

"What did you and Bob do this morning?" I say to Kyle after he returns from his outing.

"We ate mouthwatering cranberry-orange muffins at a little bakery, and he gave me a tour of the community and caught me up on its history. The energy is relaxing."

"It is. If only more of the types of people we like lived here, it would be perfect."

"Careful. I might convince your parents to sell off, and we'll move in with you."

"I don't view that as a threat."

"Do you have any plans for today?"

"I need to find José and apologize for what happened last night. I didn't have a chance to explain about Kilburn."

"I'll tag along if you don't mind," Kyle says. "I got to talk to José the other day when I did my fake bake by the pool. I can tell he's a reliable guy to have around in a pinch."

We go to the barn, and I knock on José's door. He answers, dressed in a black suit, white shirt, and tie with polished cowboy boots. Kyle raises a hand in greeting, then goes to pet my horse Ace, who lets out a soft nicker.

"Am I interrupting something?" I say.

"I'm going to a funeral."

"I'm so sorry. Who died?"

"*Mi primo fue assasindo.*"

My cousin was murdered.

"When?"

"Someone shot him in his bed a few nights ago."

"Kyle, come listen to this," I say.

Kyle joins us, and José tells us his cousin was twenty-four, the same age as him, and lived in a rented apartment with two other men. The roommates were in Mexico visiting family when the murder occurred.

"Did he have any enemies?" I say.

"I don't think so. He was a *jardinero.*" A gardener.

"Where did he work?" I say.

"Here, in Rancho Suprema, for different people. Wait. He worked for the family who was murdered."

"The Myles family?" I say.

"*Sí!*"

Kyle and I exchange glances.

"What day of the week did he work for them?" I say.

"I'm not sure."

"What was his name?" Kyle asks.

"Enrique Flores."

"Did anyone else work with him?" I ask.

"No. Enrique saved up for a truck and tools to run his own business. *Mi tía está devastada.*" José's voice cracks as he mentions his aunt.

"I'm sorry for your loss," Kyle says.

"*Gracias.*"

I apologize about Kilburn, and José assures me he's fine but is late for the service and must rush.

After he departs, I weigh this new information. "José's news skews my opinion more in favor of a pro hit of the Myles family."

"Sounds like a sanitation crew did some cleanup," Kyle says, and I agree.

I retrieve a bucket of horse treats, and Kyle gives one to Ace, patting his shiny black coat.

"Do you think José's cousin saw something?" I hand Kyle another treat.

"Hard to say. What about your connection in law enforcement? Would he know?" Kyle says as we return to the house.

"His name's Detective Montoya and he's only shared the name of the little girl who was shot and updated me on her condition. He fits in with our tight-lipped community."

"We can't blame him, but you might tip him off to the connection between the two killings."

"I didn't ask José what city the murder occurred in, so if the case isn't in his jurisdiction, Montoya might not be aware."

Once inside, I leave a message at Montoya's office for him to call me. If I were a detective, I would interview the neighbors and find out where José's cousin parked or his typical routine. Gardeners are a fixture of the community, but did anyone pay attention to them?

"Why do I want to return to the property?" I say.

"Because you're a woman of action, but do I need to remind you you're on a break?"

I give him a pretend pout.

"There, there," Kyle says. "Being a detective falls outside your job description. You're a lady of leisure."

My phone vibrates with a text from Ava Gordon.

I'm having a little party tonight. Want to come over?

What did she mean by "little?" I didn't want to know.

Me: *I have company.*

Ava: *Bring them along*

"We've been invited to a party. Do you want another taste of how the other half lives?"

"Might as well," Kyle says. "My life's been dull, except for blood pressure spikes when the weather, crops, or markets are bad."

"Be prepared for crazy, and don't say I didn't warn you."

I confirm we'll attend, and Ava texts me her address.

"It starts at six, which means we can arrive until midnight and be fine," I say.

"Would seven work?" Kyle says in a teasing tone.

"I'm sure."

"Attire?"

"Casual, which means anything."

"I'll make sure and brush my hair. I'll probably be the oldest of the group."

Kyle is forty-six but appears much younger.

"You'll be fine. Just remember not to ask any older man if the woman he's there with is his daughter."

"I'll be careful."

"What would you like to do the rest of the day?" I say.

"Want to check out the crime scene?"

"Did you catch my sleuthing bug?"

"Call it curiosity. Kilburn's hanging around, and José's cousin died. I want an up-close daytime visual of the place."

WE PARK near the entrance to the Myles' home. The iron gates are closed and decorated with bouquets, cards, and stuffed animals. I recall news coverage of relatives and friends of the family, particularly young people perhaps having their first peer die, wiping away tears as they dropped off the tribute items.

"Do you want to get out?" I say.

"I scanned the area for snipers, so I think we'll be fine."

"The disapproving neighbors will be more of a problem."

We stand by my car. The homeowners' association rules don't allow solid walls, so only a rustic wooden fence and some trees screen the house, providing a view of the front yard. Kyle points to some tall trees near the right side of the home. Black wound paint covers several branch stubs.

"What if José's cousin was up there trimming when he saw something someone didn't want him to?" he says.

The position provides an excellent view of the area.

"Depending on the day, perhaps he saw whoever scoped the place," I say.

"We might deduce the vehicle or its occupants were memorable for the area."

"The car I saw that night didn't make an impression."

"But you're not sure about the driver. Was it Markus Myles?"

"No idea."

"And you say the front door was open?" Yellow crime scene tape still crosses it.

"Yes. To me, a pro wouldn't make such an obvious mistake."

"Agreed, unless there was an urgent reason to leave."

We walk the perimeter, checking for any evidence the police might have missed but find nothing.

"What happened to the pile of cigarette butts with DNA they find in the movies?" I joke.

"I'm sure the police bagged and tagged it."

"Detective Montoya catches small details and makes logical conclusions."

As if on cue, my phone rings.

"I got your message," Montoya says. "What's up?"

I tell him about José's cousin and the tree branches.

"We don't have the case. I'll run it in the system and determine which agency's handling it. Thanks for the head's up."

"Have you learned anything else?"

Montoya remains quiet, perhaps mulling over whether or not to share. At last, he says, "Markus Myles has an interesting past."

"Yes, he does."

"You know? Why am I not surprised?"

"The info is from a third party."

"Who?"

"I can't tell you."

I would never willingly inject Kilburn into anyone's existence.

Montoya makes a frustrated noise on the other end. "I'm not

getting far with the feds, so please tell me if you find out anything else pertinent to the case."

"I will. How's Tilly Myles?"

"Still unconscious in ICU and guarded." Montoya thanks me for the information and concludes the call.

"Learn anything?" Kyle says.

"The girl's still in a coma, the feds aren't cooperating, and Montoya found out Markus Myles was a spy. So, not really."

"I wish you could walk me through what you did inside their home," Kyle says as we head back to the car.

"Are we going to stay after this?"

"In for a penny. Staying ahead of Kilburn, if possible, would be best."

"I don't think we are, but you're right. We can return tonight because no one's staying here."

"Let's decide whether or not to play private eye later. What's next?"

"Lunch?"

"Sure."

"Any preferences?" I start the engine.

"If it's not an MRE, I'm up for anything."

"What, you don't miss army rations? I'm shocked. How about a lobster roll?"

"Are we taking your jet to Maine?"

"I don't own a jet, so we're going to Lobster West in the Lumber-yard. They fly in the lobster."

"Darn. I thought for sure you kept a pilot on standby."

"Don't laugh, but many residents here do."

"Why am I not surprised?"

WE'RE five cars back from a valet station near Ava's address.

"Valet parking? Think you'll get your car back in one piece?" Kyle says.

"If you like, we can find somewhere to park along this road so I can break an ankle walking to the party in these heels." They're only three inches, but I'm working my way up.

"Want me to give you a piggyback ride?"

"Shut up."

Believing I wasn't in anyone's crosshairs, I opted for a white bodycon dress with a plunging neckline, my hair in a ponytail. Kyle wears a navy suit, white shirt, and dress shoes, so far removed from his typical attire of jeans and worn shirts; I'm unsure what to think. As we readied to leave, he said, "My little tomboy's all grown up. You're a killer, but in a different way now."

"And I don't know who you are," I replied.

After surrendering the car, we get in a golf cart ferrying guests to the front of Ava's home. Personnel wait at the entrance to assist us out of the conveyance, and Ava greets us near the front door.

"Davia, I'm so glad you came." She wears a sheer flesh-colored dress with a black lace overlay pattern, a trendy black belt, and black heels with ankle straps, her hair straight and shining.

"Ava, this is my friend, Kyle Kavanagh, Kyle; this is Ava Gordon."

"A pleasure." She puts out a hand, which Kyle takes. I catch a look of interest on her face and realize Kyle's personal life—or lack thereof—never crossed my mind.

He's attractive in a take-no-prisoners way.

A rush of guests necessitates we move inside, but Ava keeps glancing back at Kyle.

"I think someone fancies you," I say.

"For a moment, I felt like the main course, not that I'd object."

Servers offer us glasses of wine, and a quartet of musicians plays classical music. A dramatic crystal chandelier lights the foyer's marble floor, and a grand double staircase with rich burgundy and gold patterned carpet leads to a second story. Kyle's expression of absolute astonishment makes me want to laugh.

"And I thought your place was a palace," he says.

"Careful. Spending too much time here will skew your sense of reality."

We weave past the guests in the living room, take in the lush tapestries decorating its walls, and go out to a terraced patio above a lighted pool. A man approaches to inform us if we'd like to go to the lake, we can either be taken there by golf cart or walk.

After he's out of earshot, Kyle puts his hands on his hips. "Why don't you own a lake?"

Before we can dissolve into laughter, servers approach with trays of hors d'oeuvres. We make selections and drift down the spacious patio while the pink clouds dotting the western sky fade to darkness and automatic lights come on. Signs with gold lettering tout a complete dinner catered by a local five-star restaurant. Arrows point us toward a tent where white-uniformed servers stand behind a table of silver chafing dishes lit by tall glass candelabras. Black tablecloths cover round tables surrounded by chairs for guests with red flowers in vases at their centers.

"I wonder how much this shindig is costing Ava," I say.

"A pretty penny, or two or three. Is this for a special occasion?"

"I'm not sure. Ava did mention she likes to give parties. Oh, and I learned she knew Aunt Lilah in New York."

"How?"

"Social scene stuff."

"If I were anyone in New York or the world, I would've steered clear of your aunt. She believed her way was always right, which would've been fine if she kept it to herself, but she never did."

I recall Kyle having dinner with us once when my aunt visited, and his expression grew darker throughout the meal as my aunt dished out advice on how we all needed to improve our lives.

"If you wanted to move up the NYC ladder, there was no way to avoid her."

Kyle shakes his head. "Life in the fast lane."

"Want some food?"

"Sure, since I don't know what to do next."

"Story of my life in this town," I say, and we enter the tent.

After filling our plates, we find a table in a quiet corner with a clear view of the entrance. Within a few minutes, another couple joins us.

"I'm Mike Weir, and this is my wife, Brooke," a pleasant-looking man says. Brooke smiles as we introduce ourselves. Her white teeth gleam, and brown hair spills over her generous, unmoving cleavage.

"Have you tried the Wagyu beef?" she says. "This is A5. Can you believe it?"

Kyle examines the steak on his plate. "I never heard of it."

"A5 is the highest grade of beef from cows in Japan," Brooke continues. "It costs over one hundred dollars a pound. I love Ava's parties because she never stints on cost. Last month she brought in the performers from *Cirque du Soleil*, and she's had Bruno Mars and Adele come in for intimate concerts."

"How often does she host parties?" I say.

"Every month or so. Everyone clamors for invites," Mike says.

Two men join us at the table but are engrossed in an animated conversation. From the snippets I catch, they're discussing a private restaurant venture.

Mike leans forward. "Say, did you know the Myles family?"

"I didn't," I say. "Did you?"

"We visited with them at different social gatherings around town, and I'm shocked like everyone. Quite a few people here invested heavily in Maxim Myles. When the news of the SEC investigation broke, it was at the forefront of conversation; I can tell you that."

"I mean, if my wife and son were murdered and my daughter survived, nothing would keep me away," Brooke says.

"He might be out of the country," I say.

"The news is all over the world by now. I'm sure he'll return," Brooke says.

"I hope like hell he does," one of the men discussing the restaurant interjects. "We put quite a bit of money into his company, and Frederik isn't returning our calls. I want some straight answers about what happened."

To the Myles family or his investments?

"You seem upset," Kyle notes.

"Damn right I am. We're about to open a restaurant in a trendy location with an award-winning chef, which requires a considerable outlay of capital. I didn't care if Markus was in Spain, Greece, Pakistan, or wherever doing his deals because Frederik was available. But now? I want the straight scoop from both of them."

So, he doesn't care about the murders.

"How many other people think as you do?" I say.

"Plenty." Anger clouds his face. "I mean, Ava Gordon and her brother invested in Maxim Myles. I'm shocked she's throwing this bash, considering what she might have lost."

"You're speculating," Mike protests.

"Yes," Brooke says. "Not everyone puts all their money in one place."

The restaurant investor leans forward, "Who do you think we are? Complete idiots?"

His friend puts a placating hand on his arm. "Grant, let's not get into an argument."

Grant jerks his arm away, then says, "Sorry, Brad," and takes a deep drink from his wine glass.

"We open next week, so we're on edge, sorry," Brad says.

Draining his wine, Grant stands. "Let's go."

Brad shrugs an apology at us and follows Grant out.

"Do you recognize those two?" I ask the Weirs.

Mike says, "No, but I wish I got the name of their restaurant so I don't patronize it."

We laugh, relieved the minor drama at our table is over.

After finishing my food, I tell Kyle, "I need to find the ladies' room. Will you be all right here?"

"I think I can handle polite conversation on my own."

Excusing myself, I leave Kyle conversing with the Weirs about their lives. Outside the tent, I stop one of the wait staff, who points me in the right direction, and I locate a small but expensively furnished powder room. After using the facilities, I enter a quiet side room with an exit. My hand touches the door handle to the outside, when someone comes up behind me and takes hold of my arm.

I wheel around.

A tall man with blond-red hair and a closely-cropped mustache and beard holds me. He gives me a cocky smile. "You have a perfect ass, but you're more beautiful from the front."

Yanking my arm away, I say, "And who the hell are you?"

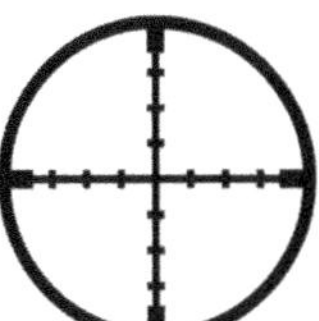

The man doesn't answer. In contrast to his conservative Italian suit, silver studs dot his left ear, and the edge of a tattoo peeks out from where his unbuttoned shirt collar sags open.

I turn to leave, but he retakes my arm.

The constraints of society are so inconvenient.

Facing him, I say, "One more time, who are you?"

"A guy who can give you exactly what you need, baby."

It doesn't take a rocket scientist to figure out what he means.

"If you don't let go, I'll—"

"You'll what?"

Break your arm? Snap your neck? Ensure you never have kids?

He takes hold of my other arm, and we stand toe-to-toe. His grip isn't tight, his actions more irritating than threatening. Three men in suits enter the room, and their bulk crowds the small space. They're all around the same age as the man before me—early thirties—and I recognize they all carry guns hidden in waistbands and shoulder holsters.

"Who are you?" I repeat. "I like to know people's names, so I have it right for their obituaries."

The newcomers tense, but my admirer raises a hand, and they relax.

"Aren't you a little troublemaker?" He bends close to my face. "Taming you will be fun."

"Oh yeah? Why don't you tell me what you'll do?" I place my body against him, a hand on his chest.

His disturbing smile becomes a full grin. "I'll train you to beg for me."

Trailing a finger down his muscular chest and tight waistline, I favor him with a sweet smile. "You can train me, but you can't tame me."

I remove his gun from its hidden holster and shove it into his stomach.

His smile fades, but mine doesn't.

The others put their hands on their weapons but don't bring them out. If I ask them to place their firearms on the floor, guests might come into the room, which would be a problem.

Calculate your moves.

"Leave," I tell them. If the men return, I can deal with them.

"Do it," orders their leader, and they back out of the room.

I push the man away from me, instructing him to sit in a nearby chair. Once he's settled, I lower his snub-nose revolver to my side.

"If you think this will put me off you, think again," he says. "I like gutsy women."

"Lucky me, now, tell me your name."

He doesn't answer or change his smug expression.

The door to the patio opens behind me.

"Alex," a female voice exclaims. "I've been trying to find you."

Ava.

"DAVIA, I wanted to introduce you to my little brother, and here you both are." She comes toward me.

What can I say about the gun?

Alex stands, and I back away from the siblings. Before we can speak, Kyle enters.

"There you are. You were gone so long I thought you drowned in the bathroom." He notes the weapon in my hand and scopes the situation.

"I got waylaid by almost more charm than was manageable." I incline my head toward Alex Gordon. "He showed me his gun."

"Gun?" Ava's eyes are enormous.

I pop open the cylinder. "Oh my, you carry it loaded."

Ava's face tightens, and Alex appears contrite, but I'm sure he's putting on an act.

"Sorry," he tells his sister, "but she's interested in guns."

I narrow my eyes when I catch his double entendre.

"Let me see." Kyle takes the weapon from me and dumps the bullets into his hand.

Alex's brow furrows, but he says nothing.

"A .22 magnum is a lot of power in a little package." Kyle puts the bullets into a pants pocket, snaps the cylinder closed, and returns it to Alex. "Be careful with that."

Alex acts unconcerned as he places the now-unloaded gun back in its holster. Ava's eyes send him a "We'll talk about this later" message, and his sister's displeasure causes him to scrape a hand through his hair, the first sign of nerves he's shown tonight.

"Have you two had dinner?" Ava refocuses on her hostess role.

"Yes," Kyle says. "I never had Wagyu beef before."

Ava begins a conversation with him about the menu and other party particulars while I keep my attention on Alex.

"Those blue eyes of yours turn as hard as diamonds in a blink," he says.

"Do they?"

"Is he your boyfriend?" Alex lifts his chin at Kyle. "Didn't peg you for liking older men. Do you have daddy issues?"

I ignore the provocation and say, "He's a family friend."

"So, you're single?"

"How this is any of your business is beyond me. I guess you prefer men? And three at the same time."

Alex scowls. "They're my bodyguards."

"You need new ones."

He comes closer.

"I wouldn't mind if you guarded my body."

"Take one more step, and you'll discover why that would be a terrible idea."

Before he can speak, Ava says, "Since you had dinner, would you like to see the swans at the lake?"

"Sounds nice," I say.

"It does," Kyle says.

"Can you take over as host?" Ava says to Alex.

"Of course." He goes to the door, raking his eyes over me before exiting.

"Sorry about him," Ava says. "He's too full of himself. I wait for him to grow up, but it hasn't happened yet."

"Why does he need bodyguards?" I say.

"They're here as security for this party, but Alex might have said otherwise to impress you. He's a successful financial advisor and wealthy in his own right, but he wants to draw attention to himself for some reason. Let's go the back way." Ava leads us down a hall, through a well-appointed study, and out a side door. A black golf cart with four tan leather seats is parked nearby. Loud music begins on the patio, replacing the string quartet.

"Calvin Harris is our DJ tonight," Ava tells Kyle.

"Will it make you like me less if I don't recognize the name?"

"Of course not. I don't think anything would make me feel that way." Ava's voice is breathy as she shoots him a sideways glance from under thick lashes.

"I'll ride in back," I say.

We jet off down a paved path with Ava driving and pass staff ferrying other carts filled with guests back to the house.

The lake is more extensive than expected, as I assumed it would be a pond referred to in grander terms. Black posts with beveled glass panels light the parking area, and other ground-level lights mark the lake's edge. Across the dark water is a bank with trees and shrubs.

Kyle dismounts and goes around to help Ava and me out.

"Want to walk to the gazebo?" Ava invites.

"Sure," I say, and Ava puts her arm through Kyle's as I trail behind.

Decorative fencing lines a wooden bridge leading to a covered structure with an ornate metal roof. It's large enough to hold at least forty people. The space is empty now, and we move to the edge of the building. A flock of swans huddle near a bank, their heads tucked under their wings.

Kyle and Ava are in a conversation I don't wish to disturb, so I stay some distance away. Booming music, loud conversation, and laughter blare from the patio far above.

A movement on the opposite bank attracts my trained eye.

"Kyle! Get down!"

A bullet cracks the railing.

15

Kyle takes Ava by the shoulders, drags her to the ground, and shelters her beneath him. Cries of *oh-OH* and *Hoo* ring out from startled swans, their wings beating the water.

I am *sick* of getting shot at in this town.

Reaching into my bag, I pull out my .22 as the *thwack* of another high-velocity round hits the structure. I picture the shooter's position at mid-bank, put my gun on the rail and pull its trigger three times in quick succession.

Only four bullets are left. Who knew Ava's party would require a large caliber gun and extra ammo? After a count of eight seconds, an incoming round shatters the wood rail above our heads

"Why is this happening?" Ava wails, hands over her ears.

"Stay down," Kyle orders as she struggles against him.

Metal sheeting lines the interior walls to match the fancy orna-mental roof. We might have a chance, dependent on the caliber of the weapon used by our unknown gunman.

I crawl to Kyle's position. "Give me the other bullets."

Kyle eases off Ava and dumps Alex's confiscated rounds from his pocket.

I eject the used casings and reload three into the chamber of my inadequate weapon. When another shot hits the pavilion, I lay down general Spray and Pray fire until the revolver is empty.

Did I hit the gunman?

While I dump the spent cartridges and reload the four remaining bullets, a shot thunks into the water. The attacker isn't clearing and reloading the bolt-action rifle with efficiency. Is it inexperience, nerves, or both?

The sound of running feet heralds the appearance of the three bodyguards and Alex Gordon. I welcome their presence this time as their guns are out and aimed at the distant bank. The men split up to go in different directions around the lake, and I run after Alex, uncaring about my lack of body armor and the glaring blank target I present. After a few steps, I kick off my shoes, preferring to cut my feet on mulch and shrubs rather than sink the spiky heels into the dirt and twist an ankle.

Astonishment crosses Alex's face as I sprint past him.

I wouldn't worry about an errant bullet in the back if he were Warden or anyone from my team.

A figure carrying a rifle crests the hill and disappears. My injured leg cramps, but I reach the peak as a man climbs into a car parked on the roadway below and drives away. Within seconds, Alex joins me.

I point at the disappearing taillights. "Any idea why someone shot at your sister?"

"Did you get a look at the shooter?"

This guy is sure bad at answering questions.

"Caught a glimpse. I'm curious why someone would start a gunfight at your sister's party and why you're armed."

"So are you."

"The gun is Kyle's. And let's go back to why this happened. Do you or your sister have any enemies?"

"No."

I weigh the time it took him to answer and recall being asked the same question by Detective Montoya in the past and lying as Alex did.

"Did you hear the shots over the music?" I say. The revelers continue to dance above us, undisturbed.

Alex pulls his cell from his jacket and points to an app. "The security system showed a breach."

"Why exactly do you need this much security?"

"We like to be careful because of the high-end talent at Ava's parties. What's your deal? You ran right after a man with a gun."

"I have poor impulse control." I head back to the pavilion.

Kyle and Ava are on their feet, and he speaks close to her face. When I approach, he comes toward me, but Ava remains frozen, her posture rigid, and her face a blank.

"Did you get him?"

"No. I saw him before he sped away in a car, but nothing definitive. At least numbnuts and his buddies didn't drill me in the back."

"I heard that," Alex says from behind me. He goes to his sister, puts a protective arm around her, and begins a murmured conversation.

Kyle lowers his voice. "What do you think this was about?"

"No clue." I describe the gunman. "He was about five-ten, wore a ball cap and dark clothing, and drove a four-door car with the license plate covered."

"Do you think it was a leftover assassin from Badger's contract on you?"

"No. Badger had some below-average hired guns, but none were this bad."

My attention returns to the patio, where oblivious partiers dance to the ear-splitting music. Did they think the shots were part of the track? What world am I in again? I retrieve my heels and hold Kyle's shoulder, raise each foot to dust it off, and put them back on.

"You didn't exaggerate about needing me for backup," he says.

"This new existence is almost more hazardous than my job."

Ava and Alex join us.

"Are you okay?" I ask Ava.

She's still pale, and a trembling hand clutches her brother's arm. "That was terrifying. Thank heavens you two were here."

"Do you know who that was or why it happened?" I say.

"I'm not sure." Ava's voice breaks, and her knees buckle. Alex steadies her.

"Let's go back to the house," Alex says, assisting Ava into the golf cart.

On the return trip, Kyle opens his hand to show me the spent casings he collected from my gun. He slides them into his coat pocket. Did the shooter also pick up his brass? Did anyone call the police?

We pull into the private parking area beside the house, and Alex helps Ava to a door leading to a bedroom. He deposits her on a couch, retrieves a water bottle from a miniature fridge, and puts it into Ava's still-shaking hands. Scratches mar her bare legs from when Kyle pushed her to safety.

"Help yourselves." Alex motions to the fridge, but we don't move.

"None of the party-goers noticed the gunfire. How did you?" Kyle says to him.

"As I showed the spitfire there, I have an app to notify me in case of a security breach. A perimeter alert triggered, and we were on our way to check."

"Did you call the police?" I ask him.

"Ava? You should decide since this is your property, not mine," he says.

"This community is already in an uproar because of the murders, and now this." Ava covers her face with her hands. "Oh, god, I thought this ended when I left New York."

"What?" I say. "Did someone shoot at you there?"

"No, but there were problems." She stares at her hands in her lap.

"Like what?" I say.

"I don't want to talk about it right now. Alex, please call 911, but ask the cops to be discreet. I don't want a mass panic."

Kyle says, "If you report someone shot at you, I'm afraid discretion won't be at the forefront of their minds."

Ava sucks in a breath. "You're right. I'm still not thinking straight, sorry."

Alex steps away to make the call, and Kyle sits next to Ava.

"Tell me if I can do anything," he says.

She gives him a weak smile. "You can remind me my life is more important than my parties."

Kyle pats her leg. "You got it."

"I TOLD you it might get crazy," I say to Kyle.

We sit at the kitchen table, hot tea before us and ice on my leg, our party duds exchanged for comfortable clothes.

"When you said crazy, I thought you meant people dancing on tables, drunks in fistfights, not a sniper on a hill."

"We did hear a man yell at a valet for not closing his car door correctly."

"Who knew that was a thing?" Kyle says. "But on a sober note, I think you should carry more firepower. Your location has changed, but who you are—a covert operative—hasn't. You're not two weeks out from defeating a terrorist who had you on a hit list, so you should stay ramped up. Pea shooters aren't what you need against someone with a scope."

"You're right. I should've brought the 9mm and extra magazines."

"And you have Kilburn to contend with, who's concerning in a different way. What happened tonight should remind you never to relax your vigilance. I mean, we handled it due to the fortuitous extra ammo from Ava's bozo brother, but it could've been much worse."

"I don't think the gunman tonight was after me, not that I'm making excuses. After battling Badger's assassins, part of me wants to carry a shotgun under a long coat, wear bandolero pistols strapped across my chest, and have a garrote in a secret ring, but hyper-vigilance can lead to paranoia."

"At least you wouldn't be dead."

"You're right, but I think this shooting tonight was something else."

Kyle sets down his tea. "Why?"

"I'm not sure, but I don't think this is Badger related."

"I counted the time between shots and thought if he was a paid assassin, he needs more time at the range."

"Did Ava tell you about her New York situation?"

"She didn't, but I hope she told the police."

We gave our statements separately to the responding deputy sheriffs, then joined the line to collect our cars. Disappointment over the party closing down and excitement about a potential shooter were the primary topics of conversation among the departing guests. Given what happened, would Ava's future parties be affected, and would she host any more gatherings?

"Ava found you attractive. What did you think of her?" I ask Kyle.

He considers for a moment. "She's beautiful, an original, and at least ten years younger. I don't foresee a future where she moves into my quaint home in the middle of nowhere, content to be a farmer's wife. I doubt she'd find any social currency in the wheat fields."

"Another reason for you and my parents to move here."

"Did you decide to give up your previous life? I thought you were waiting until the end of your year's leave before you made a choice."

"I am."

"Do you have a reason to stay?"

My injury? Making my parents' lives easier? Adair?

"You don't have to talk about it," Kyle continues when I don't answer. "Though Captain America holds your affection, he's across the country and won't quit operating anytime soon."

"Warden's at his peak and in charge of the most elite team. He wouldn't give up his job for me."

The sudden realization hurts.

Why? I wouldn't want him to quit. And if he did, would he want to live with me in Rancho Suprema?

"Has Mean Streets decided if you and Warden can keep working together after he found out you two fraternized?"

Mean Streets is Colonel Streeter's nickname.

"He's going to take the time I'm gone to think about it, although the team told him they don't care."

"What about the man from the magazine? I checked him out after the paparazzi showed up at your parents' place."

"And?"

Kyle gives me a shrewd look. "He's awfully pretty. Is there any depth to him?"

"Yes. He's self-made and kind. Something about being with him brings out a different side of me."

"What side is that?"

"He's a lot of fun and makes me laugh."

"Have you considered getting more serious with him?"

"I don't see how that would work. He has no idea about my past, and I've lied to him so many times I've lost count. With Warden, words are almost superfluous. We share the same occupation and trust each other."

"Working together and having a relationship are two separate things. Training and missions might bury potential problems. What kind of man is Warden outside the team context?"

"More relaxed, of course. We had ten days here without the pressure."

"Spend any of your time talking?"

"Ha-ha. Yes."

"Do you have anything in common with him other than the job?"

"What, like hobbies?"

Kyle gives a quick lift of his shoulders. "Any common interests besides working out, shooting, and going into the depths of hell as teammates."

"He likes to read, not just Brad Thor or Tom Clancy, and doesn't make me sit through *Apocalypse Now* or similar war films for the twentieth time," I say.

"What a Renaissance man. Did you discuss any long-term plans?"

"He's waiting for the year to be up."

"I think you should take this time and sort out your future. If you can't return to work, you'll have to consider whether it will affect your relationship with Warden."

"I think about it all the time."

"What about the other guy?"

"His name's Adair, and although he's a terrific guy, that ship has sailed." My arm shoots up like the topic is blasted into space.

Kyle considers, then says, "I don't believe you."

"It would be unfair to be in a relationship with secrets."

Kyle is thoughtful. "It depends on the man and whether he would understand."

"I'm also afraid if we get involved, he might get killed."

"You take a chance with anyone, even James Warden. You can't stop living your life because of possible threats."

I no longer want to discuss this confounding topic, so I change the subject. "Do you still want to go to the crime scene tonight?"

"Let's leave it. I think we've had enough adventure for one day."

"Are you sure? We didn't do a forty-mile hike with fifty-pound rucks," I say.

"Be glad. A regular compass wouldn't help us navigate the terrain around here."

16

Near four a.m., the vibration of my phone wakes me.

Dragging it toward me, I murmur a sleepy, "Hello?"

"You do remember we're on FaceTime, right?" Warden says.

I sit up and hold the phone out to a more acceptable distance.

"Hey, Bombshell!" Ned pops up in front of Warden, sporting his customary man bun and scruffy beard.

"I'm glad you still look like a knuckle-dragger," I say.

"Love you, too." Ned grins and disappears from view.

"Your hair's a right rat's nest, Davia." Hodge speaks from above Warden's left shoulder. He moves his mammoth body back to allow K a quick nod. K is hotter than Michael B. Jordan but would never cut it as an actor because he's a word miser.

"Hi, Dav." Savant runs a hand through his fair hair.

After returning their greetings, my chest tightens with frustration at not being with them. My attention is drawn by Warden's right eyebrow, where a bullet from a recent mission cut a jagged path, and I'm glad they all are fine.

When the rest of the team leaves, Warden says, "What have you been up to?"

I foolishly charged into a murder scene, disarmed some asshole, got shot at during a party, and kissed Adair after a candlelit dinner on his yacht.

"Oh, nothing as exciting as you, I'm sure."

"It was an ordinary job." His words are formal like he's speaking to a casual acquaintance, not me. "So everything's quiet out there?"

"No Badger blow-back, anything on your end?"

"Nothing." His eyes shift away from me, and his jaw tightens.

"Warden, what's wrong, you—"

"Nothing's wrong."

"I don't believe you."

"I'm tired." His green eyes are stony.

Deciding not to press him further, thinking perhaps their mission was worse than he told me, I say, "Kilburn's out here."

"In Rancho Suprema?"

"Yes. He's trying to locate a spook whose wife and son got murdered."

"A spy in Rancho? Huh. Guess that explains why we got a different sub on this last assignment."

"I hope the new guy didn't bungle the mission."

Would a newbie cause Warden's aloofness?

"He did fine. I'm confused about Kilburn being out there, though."

"You're not the only one. He stopped by here late one night for a chat."

"I don't have to remind you how unstable Kilburn is. He's a grenade with the pin pulled. You need to be careful."

I ignore his lecturing tone. "I am, and Kyle is here to watch my six."

"I bet Kyle's not the only one watching your six."

"What's that supposed to mean?"

A sustained silence passes, then Warden says, "Nothing."

What isn't he telling me? Why is he acting so hostile?

Now I'm awake and move off the bed to perch on an armchair facing the picture window. Outside, stars dot the sky, with wispy clouds painted across them like brush strokes. Memories of previous phone calls filled with affection surface. My battle-hardened man's deep voice repeating, "I miss you, I miss you."

His previous tenderness is gone.

Warden draws me back to the present. "Did the spy kill his own family?"

"I don't know."

"I should go. I'm wiped and need some sleep."

Unspoken questions surge through me like a riptide, but I don't say anything, uncertainty stopping me. After we disconnect, I cradle the phone to my chest as my eyes fill with tears.

As always, I blink them back.

A MERCILESS WORKOUT is the start of my morning. Despite being unable to sleep, wrenched apart by Warden's sudden animosity, I attack my lunges, deadlifts, and sit-ups. When my injured leg begins to ache, I ignore it. If it doesn't collapse, I reason, I can return to a life that makes sense.

I'm near the kitchen when the doorbell rings.

"Good morning." Sherilyn holds up a bag. "I brought you some breakfast."

She's in pink tights and a baggy t-shirt, much more casual than her typical attire.

I step aside to let her in. "I have food here."

"Only because you have a visitor. I should've texted you, but I'm working in the guest house today and wanted to catch up." She pauses. "You look awful, Davia. Do you have a headache?"

"I'm fine. Kyle's out with Bob Brooks, the realtor who sold me this house. They became friends and have been hanging out most days."

"I know Bob; he's a sweetheart. I apologize for getting here early, but I'm so busy now. I posted the photo of me with Adair Monroe at his party we attended on my social media accounts, so my business is booming."

"I'm glad." Thinking of Adair fills me with guilt since I lied by omission to Warden, something I never wanted.

Sherilyn goes into the kitchen and takes out some plates. Opening the paper bag, she places a muffin on each and fills the teapot with water.

"What's new?" She turns on a burner.

"Warden called me early this morning." I can't mask the turmoil.

Sherilyn holds a tea packet and sets it on the counter. "What happened? Did he break up with you?"

"No."

"What's the problem? Does he want someone else? When he was here, he looked at you like you were his whole world."

He had. If only I could throw myself into Warden's arms, unhampered by distance, restrictions, and Aunt Lilah's will. If only Warden never put his life in danger, and we held down regular, predictable jobs. If only.

Sherilyn comes forward to place me in a chair at the kitchen table. She sits as well and leans in. "What's going on? You're not the crying type, but you appear ready to lose it."

"I never told you, but I live here because I inherited money from my aunt, and she put some Machiavellian conditions on the will. One of them is I have to date a millionaire or billionaire once every quarter."

"Oh no. Well, I don't mean *oh no* in a bad way, except for Warden. He doesn't strike me as the type of man who would share. If a level above Alpha male exists, he's their poster boy."

"I told Warden about the requirement, and he said no one could compete with him."

"I can't imagine him saying anything else."

"But when he called last night, he was distant."

"Did he say why?"

I shake my head.

"I bet he saw the magazine cover," Sherilyn guesses. "A picture's worth a thousand words, and it might have hit Warden in a way he didn't expect. If the guy caught kissing his girl was some regular Joe, it wouldn't be much of an issue, but Adair Monroe? He's a major hunk, besides being ungodly rich. Perhaps Warden considers Adair a threat."

Warden? The man who can take on a terrorist cell by himself?

Still, Sherilyn's theory sounds like a reasonable explanation of why he went from caring and cuddly to sullen and sarcastic. The teapot's whistle sounds, and Sherilyn turns off the burner. She returns with hot tea and muffins.

"You might be right." I remove the muffin from its wrapper. "But a vulnerable Warden is hard to imagine."

"Oh, Davia. Men are full of bluster and swagger, declaring they can handle anything in the world, but their act is a total lie. I bet inside Warden's hard body is a man terrified of losing you. I'm sure he wouldn't worry a second if he lived here. There would never be a problem if you woke up with him in your bed daily, but he's in Virginia, right?"

I nod.

"Long-distance relationships are difficult, as I'm sure you realize. Did he say he loves you?"

"Not yet. We worked together for three years, but only kissed right before I moved to Rancho Suprema. The sum total of our time together as a couple is the ten days he was here. Our relationship is too new for those sentiments."

Sherilyn forces a mug into my hand and instructs me to take a drink, which I do.

"You told me your life was complicated, and you were right," she says.

"I naively thought if I dated men I didn't care for to comply with the will, it wouldn't be a problem. Then I met Adair. No matter how much I care about Warden, something draws me toward him when we're together. I returned the comb to close things off, but we kissed, and I lied to Warden. My life is off the rails."

Sherilyn puts down her drink. "Davia, stop. You're a woman, not a robot. Life presented you with an unexpected choice and a damn fine one. You're young, single, and can take time to discover if either—or neither—of these men is what you want."

"I guess."

"Now, eat some breakfast. You can't figure out your whole future on an empty stomach."

I take a bite of the muffin. Was this what having a close girlfriend meant? Confidences were foreign to me, emotions a distraction. Had I ever talked about man problems with another woman? Never.

Am I suddenly in one of those rom-coms where all women do is complain about their love lives?

"Has your visitor enjoyed being here?" Sherilyn asks.

"Kyle's been playing a lot of golf, and I took him to a party at Ava Gordon's last night."

"Did he like it?"

"It was a mixed experience." I'm not in the mood to discuss the shooting.

"Ava spends a fortune on her events, and people brag if they're invited. Was her brother Alex there?"

"Yes."

"I saw him at a party. He's eye candy with a bad boy vibe." Sherilyn waggles her eyebrows and I laugh.

"He possesses an ego to match."

"Many men do."

"Has Detective Montoya called you?"

"No."

"I passed on your number, but he's handling the Myles murder case."

"He is? The murders are the biggest story in Rancho and beyond, so now I won't be as upset he hasn't contacted me."

"Did you ever meet the Myles family?"

"I met Stephanie Myles once. She asked me to turn a bedroom into a nursery but didn't hire me. I was glad."

"Glad? Why?"

"I don't like to speak ill of the dead, but she was so particular about everything and super aggressive with her demands. She initially wanted a crib made of solid gold costing nearly seventeen million dollars."

"Seventeen what?"

"Million. She then considered a sixty-thousand dollar crib like Kim Kardashian used but decided she didn't want to be a Kardashian imitator. She also told me to order two dozen onesies costing $200 a piece, a $4,000 stroller, and a baby wrap made from Vicuña fiber. If you don't know, a Vicuña is from the camel family and only lives in the Andes in South America. The wrap alone costs $8,000! The list of expensive items was never-ending, and she kept changing her mind because she wasn't sure whether the baby would be a boy or a girl. I doubt she would've been happy with the results, even if they were perfect."

"I can't begin to imagine spending those amounts. Did you meet anyone else in the family?"

"Her husband came in, but there was some sort of animosity between them."

"Like what?"

"Oh, nothing overt, just those side-eye glares couples give each other when they're not getting along, which kind of surprised me if they were planning on another baby. He picked up some paperwork from the counter and left the room. Neither spoke."

"How long ago did this happen?"

"I have to check my calendar, but—oh my god. The murders were three or four days later. I can't bear to think about it! Now I'm thrilled I didn't get the job."

The gate buzzer rings, and I excuse myself to check the monitor.

"It's Bob and Kyle."

We go out through the courtyard as the duo drives up. Bob rolls down his window and greets us as Kyle retrieves his golf bag. "I picked up a new listing, so I must run to a showing." He drives off with a cheery wave.

I introduce Kyle to Sherilyn, and she opens the trunk of her white Mercedes and lifts out two hefty bags bulging with something.

"Do you need some help?" Kyle says.

"Yes, thank you." She hands him one of the bags. "I'm almost done in the guest house. Sorry that I didn't finish it, but I needed a few items still on backorder. I mean, like, how hard is it to obtain luxury window treatments? I ordered them *weeks* ago. I should have done more research to find the material and made them myself, but I wanted this one type of expensive linen, and— "

"The house has plenty of room," Kyle interrupts.

"Yes, but I wanted to finish before Davia had any company. Davia's man, Warden, showed up out of the blue, and I waited for those darned curtains the whole time he was here, not that he would have used the guest house or anything, but still. How do you two know each other, by the way?"

"We were neighbors in South Dakota. I met Davia when she was eleven," Kyle says.

"Around sixteen years ago now," I say. "Hard to believe it's been that long."

I was thirteen. Kyle wore protective padding and handed me an airsoft pistol.

"Shooting at a person who's moving while you're also in motion isn't like stationary target practice," he said. "I want you to aim for my torso and continue firing until you run out of rounds. Soft knees, okay?"

Kyle put on protective eyewear and a padded helmet and moved away, aiming his gun at me, pretending he would fire. Though he hadn't had the prosthetic leg for long, his movement to the side was smooth and fast. I pulled the trigger and missed. My arm bounced as I sprinted to catch him, and I realized a running gunfight was harrowing.

"I can't wait to learn more about Davia as a child," Sherilyn says. "You'll have to tell me all about her. Oh, Davia, I forgot to ask you earlier, but we got sidetracked. Have you thought of anything you need for the house?"

"Now you mention it; the master needs a comfy chair, a reading lamp, and some books to fill those built-in cases."

"How many books do you want? For 300 feet of bookshelf space, I can order one-hundred feet of classics, fifty of general fiction, fifty of science fiction or fantasy, and—"

I put up a hand. "What are you talking about?"

"Nowadays, people order categories of books by the foot."

"By the foot?" I echo. "No, just no. I prefer to go book hunting on my own."

"Okay, if you want."

"Ready to go to work?" Kyle says to her.

"Yes. I'll text you photos of chair possibilities."

"Thanks."

Kyle follows Sherilyn to the guest house as she peppers him with questions about South Dakota.

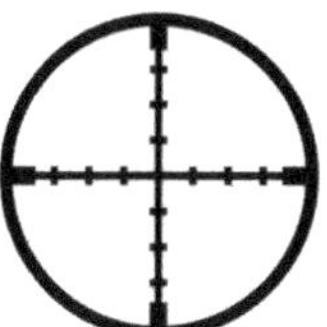

Kyle comes to find me. "I need to borrow some ear protection."

"Going shooting?"

"No. I might have to spend more time with your designer. That young lady sure can talk."

"She can, but Sherilyn's become a friend."

"I'll trust your judgment. Besides, we men have monopolized your time for too long." He refers to my all-male unit and his operator friends, who added to my training over the years.

"I'm still not used to her, but having a close girlfriend is a first. Anything you want to do today?"

"You don't seem up to par. Did all the excitement last night interfere with your sleep?"

"I'm fine."

Kyle lifts a skeptical eyebrow but doesn't question me. "I'm up for whatever you are."

We decide on a trip to Balboa Park, a 1,200-acre space near downtown San Diego. After parking, we walk past the Spreckels Organ Pavilion, where a sign indicates it was constructed in 1914 in preparation for the Panama-California Exposition. It houses the largest outdoor pipe organ globally in an ornate, carved structure. No one is playing, so we continue past rows of empty metal seating and toward a Japanese Friendship Garden. We stop to consider if we want to visit any museums.

"We might have picked up a tail," Kyle says.

"Is it Kilburn?"

"No. Maybe it's my usual paranoia."

"Want to do some dry cleaning?" I use a spy term for taking action to check for followers.

Kyle indicates a cart serving beverages and snacks. "I'll order some coffee, and you can verify."

While he waits in line to order, I lean against a pillar, a natural turn-around for counter-surveillance. I pretend to be bored, gazing down and scuffing the toe of one tennis shoe against the sidewalk as I scan the area over the top of my shades. A man in nondescript clothes across the parking lot is too interested in his phone.

Is it someone from Badger's crew out for revenge? Perhaps Warden and I were wrong to conclude no one would take over Badger's vast terrorist organization.

Kyle returns and hands me a bottle of cold Perrier.

"What's the verdict?" He takes a swig of his coffee.

"One guy. He's more super snooper than assassin."

"Describe him."

I do, and Kyle says, "I spotted one more, same profile."

"What did we do to merit this?"

"I think you can remove me from the equation. What did *you* do?"

"I'm not sure unless this has something to do with Markus Myles or Kilburn."

We walk past a long reflecting pond filled with lilies and koi. A building made of slatted wood with a sign indicating the structure contains a botanical exhibit sits at its end and has two entrances. Inside, sunlight filters through the ceiling, and the space brims with orchids and mixed tropical plants. People fill the narrow walkways, stopping to admire the foliage.

"On the end." Kyle indicates a basket of blooms near the ceiling. I pretend to be interested but let my eyes drift to pick out one of the followers. I spot the other man propped against a bridge outside.

"Let me take your picture." Kyle pulls out his phone, and I pose in different locations so he can snap both men in the background. We link arms and put our heads together.

"Get them?" I say.

"Think so."

"I'd like to find out their identities."

"Want to corner them?" Kyle says.

"If they step a hair out of line, I'm game."

"Roger that."

We leave the building and make our way to the Art Village. As we browse paintings, jewelry, and pottery made by artists in individual shops, two men draw my attention. I nudge Kyle.

"Is there a problem?"

"I think we picked up more followers."

"More?" Kyle continues to examine the piece of pottery in his hand.

"Middle Eastern, two of them."

"Are they following our followers or us?"

"I can't tell."

"Badger's people?"

I shrug.

A holster containing my 9mm Sig Sauer is tucked securely in my front waistband. In Kyle's jacket pocket are my .22 and two speed loaders. Not altering our rambling course, we cross the multi-colored tiled courtyard and drift in and out of more shops.

"I want to buy something for your folks but need my hands free," Kyle says.

"We can ship," a helpful salesperson offers.

Kyle selects a cerulean blue blown-glass vase. After paying, we join a crowd of people on a sidewalk leading toward the San Diego Zoo.

"The second set of guys are in their late twenties, average height and build on both, and wear dark jeans and jackets," I say.

"One's in front of us, one behind, a smart technique. I'd put them down as tourists if they didn't have such hardened demeanors."

"The funny thing is, the other two don't appear aware of them."

"I'm beginning to suspect the first two are FBI."

We pass a miniature train with parents and children riding in orange and white striped carriages. A conductor travels in the front near the engine wearing a jaunty blue cap and leather gloves.

"Would you like to buy a ticket?" Kyle says.

"The kid in me does, but I don't want these people enjoying a day out to become collateral damage."

"So, what's our plan?"

"I wish I knew this area better, but I don't, which makes rousting our tails more difficult. We can tour the San Diego Zoo and find out if they will continue to follow us."

"And here I thought this would be a vacation," Kyle says, but I know he's teasing. I can tell he enjoys using his old skills.

We buy tickets to the zoo, the musky smell of exotic animals scenting the air. Our followers choose to wait outside, and the tension in my shoulders eases a fraction. Kyle points to an enclosure filled with bright pink flamingos. "In case you're interested, a group of flamingos is called a flamboyance."

"If my parents ever host a trivia night, you're my partner."

After a thirty-five-minute bus tour on a double-decker, we study maps and follow paths lined with exotic plants and trees. We pass enclosures with tigers, hippos, and other animals and descend through an immense aviary. Several hours later, Kyle limps, and my leg shoots lightning strikes of pain down its length. We catch the Sky Tram so we don't have to walk back across the zoo, and enjoy the view of the Laurel Street Bridge and the Museum of Man's distinctive tiled tower. The ride deposits us near the front entrance. Before departing, we stop for ice cream cones and a rest.

"What do you think? Check out the Reptile House, and call it a day?" I say, and Kyle agrees.

After we peruse the assorted reptiles, including some poisonous vipers, we square our shoulders to confront any real threat outside the gates.

"The zoo only has one exit," Kyle says. We have our hands stamped for re-entry should we need a quick line of retreat but don't spot any of the men tailing us outside. Flagging a pedicab driver to bike us in a shaded cart, we head back to the car.

"Think we lost them?" I ask Kyle when we arrive at the Rover.

"Not sure."

I pay for the ride while he checks our surroundings.

"The coast is clear," Kyle says as I unlock the doors.

"The first two were FBI, not Company guys." My covert black ops unit is an operation based with the CIA, and I'm familiar with their tactics.

"They did appear to be fumblers," Kyle agrees. "But what about those other two?"

"I can't tell if they're from a middle-eastern counterpart to our secret agencies or assassins."

"At least they aren't paparazzi."

Checking mirrors as I drive, I don't pick out any tails.

"We've gone black," I tell Kyle.

"Agreed."

When we near the turn-off to Rancho Suprema, Kyle says. "As time grows closer to me leaving, I want to reiterate my concerns. You conquered near-impossible tasks training to make it into your unit, but out here, something's missing. Today you spotted those additional men following us, but you're distracted. What's going on?"

Kyle recognized something was wrong earlier and spent the day observing me. My thoughts are in such turmoil I almost miss our exit.

"Warden's back and called early this morning. He talked to me like we were casual acquaintances."

"Did something go wrong on their mission?"

"I thought of that first, but the other guys said hello, and acted the same as usual. Sherilyn thinks the magazine cover upset him."

"If he's like the men I know in our line of work, the cover wouldn't go over well at all. Warden might be having an internal tantrum because he got jealous and hates himself for it," Kyle says. "Still, you're more unsettled than some spat with your man would make you."

Frustration twists my lips. "Most people would accept the life Aunt Lilah provided without a thought, but the duality of my existence is tearing me apart. I try to fit in here, but I don't. I miss my team and want to return to action, but I might never be fit enough to pass a physical with my leg acting up. If I don't pull my weight, I'll endanger the whole team."

"Nerve damage takes time to heal, and you need to give it a few more months at the least. Don't push yourself and make it worse. To recover, you need to rest."

"Rest? I don't want to rest. I need to figure out which way my life will go."

"You can't afford to be distracted by what will or won't happen in the future, because inattention might kill you in the meantime."

I pull into my drive. "You're right, but it's ironic that I live in one of the most exclusive communities in the country and must stay prepared for the worst."

"And you live in one location. Patterns and predictability are killers."

"I know."

The gate swings open.

"Until you have an answer to your dilemma, remember to live by our motto," Kyle says.

"I will."

Stay alert, stay alive.

18

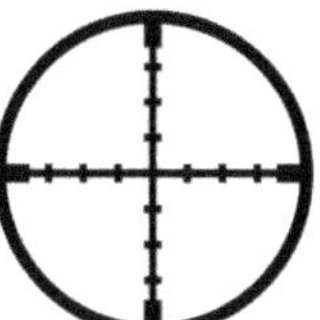

An unfamiliar car fills a space near my garage, and José and Detective Montoya stand near its front.

After parking, we approach them. "Didn't expect to find you here, Detective," I say.

I introduce Kyle to Montoya, and they shake hands. He greets José, then excuses himself to go inside and rest.

"I'm talking to Mr. Macías about Enrique Flores's murder," Montoya says. "I stopped in to ask him for more background information since the deceased's immediate family is still too distraught, plus the case isn't in my jurisdiction. There are no leads so far."

"I told the detective I can't think of any reason someone would kill Enrique," José says. "I hope they catch whoever did this, and soon."

"You guys want to come in for something to drink?" I invite.

José declines. "I'm going out for dinner."

Montoya says, "Would you mind if I stick around until dark so you can show me where you were when you saw the gunfire?"

"Of course. Let's go inside." We enter the house. "What would you like to drink?"

"Water's fine, but you own a fancy espresso machine. Were you lying to me about not drinking coffee?"

"No. The rest of the world drinks the stuff, so I bought one, but I've never used it."

Montoya runs a hand over the appliance. "I'll figure it out if you have any coffee."

"I bought some for Kyle's visit."

I locate the coffee bean container and grinder, hand them to Montoya, and he sets them on the counter.

"I think we should let this heat up, so I'll take some water," he says.

We go out to the back patio and sit in lounge chairs. Three colorful hot air balloons dot the sky and make whooshing sounds when the operators hit the flame to cause them to ascend.

"You have a magnificent view," Montoya says. "It's so peaceful here."

"It is." *When assassins don't attack me, Kilburn doesn't pop in for a visit, and no one is murdered.* "Any updates on Tilly Myles?"

"She regained consciousness but doesn't remember anything about the murders. She might, with time, but I don't want to press her. Relatives are with her at the hospital."

The sky fades from blue to pink, red, and yellow shades, and the temperature dips.

I stand. "Ready to check the espresso machine?"

While Montoya preps the coffee, I find him a cup and lean against the kitchen island. Kyle joins us, his eyes on the dark liquid pouring into Montoya's mug.

"Didn't expect you to be up," I greet.

"The aroma is irresistible," Kyle says.

"I'll remember to use it as a lure," I say. "How are you?"

"I just needed to lie down and reset."

Montoya fills another cup for Kyle. They sip their brews, contented smiles spreading over their faces. We go outside, and I show them my position the night of the murders and the window of the Myles' home. Montoya and Kyle stand shoulder to shoulder, staring at the now-dark window across the valley.

"You would have heard unsuppressed gunfire," Kyle says. "Think the shooter used a suppressor and subsonic rounds?"

"Most likely," I say.

"Are you familiar with guns?" Montoya asks Kyle.

"Somewhat."

The detective's penetrating gaze goes between us, and I imagine the gears in his mind whirring with suspicion.

Kyle taps Montoya's arm. "Do you have the keys to that place, by any chance?"

"I put them in my car. Why?"

"I'd like to look at the scene."

Montoya studies him. "And your reason is?"

"I'm curious, that's all."

"Uh-huh." Montoya's brows draw together. "Curiosity killed—"

"You'll both be amped all night because of your caffeine dose," I interrupt.

Montoya weighs this. "I wouldn't mind going over your path that night, but you do what I tell you."

"Of course," I say, and Kyle nods.

We take separate cars, Montoya in his plain wrap and us in the Rover. Once parked, we wait for Montoya to clip a radio to his belt. He unlocks a pedestrian entrance next to the driveway as a dense fog creeps in, its thick moisture creating ground clouds that obscure the property.

"After you," Montoya says. I step into the haze, point out where I parked my car, and make for the side gate with the men behind me. The pool's water is still, and I think about how it won't be used by the Myles family again. Stopping outside the door I entered, Montoya finds the correct key.

We step into the laundry room and move toward the kitchen, pausing to let our eyes adjust to the scant light. We don't speak, the tragedy of what occurred muting our words. The men follow me across the living room to the corridor that leads to the bedrooms. The master lies to the right.

I don't move.

In a room at the opposite end of the hallway, a flashlight clicks off.

<h1 style="text-align:center">19</h1>

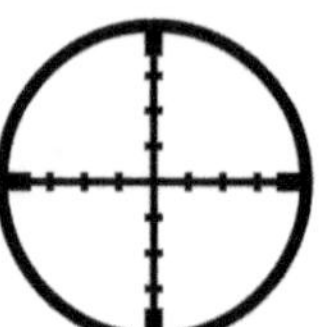

"Someone's in here," I whisper. "Last room on the left."

Montoya removes his weapon from his shoulder holster and clicks on a small flashlight.

"Stay here," he mouths, moving toward the room. He's in a vulnerable position, at the front of a funnel, and isn't wearing body armor.

Wait, Ms. Hypocrite. Last night, I wore a white cocktail dress while pursuing a shooter.

When he's about five feet away, I trail him. Kyle stays at the intersection.

"Who are you, and what are you doing?" Montoya calls as he nears the door.

Something sails out of the room, Montoya ducks, and a metal trashcan crashes to the floor.

"Will you stop throwing things? I'm from the Sheriff's Department, and you should come out and talk to me."

A clamor from within the room is the response.

"Aw, man. Don't go out the window," Montoya says with exasperation.

I rush forward, but he stops me. "The dude can't outrun a radio."

He puts out a description that matches the gunman's profile from the Gordon's party. I wheel around and run for the front door. Montoya yells for me to stop, but I don't. If this is the same person who shot at us at Ava's, I want to catch him. I pull open the door, duck under the evidence tape, and bolt down the stairs.

Thick gray ground clouds distort the scene, but footfalls alert me to the escaping intruder's route. A dim shape scrambles up a side embankment, and I sprint in his direction.

"Davia, don't." Detective Montoya closes the distance between us.

I scale the hillside, vault over a short wooden fence, and find myself on the street. A vehicle speeds straight at me. I leap out of the way and crash to the asphalt.

Taillights disappear into the heavy mist.

Montoya is beside me in seconds. "Did you get the plate?"

"The fog's too thick. The car was a late model sedan, dark." I take the hand he puts out, and he pulls me up.

Montoya relays the information on his radio as distant sirens grow louder. When he finishes, he says, "What is it with you? You're not law enforcement."

"Why didn't you go after him, then?"

His nostrils flare. "Experience tells me a radio's faster."

I never worked Montoya's job, plus I knew things about the intruder he didn't; if it was the same person who shot up Ava's gathering, that is. As we head back, his radio crackles. He steps away to speak, and I remind myself I'm a civilian in this setting, nothing more.

Kyle waits for us on the front steps. "Didn't catch him, eh?"

"No, but he thanked me for chasing him by trying to run me over," I say.

"Are you okay?"

"Yes."

"Did you touch anything in the office?" Montoya asks Kyle.

"No."

"I requested an evidence team to recheck it," Montoya says.

Sorry for the words I exchanged with him earlier, I say, "Did you receive a call last night about a shooting in Rancho Suprema?"

"All shootings are in our briefings, and I told Detective Worth from my team to look into the matter."

"I think you need to check yourself. Kyle and I were at a party where a man with a sniper rifle matching the description you put out on the radio began shooting at the host."

"Only the host?"

"Well, Kyle and I were in the line of fire."

"Is someone after you again?" Montoya bore witness to the consequences of previous assassins trying to kill me.

"Not at the moment, and I'm telling you the truth."

"I take it he got away?"

"Yes."

"And I bet you chased him." The statement isn't a question.

My expression conveys he's correct.

"Whose party?"

"Ava Gordon's."

"The name's not ringing a bell." Montoya tips his face up to stare into the sky, lost in thought.

A patrol car pulls in, and Montoya goes to speak with the deputies. When he returns, he says, "No one's found a vehicle or person matching the description. The fog complicates visibility, and he might have parked or taken a side road. They're still searching."

"If someone is familiar with the area, it might be a clue to his identity," I say.

"Possibly."

"Do you still need us?" I say.

"Actually, yes. Let's go back inside and continue from where we left off."

We return to the hall intersection, and I describe the state of Tilly and Eric's bedrooms, then go to the master.

"Was the door open or closed?" Montoya gestures to the threshold.

"Partly closed."

"What made you enter?"

"A cry from someone in distress."

After viewing the dark room, Montoya touches a wall switch. Lamps on either side of the bed come on, leaving me to stare down at the bloody carpet where Stephanie Myles died. Kyle leans on the doorframe, expression impassive.

I recall both pillows on the bed holding indentations, the covers thrown to the side like someone got up in a rush. The bedclothes are gone, but I tell Montoya and explain how I checked Stephanie's body, started to leave, heard a faint noise, and went to the opposite side of the bed. I demonstrate my position, staring at more bloodstains darkening the floor.

"And this is when I called 911."

"Got it," Montoya says. "Do you remember anything else?"

I indicate the window facing my house. "Those curtains were open."

"We closed them to stop lookie-loos."

"Did I mess up any evidence left by the killer?"

"You, the paramedics, and a deputy did a number on any possible footprints trying to save Tilly."

"How about DNA?" I say, and the detective shakes his head.

"Did you find any brass?" Kyle says to Montoya.

"No."

"Care to share the caliber of the murder weapon?" I say.

Montoya hesitates, then says, ".45."

"Not mine, as I'm sure you know by now."

Montoya nods, and we go back outside.

"Do you still need us?" I say.

"No, but if you think of anything else, call or text."

We make our farewells, and Kyle returns with me to the Rover.

"Tonight's intruder description is similar to last night's shooter, but it doesn't mean they're the same person," I say. "One gunman had a sophisticated setup with a suppressor, subsonic rounds, and tightly grouped shots; the other had a bolt-action rifle and subpar skills. It argues against any Myles and Ava Gordon connection."

"Unless they both ran afoul of the gunman or gunmen."

"Montoya will find any connection if there is one."

"After you two ran out, I shined my phone's flashlight at the surface of the office. On the carpet were footprints of a man's shoe, size nine or ten."

"Anything distinctive?"

"They didn't penetrate the carpet with a heavy tread, so the person's average weight."

"The fog made it difficult, but the glimpse I got backs up your conclusion."

We're cautious on our return. I park down the road and walk to a vantage point to scope for enemies while Kyle checks in the opposite direction, but we find no one. As we drive toward the gate, I say, "I should sell this place and buy another every few months to mix things up."

"Wouldn't be a bad idea, but vigilance is a priority no matter where you are."

20

"**Y**ou're doing what?" Kyle stops buttering his toast.

"Taking a lesson in how to walk in five-inch heels. It will be more difficult than anything you've taught me."

"And you have an instructor for this sort of thing?"

"Yes. After all the perils I survived in my life so far, I don't want to die falling off a catwalk."

After breakfast, I head to Bryce's Boutique, dreading the one hour we've set aside to practice before he opens for business. He rushes up to where I wait by his locked door.

"*Bonjour!*" After turning on the lights, he secures the bolt so we won't be disturbed. Hurrying to the rear of the store, he shoves several revolving racks to the side and picks up a shoebox. When he returns, he puts it into my hands.

"Here, put these on."

"I'm scared."

"*Tu blagues.*"

"No, I'm not joking."

I open the lid to reveal pumps with towering stiletto heels. Finding a chair, I change into them and stand. The shoes force my body into an awkward angle, and pain shoots down my leg.

"Are you all right?" Bryce puts his hand under my arm.

"Yes."

"Then why are you pale as a ghost?"

The pain subsides. "I'm nervous."

After Bryce gives me some preliminary instructions and a quick demonstration, I make my first attempt. When I reach the end and turn, Bryce's hand is over his eyes.

"*Non.* Eyes forward, shoulders back, one foot *before* the other, not *beside* the other."

For the next fifteen minutes, I make a complete fool of myself. Who knew walking in a straight line was so tricky? When I achieve a few semi-acceptable run-throughs, we take a break. I sink into a chair, take off the heels, and rub my feet. Bryce disappears into the back of his store and returns with a roll of shiny material.

"What's that?"

"What they use for the fashion show walkway." He spreads it out and begins to secure the piece. "I forgot to ask, how did your date with Mr. Monroe go?"

"It wasn't a—I gave him back his gift."

"Where did he take you?" Bryce tapes down a corner.

"His superyacht."

He stops. "Tell me everything."

I describe Adair's helicopter and the features on his yacht as Bryce continues with his project.

When I finish, Bryce says, "And what aren't you telling me?"

"What do you mean?"

"You didn't tell me what happened between you and Adair." He puckers his lips and makes smooching sounds.

"We—" I almost blush at the memory of Adair's insistent kisses. "We aren't going to see each other anymore."

Bryce lifts an eyebrow. "Does *he* know that?"

"Don't you think we should finish practicing? You need to open soon."

Two steps in on the new surface, my feet slide in different directions, and I fall with a hard thump.

"*Quelle catastrophe*," Bryce exclaims.

The second time goes as well as the first, but the white surface of the makeshift runway triggers a memory of training for winter warfare.

Our plane flew over blinding white terrain, the back ramp open. I jumped out. The frigid air was a hard slap to my system as the canopies of my teammates' parachutes floated below me. I landed, the force from my drop burying me in snow up to my chest. Struggling to breathe, I twisted and dug to reach the surface.

It took almost an hour for us to free ourselves. We gathered our equipment, donned skis, and headed for our destination without speaking. Making camp, we didn't light a fire since it might give away our position. Instead, we tunneled into the snow and did some tactical spooning to share our body heat.

Reflecting on this puts the runway's surface into perspective. After several more inelegant attempts, I manage to traverse it. Before I can celebrate, Bryce uses some padding to give the material a slope.

I frown. "Will the fashion show be like downhill skiing at the Olympics?"

"The ramp always slants. Again."

A few steps in, I slide toward the back wall and slam into a clothes rack, knocking it down.

"*Mon Dieu!*" Bryce is back to covering his eyes.

Righting the rack, I return to where he stands and start over.

Bryce unlocks the shop door when our time is up and lets several impatient women enter. After thanking him profusely, I head to my car as a text comes through from Kyle, notifying me he's off to play a final round with Bob. I settle in the driver's seat when my phone displays a video call request from Warden.

How will this go?

"Did I catch you at a bad time?" His expression is relaxed, unlike the previous call. His black t-shirt is stretched tight across his chest, and his developed biceps bulge.

"Your timing's perfect. Did you work out?" I ask.

He grins. "How'd you guess?"

"Pumped up there, big boy," I say.

"What have you been doing?"

"Nothing as fun as you. I just finished a lesson in how to walk in five-inch heels."

"For real?"

I nod.

"Why?"

"More Ladies' League lunacy. I'm on their board to satisfy another of Aunt Lilah's will conditions, and one of their requirements is I model in their fashion show."

Warden's eyes fill with mirth, and I wait for him to erupt into laughter, but he composes himself and says, "You'll have to give me a private showing of your new skills."

He's back to being the man who can leave me breathless with a look.

"Davia, I need to apologize. The last time we spoke, I was a complete ass."

No kidding.

"I said I could handle you dating other guys, but Ned brought in a copy of a magazine with you on the cover kissing the Brit I met at the gala. He read the article aloud to the team, emphasizing how rich the guy is and how he's one of the world's hottest bachelors. The team's comments of 'You can't compete with him,' and 'Bombshell's going to dump your ass,' got me. I didn't have a handle on my feelings when I called you."

I understand how much this admission costs him. "I'm sorry."

"Don't be. You told me you had to date other men. At the time, I thought of it as a job like any of our assignments."

"I view it that way, too."

"Do you? Davia, I can't compete with someone like him financially. If you want a different life, I won't blame you."

"I intend to place Adair in the rearview."

"Honestly? Distance separates us, and I won't be there if you need someone. You know my position doesn't allow much time for travel to California."

"I'll be back as soon as my leave ends."

"Will you? For sure?" His face fills with hope.

"I want to, but I can't promise."

"Why?"

"Right now, I couldn't pass a physical because of my injury."

Warden frowns. "How bad is it?"

"Not good." Not good in our lingo translates to it hurts like being run over by a dump truck and set afire.

"I didn't note any issues when I was there."

"If I recall, we spent most of our time horizontal."

He chuckles. "True."

"I won't find out whether this is a permanent problem for at least three or four months."

"What's been the issue?"

"Sudden, extreme pain to the point I almost collapse. I can't predict when it will happen."

"I won't insult you by pretending you'll be fine, but I wish I were there to hold you. I want to be with you instead of getting by on calls, texts, and memories."

I recall the heat of his bare skin, his rough hands running down my body, and the passion burning between us as he placed me against any surface where we indulged our desires. Then there were contrasting moments when I propped my head against one of his muscular thighs on the couch while we both read books, or he reached for my hand as we walked on the Rancho Suprema trails.

Fighting the rush of longing, I say, "What do you think we should do?"

"I know what I want to do."

"I think I can guess."

He gives me a slow smile. "Tell me."

"You want to try to beat me at knife fighting."

Warden sits back. "All right, smartass. I shouldn't tell you what else I was going to say."

"What?"

"Something I should've told you before I left." He hesitates. "I know you're required to date other men, but I want you to be all mine. I'm not sure I realized how much you meant to me until that magazine cover hit me harder than a mortar shell."

His eyes are soft and full of his feelings. I want to run my hand down the planes of his high cheekbones and kiss him. I want to block out the world so we can be together, and I don't pretend to be someone I'm not and lie to almost everyone around me.

Nothing is easy is the mantra of my life.

"What if my leg doesn't improve, though?"

"You can move in with me. We can find a different apartment and replace my thrift store furniture, but it would be quite a step down from your current lifestyle."

I picture the situation. Me, a stay-at-home—what?

A door opens, and a man I recognize as aide Luke Upton says, "Warden, Colonel Streeter needs you in his office immediately."

"Be right there." The door clicks shut, and Warden says, "I'll call you tonight."

BEFORE I DRIVE HOME, I think of Ava and text her.

Me: *How are you?*

Ava: *Want to get together for breakfast?*

We arrange to meet at a nearby restaurant. Ava joins me at a table on a covered patio, and sits across from me. "Where's Kyle?"

"Playing golf with a friend; he leaves tomorrow."

"Will he be back anytime soon?"

"I don't think so. He's a farmer with a lot of responsibilities."

"Remember the old saying, good men are hard to find, and hard men are good to find?" She giggles. "I wish he lived here."

"Uh—"

"You don't think of him that way, do you?"

"We met when I was young, so I never considered his love life."

A server brings menus and takes our drink orders.

"Are you dating anyone other than Adair Monroe?" Ava teases.

"Yes, but he doesn't live here."

"Too bad. My brother's interested in you. Most women don't turn him down, so he views you as a challenge."

Just shoot me.

Anxious to change the subject, I say, "How are you doing? Please be honest."

Ava's grip tightens on the sides of the menu. "I left New York due to death threats, so when the Myles murders came up on our trip to L.A., memories I kept repressed flooded back.

"Did someone follow you out here?"

She lifts a shoulder. "I didn't think so until the party."

The server interrupts our conversation to take our orders. After he leaves, I say, "Why don't you have bodyguards? You're the one who needs them, not your brother."

Is it a Rancho rule that only people who don't need bodyguards are allowed to employ them?

"I told myself I'd never endure living in fear again," she says. "I set the security system whenever I'm home and hire extra protection for my parties, but a bodyguard is a reminder of something I want to put out of my mind."

"What happened, if you don't mind me asking?"

Ava's hands curl into fists, then she gives a quick head shake, and her hands relax.

"You don't need to talk about it," I assure her.

"I'll be all right." She blinks several times. "I was about your age and on top of the world. I made money, went to parties, and lived a thrilling existence against the backdrop of New York. A person from work told me about an opportunity to volunteer at a charity for foster children, and I thought it would be a needed balance for my life."

Our meals arrive, and I don't push Ava to tell me anything else. She takes a few bites and says, "I attended classes to learn about being a volunteer, met others from the organization, and volunteered once or twice a month. I became friends with another woman who worked there. One day, she invited me out for lunch, and her husband was in the area and came by. When he found out I worked on Wall Street, we talked about investments and had much in common. The woman was upset by this, and weird stuff began to happen."

"Like what?"

Ava swallows. "First, it was texts. I didn't know who sent them, but they were unsettling. Like, *I saw you near the carousel in Central Park,* or *I love your new haircut.* After the texts, there are calls from an unknown number, and someone breathes into the phone."

"That sounds disturbing."

"It got *much* worse. At times, my neck's hair stood up, but I saw no one."

"Did you ever find out who was doing it?"

"No, but I met loads of people, so it was hard to be sure." Ava straightens, chest raised. "One time, someone broke in. They took all the makeup, dumped it in the sink, and wrote in red lipstick on the mirror, *Die, Bitch.* The phrase was a horror movie cliché but still scary. Took all the clothes from the closet, poured bleach on them..." Her voice trails off like she's hiding from the memory.

"Did they ever find out who did it?"

"No. The doorman was on a lunch break, and there were no security cameras and no witnesses."

"Is that why you moved?"

"Yes, I needed to begin anew."

"And now the problem's escalated from bleach to bullets."

Ava picks up her coffee cup, holds it in front of her, and contemplates the contents before answering. "I don't understand how the shooting connects to what happened in New York."

"The shooter was a man. Can you think of a man who might want to harm you? A jealous ex-boyfriend?"

"No."

"Is there a reason whoever killed Stephanie and Eric Myles might be after you?"

"A detective came by and asked me the same thing."

"A man or a woman?"

"A good-looking man, a little too intense for me, but I'm a bundle of nerves anyway."

So, Montoya followed up. "What did you say?"

"I didn't know what to say. I invested in Maxim Myles, like lots of people here. Defense contractors will always be in business given the state of the world, so their company was a safe bet, but I'm like any other investor."

"Quite a few people were angry, and some were violent, about the stock price decrease. How about you?"

"The market has ups and downs. I don't waste time getting emotional about stocks since fluctuations occur daily."

"Makes sense," I say. "Please continue to be careful, though. I don't want to lose one of my few friends."

"Don't worry. We need each other to survive that wretched fashion show."

21

Kyle drives up in the Rover as I park in the garage.

"How was your game today?"

"I hit a neat backhander and stayed out of the cat box."

"Those terms are Greek to me."

"And I'm sure you don't want to learn the definitions," he says.

"True."

"How was your lesson?"

"That's another subject we shouldn't discuss."

Kyle laughs. "I'll leave my clubs in the back since I'm flying out tomorrow."

"I can't believe you're leaving already."

"I wish I could stay longer, but I'm due in Washington to testify in front of the Senate Committee on Veteran's Affairs. We're losing twenty-two veterans a day to suicide, and I'm an attempt survivor, so speaking up is more than my duty."

"I'm proud of you," I say as we enter the house.

"Besides the high-heel lesson, is there anything else you don't want to discuss?"

"You're so funny. Warden called and apologized, and I had break-fast with Ava. She asked about you."

"And?"

"She's disappointed you're leaving."

"Me, too, but the situation's complicated."

At last, someone besides me who uses the word complicated regarding the opposite sex.

As if on cue, my phone sounds, and the caller ID flashes, "Adair Monroe." I hesitate, then answer. "Hello?"

"What do you want from me?" His voice comes from a distance.

Is this a butt dial or something?

I catch bits of what appears to be a tense conversation between Adair and a man whose voice I don't recognize. Although the stranger's words are indistinct, their tone is threatening. Kyle notes my perplexed expression, and I put a finger to my lips and hit the speaker button.

"I told you, the photographer caught us in a kiss. So what? Nothing's going on with us. Davia's another fit bird." Adair's tone is dismissive, but stress underscores his words.

"Liar," the unknown man's angry voice barks, followed by the sound of what is sure to be a fist striking Adair.

A grunt of pain bursts from the phone, and we exchange looks of alarm.

"You did business with Markus Myles, and you're in a relationship with Davia Glenn, no matter what you claim. She went to his home and Markus disappeared. Don't you know she's a trained killer?"

Adair coughs and spits what is sure to be blood.

"I think you got bad intel. Davia's a party girl."

The other man roars with frustration, and the sound of punches hammering into what I'm sure is Adair's face echo through the phone.

An assortment of emotions fill me. I'm angry Adair blew off hiring bodyguards, terrified he might die, and consumed with guilt for putting him in this position.

Static and a crashing sound emits from the phone.

"What's this?" The nameless man says. "Ah, just who I wanted to talk to." There are muffled noises, then a clear voice says, "Hello, Ms. Glenn."

He speaks with a Middle-Eastern accent.

I skip the niceties. "Who are you, and what do you want?"

"This young man lies to protect you, telling me you don't mean anything to him, but he calls you on the sly. He must care about you quite a lot."

"He goes out with a different woman every week, so—"

The man cuts off my words. "Where's Markus Myles?"

"How should I know?"

"Rancho Suprema's had a congregation of high-level operatives. You, the man staying with you, and *Mout*."

I narrow down this man's region to Pakistan, as he uses the Urdu word for death, which must be his nickname for Craig Kilburn. Was he one of those men shadowing us at Balboa Park? No, he sounds older.

"I live here, my friend is visiting, and I don't know who *Mout* is."

A visceral cry of pain explodes through the phone as an answer. When the man comes back on the line, he's out of breath from exertion. "The paparazzi and federal agents would make my presence too public to ask you these questions in person. Where's Markus Myles?"

If I tell him I don't know, Adair will die. I picture his life draining away because I rushed into a situation with unforeseeable fallout.

"I'll tell you only if you let Adair go—alive and no worse off than he is now."

"Where's Markus Myles?" the man repeats.

"Again, I won't tell you unless you let Adair go."

The man doesn't answer, and the only sound is Adair moaning.

A deadly calm covers me.

I am going to kill you.

"Although numerous resources are available to you, if you enlist an agency or agencies as reinforcements, he dies. I'll be in touch."

The line disconnects.

"We need to find Adair," I tell Kyle, and he follows me into the garage.

I start the Maserati's engine and open the garage door while Kyle settles in the passenger side. "How can I help?"

"I don't think you can yet." I find the local number of Adair Monroe, Limited. Routing the call through the car, I put it in reverse. A receptionist answers, and I ask to speak with Jason McCall, emphasizing the urgency.

"I'll transfer you."

Two rings. "This is Jason McCall."

I speed down the drive. "A hostile has Adair."

"*What?*"

"Can you track Adair's phone?"

"Yes." Jason's all business in an instant.

"Where are you?"

"I'm at Adair's estate in Rancho. He went to a business meeting this morning and was supposed to return hours ago." Jason talks fast, and keys click. "I didn't think anything of it—"

"Where is he?"

Jason will track Adair through his phone as any trained agent would. He reads me an address. "He's not in motion."

I pause to program it into my GPS. The location is only about fifteen minutes east, and I'll break every speed record on the trip.

Will I get there in time?

"I'm leaving it to you to call the authorities," I say to Jason, "but whoever kidnapped Adair said he would kill him if I call for backup. I'm driving there now."

The line to Jason goes dead, and I can't waste time thinking about what he'll do.

Kyle places his hand on the door to brace himself as I accelerate out of the drive and hang a right, tires squealing. Winding, narrow roads stand between Adair and me.

"The Adair Monroe of the magazine cover?" Kyle asks.

"Yes. He's gotten in the line of fire because of me once already. That was his right-hand man Jason McCall, former MI6."

Kyle takes my .22 out of his jacket, checks the ammo, and a

composed expression settles over his features.

The manicured flowers and trees of Rancho Suprema stream past in a blur as I push the limits of the Maserati MC20, going well over 100 mph. I zoom around any slow-moving car on the two-lane roads without thought. Once I'm out of town, we speed past a lake with homes set into the mountainside around it. Despite the uphill journey and blind curves, fate is on my side, and no vehicle obstructs or delays me. We near the location, and I burn a hard left onto a narrow, paved road and pull to the side.

"He's a quarter-mile ahead. Will your leg hold?" I say.

"Pain is pain, and extreme pain is exquisite. What's the plan?"

"Let's go in from separate directions."

A meadow dotted with live oaks surrounds us and will provide some cover. Dry grass and brush make up the terrain, and I step forward with care in case of snakes. Kyle moves to my right, only a slight limp in his gait.

The trees shelter a one-story wooden house painted brown. A front porch contains two empty chairs, solar panels line the roof, and the yard consists of dried mulch.

We halt and listen.

There isn't a vehicle in the driveway and no garage.

Did they park in the back?

Soft footfalls sound behind me, and I wheel around, gun pointed.

Jason McCall moves fast, holding a firearm. He wears an immaculate suit, but his hair is disheveled like he's repeatedly run a hand through it. I give Kyle the okay, and he lowers the gun barrel sighted on Jason.

When he reaches me, I whisper, "Did you call the police?"

"No. I'm going to kill whoever did this." His eyes don't move from the structure.

"You'll have to beat me to it."

We proceed forward and avoid stepping on dry leaves or anything that will make noise. The trek stretches into eternity as concern for Adair roils through my system. Slow is smooth, smooth is fast, I remind myself.

Kyle signals he'll check the back, and I sign I'm going with him. Jason holds up his left hand showing three fingers, and I acknowledge him. Jason will come in the front in three minutes, and Kyle and I will enter through the rear.

The backyard is flat dirt with tufts of dead grass and a horseshoe pit. I scan the roofline and area around the solitary back door for any security cameras, but there are none. I put my hand in a fist by my head in a *cover me* sign to Kyle and continue my careful tread across the yard. I peek through a window, but the curtains are closed, so I stealth move to the back door. A turn of the doorknob reveals it's unlocked. Kyle comes into position opposite me, waiting.

Three-two-one

I enter. On my left is a small, empty kitchen and dining area. Kyle is right behind me and waits at the living room and kitchen intersection. Jason joins me, and we move down a short hall with three closed doors.

A shooter might be behind each one.

We aren't in tactical gear, protected by vests and helmets.

I don't care.

Crouching to the side, I throw open the first door. The small room contains a single bed, dresser, and lamp. Jason opens the door to another basic bedroom and clears the space.

One to go.

The final door's locked knob lets out a squeak, and I expect gunfire to come right through the flimsy wood.

Nothing happens.

We switch positions so Jason can put his shoulder and heftier weight into the door. He raises three fingers, counting them down to one, then hits the barrier.

The wood splinters, and we burst in.

The room is small. We spin in the space and check the closet, but it contains only a few wire hangers. On the floor is a broken chair, a blood stain coating the carpet beneath it. Lying next to the chair is a cell phone with a shattered screen.

Adair is gone.

22

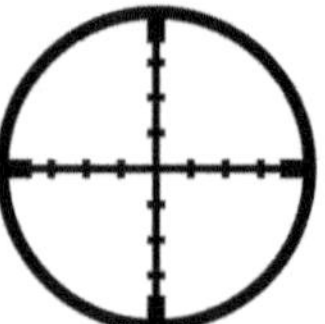

We search every inch of the premises and grounds for clues. Jason clenches and unclenches his hands, his neck corded from suppressed fury. I can't blame him. This is the second time Adair has been in danger because of me, and now he might be dead. Only my training keeps me from screaming.

We congregate near our cars, and Kyle rests his leg while I give Jason a quick overview of my participation in the Myles case and what the hostile told me.

Jason is incredulous. "What were you thinking, going into that situation alone?"

"Does it matter? I can't change it. Have you met Markus Myles?"

"He attended a few business meetings I went to with Mr. Monroe. Nothing about him stood out, a plus in our business. His partner, Frederick Maxim, did most of the talking. He bragged about business deals or touted investment opportunities, but Markus was quiet."

Jason's mobile rings, and he answers. He finishes the brief conversation and says, "This property is an Airbnb, owned for the past forty years by the same person, an elderly widow who uses the extra income to support herself. The renter is an Ali Singh, and my people ran a more thorough background than Airbnb did but hit a dead end.

His cover is deep, so I think we can assume he's from a high-level organization or is a well-funded mercenary."

"I recall someone saying Markus traveled to Pakistan for some of his arms deals. Maybe it's ISI," I speculate.

"If so, you recall their reputation."

ISI, or Inter-Service Intelligence, is Pakistan's equivalent to the CIA. It was created in 1948 and played a significant role in thwarting Russia in Afghanistan. Although their resources are less than many other countries, their covert operations and intelligence gathering are highly effective.

"Why would ISI be here?" I say. "Two Middle Eastern men trailed Kyle and me when we went to Balboa Park, so there might be a team."

"Possibly, but speculation is useless."

I'm not offended by his abruptness. Time is running out.

"An operative is here searching for Markus," I say. "His primary function is wetwork, but he owes Markus and wants to find him. I'll tell him to meet me to find out if he's made any progress."

We go to our cars without further words or promises. Our straightforward task is to expend every resource at our disposal to find Adair.

I text Kilburn.

Meet me at my house in fifteen.

Kilburn: *Can't. I'm running down a lead.*

Me: *It's urgent.*

Kilburn: *Be there when I can.*

"Damn it," I mutter as I turn the car around.

"What?" Kyle says.

"Kilburn's got a lead, which is good, but he can't meet until later. I hope he finds Myles so a swap, even a pretend one, can be set up."

Kyle can tell how upset I am and says, "You couldn't have predicted this."

He's right, of course, but guilt is kicking the crap out of me.

"This is my fault for getting involved with a guy like Adair."

"Fault isn't important right now. You need to keep your mind set on a rescue. Since we didn't find a body, he must be alive."

"I need to believe he is. I hope when Kilburn meets us, he'll have Markus Myles with him, but if he doesn't, I'll help try to locate him since our goals align."

"A strange bedfellow's situation for sure."

Once home, I leave both security gates open.

All I can do now is wait.

It's nearing 10 p.m. when Kilburn arrives, and I hurry out to meet him.

"Did you find him?" I ask, but he shakes his head.

"Nope. He's a slippery bastard, that one. Every time I think I've found him, the trail goes cold. What's so urgent, by the way?"

"Come in, and I'll catch you up."

When Craig sees Kyle, his expression goes cold. We all settle at the kitchen table, and Kyle and I leave our guns in our waistbands this time. When I finish filling Kilburn in, he lets out a whistle.

"So, someone scooped up your boy toy and tortured him to find Markus through you? This sitch is more critical than I thought."

"Do you have any more leads on where Markus might be?" I ask.

"No. I can't exactly torture the folks in this community to get information. I think he's still in the area, though."

"I'll help you find him because our goals now intersect."

"Are you going to tell me who *he* is this time?" Kilburn motions to Kyle.

"I'll let him introduce himself."

After Kyle does, Kilburn tilts his head to the side. "Kyle Kavanagh? No wonder you were Deadeye Dick the last time. Your reputation precedes you."

"And?" Kyle says.

"I recall your impressive but notorious record, so I'll try to behave myself. At least a little."

During this exchange, I'm antsy, not wanting the conversation to take off down a side trail and derail our progress.

"Tell me everything about Markus," I say.

"You must be worried about this kidnapped guy. You haven't offered me anything to drink," Kilburn says.

Kyle goes to the fridge, grabs a water bottle, and tosses it to Kilburn. He snatches it from the air, twists off the cap, and takes a long drink. He's aware of my impatience and doesn't hurry, then settles in to begin his story.

"First, Markus Myles isn't the name I knew him by twelve years ago. He worked in Pakistan, monitoring the cash flow between us and the Afghan paramilitary units we ran to eliminate Taliban leaders and bring peace to the country. We all know how well that worked out. Anyway, I was out solo to a meeting with an informant who claimed to possess some vital information. It wasn't protocol, but I don't like babysitters tagging along. The standard procedure was for informants to come to the base, where we performed a full-body search. We would stick them in a room with cigarettes and cashews for their enjoyment with a terp present to translate."

I nod, and Kilburn continues. "This guy said he had details about an attack on our consulate in Peshawar where a suicide truck bomb and armed Taliban hit the building. He claimed to possess the ring leader's identity but refused to come to the base. Brass told me not to meet him alone, but I figured the info was worth the risk since whoever ordered the attack was an HVT. I arranged to meet the informant in the wee hours, with fewer people around."

"What happened?" I say.

"I verified as much as possible, as going off the range was dicey. Pakistan's sentiments toward Americans weren't friendly because of some unsanctioned killings by our military. We set up a meeting in the slums of Islamabad, a narrow maze of streets and alleys stinking with decaying trash mixed with human and animal waste. Hell, they burned it for fuel, so the air was thick with the smell. I wore the traditional *shalwar-kameez* outfit with a shawl to cover my bald head and most of my face. Do you know anything about Pakis?" Kilburn directs this question to Kyle.

"Some pretend to be compatriots but sell you out if they think they'll gain more."

"Bingo!" Kilburn takes another slug of water. "One of the many reasons most plans don't survive contact with the enemy."

"And?" I cut in, conscious of time draining away as quickly as Adair's life might be.

"I got double-crossed. Five hostiles came out of the shadows in front of me at the meeting place, and a few more popped up on the rooftops. Nothing will kick you into high gear faster than being surrounded by armed people who don't like you. An instant run-and-gun battle ensued. It was me versus a posse on terrain I scoped but didn't know like the back of my hand. I cut in and out of side lanes, ran straight into more hostiles, bowled them over, and crashed through houses trying to escape. I thought this was the end—but here's where Markus Myles comes into the story."

Kilburn takes another drink of water then continues.

"I blazed down a path when someone jumped in front of me, and before I hit or shot whoever it was, the person grabbed my arm and called my name. It was Markus. The little spook pulled me into a house, and we hunkered down, listening to shouts and the sound of running feet passing by outside. A Pakistani family was inside with us, eyes wide. They were cooperative, and I'm sure Myles expended a lot of cash to ensure they stayed that way."

"Quite a tale of luck," Kyle comments.

"It was a happy coincidence Myles was in the area running intel. After I learned his family had been whacked with him not among the victims, I thought it was either a warning or a way to bring him out of the cold."

"Why do you think this is happening now?" I say.

Kilburn shrugs. "Not sure, but it might tie into the recent publicity about his company. He's been living under a new identity, and might have thought no one from his past would remember him because his face doesn't stick in your mind. He's a guy you pass and forget a second later."

I think about the photos of Markus from my Internet search. The men surrounding him stood out more than he did, but the headshot used for recent press might have triggered someone's memory.

"Did you learn anything else that might help?" I ask.

"No, but I did pick up clues on who might be behind this."

"ISI?" I say.

"Another smart conclusion, Bombshell. This is either an official agency move, a former rogue agent, or a shadowy terrorist organization."

Kilburn's thoughts mirror mine.

"Do you recognize these guys?" Kyle hands Kilburn his phone open to the photos we took of the first team in Balboa Park.

Kilburn checks them. "Their clean-cut appearances scream feds."

"Our conclusion as well," I say. "Two agents stopped by for my statement after the murders, thinking I might know Markus's location."

"And these?" Kyle swipes forward to photos of the other men.

"They're either ISI or some mercs or terrorists, as I said." Kilburn slides the phone back to Kyle, then turns to me. "The Badger leak might give them information about you."

"You think the leak went beyond Badger's group?"

"I'm sure those juicy tidbits about the members of your much-feared team made the rounds of the rogue cesspools of the world, because Badger had his finger in a load of fetid pies. Your current location and injured status are also out there."

"I helped take out Badger, so any enemies should think more than twice about coming after me. The kidnapper I spoke with knew you were here. How do you think they got onto you?"

"Maybe I killed their best friend from second grade, and my identity stuck in their craw. I have my share of haters."

"Did you learn why they're after Myles?" I say.

"Myles negotiated numerous arms deals in Pakistan. The U.S. calls Pakistan a supporter, but we can leave the debate for another day with a lot of alcohol involved. Markus might have bought defective weapons from a scrap auction and sold them for a lot of money to thwart their plans. If they purchased a shipment of SAWs with cracked bolts or the like, they'd want to speak to the seller about it."

SAWs are M249 Squad Automatic Weapons, light machine guns notorious for having operational problems. Receiving defective weapons for a considerable amount of money would tick anyone off.

"We can't know what happened," I say. "We have to set a trap for whoever took Adair."

"This again? Your billionaire's dead by now. And if he's still alive, what will he think if you save him and tell him he got kidnapped and tortured because of you?"

"I won't believe Adair's dead, and I won't care what he thinks about me if I can save him. I'll help you find Markus, but I want to be ready if or when this Ali Singh calls me back. Do you agree to work with me or not?"

Kilburn sits back further in his chair. "Sure, Bombshell, I never got to play in the sandbox with you."

The sandbox usually refers to a desert deployment, but I don't correct him, thinking he might frame his life as a childhood adventure.

"Do you have a gun?" Kyle says.

Kilburn breaks into a smile. "I always have a bit of kindness with me."

"What do you mean?" I say.

He removes an automatic from a hidden holster and brings it to his lips for a quick kiss. "My mom told me you get more out of life if you kill people with kindness, so that's what I call all my guns."

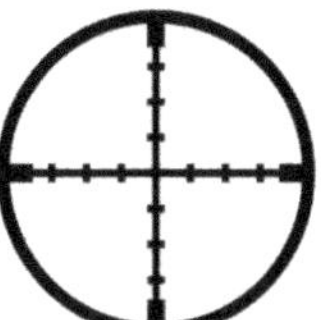

23

We talk late into the night.

My team drilled for years, entering rooms and shooting near each other, yet Kilburn and I never worked together. I think of the times I sat in a hostage seat in a shoot house. The door to the room would explode with jarring force, followed by a flash-bang grenade thrown at the ceiling. Men entered, yelling and shooting at bad-guy dummies mere inches from where I sat. It was an act of organized mayhem.

I trust Kyle, but he's leaving. Kilburn marches to an irregular beat, and Jason is an unknown quantity.

Do what you can, with what you have, where you are.

My dad was fond of this quote from President Theodore Roosevelt, and I thought of it whenever our missions took an unexpected turn, and it fit the situation now.

When we finish exhausting scenarios that might never happen, I show Kilburn to a guest bedroom, and he closes the door in my face. His lock clicks, and I do the same at my room. How can I work with Kilburn on a rescue when I'm not happy having him sleep in my house?

Warden's words surface.

I don't need to remind you how unstable Kilburn is.

I crawl into bed when Warden texts, *You still up?*

In response, I do a video call, and his face brightens when he answers.

"Hey, Night Owl, why are you awake? Can't sleep without me?"

What should I tell him?

"I have a bit of a situation out here."

"What's happened?"

Not holding back, I tell him about my involvement with the murders, Adair's kidnapping, and allying myself with Kilburn. I finish, and Warden is disbelieving.

"What the hell, Davia? Why didn't you call 911? And why do you need to be involved in a rescue with Kilburn as a partner?"

"I—"

"Call Agent Wills at National Security and back out of this mess. If they're ISI or some terrorist group, how are you supposed to handle this alone?"

I blanch in the face of his harsh tone. "Bringing in unknown forces would worsen this as most don't have our training. Besides, whoever took Adair told me not to get any agencies involved."

"How can you not? Hostage rescues are a crapshoot at the best of times. You don't know where he is, how many opponents there are, and what type of weapons they possess. When we do missions, we have an intelligence picture, and even then, the chance of failure is high."

"Everyone's been hunting for Markus Myles since the murders. My money's on Kilburn bringing him in."

"But then what? Will you hand him over and expect the hostile to cooperate? I bet that Brit's dead or sold off to some terrorist organization that likes to ransom people or kill them to make a statement. You know the drill."

"I do, but Adair was on their radar because of me, so no matter the odds, I need to try and save him."

"With our identities leaked and bad guys gunning for us, did you ever consider letting a regular guy kiss you might cause problems?"

I recognize his concern for me drives his caustic words. "Of course, but I can't change the past. If the shoe were on the other foot and someone got caught up in something like this because of you, you would do everything to find them."

"Perhaps, but you could die doing this alone or with Kilburn as your backup. I can't lose you, Davia." His drawn face and beseeching tone shake me to the core.

"I can't turn away now."

"Please, please don't get hurt." Warden's voice breaks.

"You need to trust me and my training."

"You're beyond capable, but you're not invincible. Remember that."

5 A.M. I LIE AWAKE, unsure what to do. Warden was right, but not about everything. I would involve Agent Wills and the NSA or FBI once we found Markus Myles and set up a trade. I think about Kilburn's nickname for his guns and consider that my affection for Adair, a symbolic kindness, might lead to him getting killed just as sure as a bullet.

Bang! Bang! Bang!

Someone hammers on my door as loud as a battering ram.

"Wake up, sweetheart," Kilburn says. "Time to hit the road."

Throwing back the covers, I'm thankful I slept in my clothes.

I open the door. "What's up?"

"I got a lead on Markus, so we need to go catch him."

"Let me put on some boots."

Kyle comes down the hall, dressed. The gun he holds points to the ground, but his eyes are on Kilburn. "What's the deal?"

"Tell him," I say to Kilburn. "I'll be ready in a sec."

I do a quick bathroom run, pull my hair into a ponytail, and draw on boots and a ball cap. The men are in the kitchen drinking coffee. I chug down a glass of water and inhale a protein bar.

"My plane's at ten," Kyle says.

"Take the Rover." I reserve a spot via a long-term parking app and text Kyle the info.

"You sure?" The tension on his face tells me he doesn't want to leave.

"You can't blow off a Senate committee. I'll be fine."

"I'll wait in my car," Kilburn says, and I open the garage door for him to exit.

Kyle steps close and hands me my .22. I place the gun in my ankle holster. My 9mm is secure in a holster tucked into my front waistband, and I carry extra magazines.

"I don't like this," he says.

"I'll be fine."

"Yes, but Kilburn qualifies for Section Eight."

"We can't change the circumstances, only our reaction to them."

Kyle nods when I quote one of his training points, then pulls me in for a hug.

"Call or text when you can."

I ignore the lump in my throat. "I will."

Outside, when I pull the car door closed, Kilburn drives off.

"Where are we going?" I put on my seatbelt while he waits for the security gate to open.

"When I began shaking trees, I hit up a contact to assist. Early this morning, he texted me that our man went by the hospital to check on his little girl. As it was the only place Myles might risk showing himself, I had my guy there on surveillance."

"Makes sense, but the police guard Tilly and the FBI are also on a stakeout. Did they spot him?"

"Of course not. Markus might be many things, but he's not a fool. He wore a disguise and blended."

"How far did he get?"

"Waltzed right past security and police, glimpsed his kid through the door, and continued outside to his car. My guy's skilled, and Markus didn't spot his tail. Followed him to a rundown apartment where he likely bypassed questions with substantial cash."

"Is he there now?"

"Yes, at least he was."

I won't be happy until we have our hands on him and can devise a solid plan to save Adair. Cars pack the southbound freeway, and I text Kyle to remind him to allow time for delays.

Kilburn glances over. "Are you telling Kavanagh you're still alive?"

"I'm advising him about the traffic. Should I tell him you're planning to kill me?"

"Why would I tell you if I were?"

I place my hand near my gun. "I wouldn't expect you to because we're on the same side, but I wouldn't let you.

"You think you're bulletproof, don't you?"

"I don't. Do you?"

Kilburn's relaxed, a hand at the bottom of the wheel. "I survived some significant injuries through the years."

"How many targets have you assassinated?"

He sucks air past his teeth. "Too many to count. They're not assassinations, though, merely us fighting wars and demoralizing leadership."

The CIA hasn't used the term assassination since its failed attempt to take out Fidel Castro in Cuba in the 1960s, and Congress passed laws against such acts.

"No matter what label we use now, I imagine what you did is hard to live with," I say.

His hand twitches, and we drift into the next lane.

"Careful," I warn.

Kilburn wrenches the wheel back and almost overcorrects into the opposite lane.

"Are you okay?" I say.

He doesn't answer. Instead, his body goes rigid, and he takes his foot off the gas.

The vehicle fades to a stop.

What's going on?

"You need to pull over," I say with urgency as cars brake and veer around us.

Kilburn is oblivious. He stares straight ahead, unresponsive.

While I consider what to do, a loud honk jolts him back into reality. I repeat my command to pull over, and he gulps in a breath before maneuvering toward the shoulder. I hit the emergency blinkers when we're off the road and stopped. Kilburn slumps over the wheel, a tear sliding down his cheek. After several moments, his body shakes from convulsive sobs. I keep a hand on my gun, bewildered by his sudden mood swing.

"What the hell?" I'm at a loss.

He doesn't answer. Cars slow as they pass, and people stare.

At last, Kilburn raises his head and draws a forearm across his face.

"Sometimes thinking about my work triggers me. When you asked about killing people, I flashed on a time I had orders to take out a group of people slumbering near a campfire. Using a suppressed gun that made as much noise as a slight cough, I moved around the circle as the flames flickered, hoping no one woke. One moment they were in a dream world, and the next in the afterlife."

"I'm sure that was difficult," I say. Being tasked with the same mission is something I can't imagine, but now isn't the time to consider the subject. I worried about working with him before. Now what?

Time passes, and neither of us speaks or moves, then Kilburn exhales.

"I guess my meds need adjusting."

Meds? We aren't allowed to take anything that can affect our perfor-mance. As I think this, Kilburn fixes me with an icy glare, and I'm glad my hand still hovers near my gun.

"Going to rat me out?" He points a small revolver at me, and his implacability has returned.

"We have a job to do."

"And after?"

"This isn't official, so I don't care what you're on, as long as it doesn't interfere with us finding Markus and saving Adair."

He considers me for a minute and then puts the weapon in a coat pocket. "You wouldn't have gotten your gun clear before I shot you."

Kilburn turns to check the freeway before pulling out, and I bring my left arm back from where it rests across the seat behind his head. I slide my combat knife back into its hiding place in my jacket sleeve.

TRAFFIC PICKS UP. We pass downtown San Diego and continue south until we near Mexico, exiting the freeway at San Ysidro.

"Why would he pick this town? Almost everyone's Latino, so he would stick out," I say.

"We're one exit from the border, so he has a quick escape route." Kilburn turns into a residential area filled with apartments and parks on a side street. He points out a worn, brown building with a sign indicating the Las Palmas Apartments.

After we park, he takes a flight of stairs to an upper walkway leading to a second-floor apartment, and I stay at ground level at the opposite end of the building. The target apartment's window curtains are closed, but Kilburn's path doesn't take him past it. He stops near the edge of the door.

Kilburn catches my eye, signaling he will enter. He gathers his bulky frame to break through the barrier, but the door flies open. A man tears out of the room, ducks past Kilburn, and makes for the stairs. Kilburn grabs for his shirt but misses.

I run through the parking lot in pursuit. A car with an inattentive driver shoots out of a slot, and I slam into its side, the force throwing me backward to the asphalt. I push myself up and duck around the vehicle as familiar pulses of pain shoot down my leg. Kilburn hurdles down the stairs and joins me as I pass. Ignoring curious bystanders, we race after the escaping man.

"Was it him?" I say.

"Think so, not sure."

The person we pursue is almost twenty yards ahead of us, fleeing at full speed. He stops at a nondescript dark sedan backed into a space, and a beep sounds as its doors unlock. I ignore the pain for a final burst of speed, unwilling to let him escape. The car starts, and the man revs the gas to speed off.

The engine stutters and dies.

Face creased with panic, he jabs the ignition switch until the motor turns over, but it groans with protest and cuts out. Kilburn has fallen behind, so I take out my firearm and point it through the window. The man ignores me, still trying to start the car. Kilburn comes to stand near the passenger side.

"He's not going anywhere," he says. "My contact disabled his engine."

"Is it Markus Myles?" I leave my muzzle aimed at the man's head.

Kilburn ducks to check. "Yup."

The former spy bangs his hand against the wheel, then drives his body weight into the door as he opens it, sending me sprawling into the car next to his. He makes like a rabbit and jets off with the two of us in pursuit. We run past people sitting at cement picnic tables, navigate through and around trees, and find ourselves pounding across a grass lawn near a fenced baseball diamond and children's playground.

Markus glances back, trips, and almost goes down. Catching his balance, he starts forward again, but the slight delay enables us to gain on him. Kilburn accelerates, bends, and aims his shoulder at Markus's back. He hits him near the waistline, and the men slam to the ground. Kilburn has the size and weight advantage, but Markus is lithe and motivated. He twists away, scrambling to freedom, but Kilburn seizes his ankle, halting his escape.

"Stay where you are," I say, gun out. Kilburn keeps a firm grip on Markus's arm as the men rise. We huddle, bent over and breathing hard.

"Let's go back to your apartment," Kilburn tells Markus. "And if you put us through a repeat of this little misadventure, I will break something no doctor will be able to repair."

Markus's eyes dart side to side despite Kilburn's threat, sizing up his chances. He's dyed his hair dark and grown a beard and mustache to change his appearance. Sunken eyes and a worn cast age his face. Is his pallor caused by shooting his family or something else?

When we enter Markus's apartment, Kilburn tosses him into a chair. I close the door and place my back against the exit. Markus's legs jiggle, and his eyes flit around the room. He's so agitated, he might attempt to escape by pitching himself straight through the glass window.

"Long time no see, Patrick Ross," Kilburn says, and I deduce this was Markus's operative alias. "If the Company gave me a chance to live the pampered existence you have, I don't think I would put myself back in their crosshairs."

Markus wears a mulish expression. "What are you talking about?"

Kilburn pulls another chair in front of Markus, spins it, and sits. "Did you think no one would realize you snagged some advanced military tech mistakenly put up for auction that makes us vulnerable? You made the situation worse when you sold the merch to a group of terrorists for a sizable sum of untraceable money. You must realize this made you super popular with us."

Kilburn's words startle me. What does this have to do with him wanting to help the man who saved him in Pakistan?

Lies. All lies.

When I first questioned Kilburn's humanism, I'd been on the right track. Now, Kilburn threatening me in the car after his admission about the meds makes more sense. Will he view me as expendable? I double-check my weapon.

Markus says, "How did you find me?"

"How else? I set someone on your vulnerable spot, the kid in the hospital. I figured if you had a shred of conscience left, you might pop by for a visit. Did you plan to bail out of the country? Is that why you killed your family?"

Markus's face flushes red. "I didn't think it would go down like that."

Kilburn sits back. "Don't worry; I'm not here about whatever you did to your dearly departed. You need to answer for much more than that little debacle. The local law might want to chat with you later, but you're coming with me first."

Markus's face doesn't change. Is he locked in the past, reliving the murders?

Kilburn turns to me. "Thanks for the assist."

"You need to return the favor."

"I don't. This loser and I are due for a plane ride."

"You can't leave without helping me."

"I can. Rescuing a hostage isn't why I'm here."

"You promised to assist me, and we spent most of last night discussing rescue scenarios."

"I did it for my benefit, to learn more about you. I appreciate your problem-solving creativity, but I never intended to stay. My mission is to bring in this pain in the ass, nothing more."

"Are you kidding?"

If he takes Markus, how will I save Adair?

"You're sure worked up. When I stopped by your place and you got home late, I detected the scent of some guy's cologne on your clothes. Should I tell Warden he has competition?"

His words make me want to close the distance and crack my gun across his face, but I remind myself to stay calm.

Kilburn pulls Markus to his feet, produces handcuffs, and snaps them on both their wrists. "If you want to bail out, think of me as an anchor."

They start for the door, but I continue to block the exit.

"Don't make me hurt you," Kilburn warns.

"I'm not letting you leave. An innocent man's life is at stake here."

"How many times must I repeat he's dead? D-E-A-D. I don't want to report you got in the way of me bringing back the target of this mission."

I realize what will happen to my tenuous career if he does. "Are you on a specific time deadline or something?"

"No, but I accomplished what I needed and am ready to leave. Although—" Kilburn pauses. "Because you helped me out and have been so sweet about it, I'll text you the location of a cache I set up.

There might be something in there you can use during your futile rescue attempt."

"Text it now."

Kilburn taps his phone while Markus stands beside him like a deflated balloon. A text vibrates, and I check the contents.

Not moving, I say to Markus, "Who killed your wife and son? You? Those terrorists who are after you?"

Markus's mask of pain and humility drops like a snake shedding its skin. His cold eyes meet mine, but he doesn't answer.

I step into his space, unfazed. "Did you try to run me over?"

Markus doesn't drop eye contact or answer. Kilburn stares down at him. "Were you a naughty boy?"

Markus's lips curl into a mocking sneer.

"Promise me you'll get some answers," I say to Kilburn.

"My pleasure."

I step aside, unhappy. Kilburn maneuvers Markus out, down the stairs, and back to where we parked, me following. Kilburn opens the passenger door and instructs Markus to sit. He removes the cuff connecting them, puts it around the roof handle, and closes the door.

Kilburn hands me a hundred-dollar bill.

"What's this for?"

"Uber. I'm done lounging around Rancho Suprema."

I hand it back.

"Your loss." Kilburn goes to the driver's side and is gone.

24

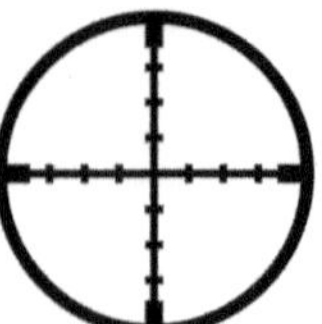

On my return trip, I read a series of texts from Kyle telling me Bob Brooks gave him a ride to the airport, and he boarded his flight. After responding, I consider Markus's comment about the murders.

I didn't think it would go down like that.

What did he mean? Was it a weapons deal with the man who holds Adair captive, and it went wrong? Did Markus flee from them and go into hiding? Was he the person who tried to run me over? He was similar in height and build, but I wasn't sure.

More pressing than solving the mystery of the murders was the fact I no longer had backup or a bargaining chip. After much debate, I text Jason McCall.

We need to meet.

Jason's reply is instant. *Did you find Adair?*

No.

Breaking the news Markus is out of the picture isn't something I want to do by text, so we set up a meeting at my home. After the Uber driver drops me off, I enter the courtyard where José waters succulent-filled Talavera pots near a three-tiered fountain flowing into a basin lined with colorful tiles. He wears headphones and bops his head in time to some music.

"*Como esta?*" he inquires, removing one of his earbuds.

"Do you remember the guy who tied you up?"

He scowls. "*Sí.*"

"I got to spend a fun morning with him. He left me in San Ysidro, and I had to catch an Uber back."

José mutters a few choice descriptors about Kilburn in Spanish as I unlock the front door.

"A man will be here later today. He's—" What was Jason? "An ally."

For now, we're united in purpose, and I can't waste time speculating what will occur afterward. José nods and returns to his task.

Closing the front door, I sag. Not sleeping, dealing with Kilburn, and catching Markus have zapped my energy. I pull off the ball cap, throw it on the kitchen island, and consider what to do next.

A call comes through from Kyle, and I pick up.

"Read your text but wanted to give you a quick call. We're in Denver on a layover. What happened?"

I fill him in. "Who knew Kilburn would be two different people in one car ride?"

"I'd laugh if the situation weren't so alarming. What's next?"

"I'm going to check out the cache Kilburn left. The upside is I won't be forced to split my attention between any hostiles and him."

"What about Adair's right-hand man?"

"He's meeting with me soon, but he's another mixed bag. He might be motivated to try and take me out of any future equation."

A voice from the plane's speaker announces the aircraft is ready for departure, and Kyle says, "Keep me updated."

"I will."

I eat some lunch, ice my leg, and take a shower, which revives me somewhat. Pulling on clean clothes, I take the Rover to the address from Kilburn's text. A narrow drive leads to a rambling ranch-style home on a hill near Rancho Suprema. The 2,500-square-foot abode appears tiny after living amongst mansions.

I need to get back to reality, and soon.

When I turn off my engine, a fit man nearing forty is out his front door. He moves with the casual ease of a highly-trained operator, and I keep my hands visible and don't move.

He approaches the driver's window, and I roll it down.

"I'm Davia Glenn."

Polarized shades hide his eyes. "Nickname?"

"Bombshell."

"Come with me." He makes for a gate into a fenced backyard, and I follow him to a padlocked shed. A Doberman on a shaded porch stands, but the man puts out a flat hand, and it doesn't move. He unlocks the metal shed's door and pulls out a black polypropylene case with wheels, which he transports to the back of my vehicle. I open the tailgate, and he sets it inside.

"Thanks." I close up.

"Good hunting." He returns to his house.

When I pull back into my garage, I open the trunk to survey the war kit left by Kilburn, and my spirits lift for the first time since I learned Adair had been kidnapped. I'm happy to find a thirty-round submachine gun with an integrated suppressor, a 9mm pistol with a 15-round magazine, all necessary ammo, tracking devices, a transponder, a hooligan entry tool, and a plate carrier protective vest.

The gate buzzer stops my inventory.

Jason steps out of his Audi and joins me in the garage. I show him Kilburn's cache to try and soften the blow about Markus Myles.

"What did you need to tell me?" he says, impatient.

I fill him in.

"He did what?"

"Kilburn was here to find and retrieve Markus. I couldn't interfere since it was an official operation."

A vein in Jason's neck pulses. "If Adair dies because of you—"

"He won't, but if he does, we can deal with it then," I interrupt. "We need to concentrate on preparing for a rescue. Let's go inside and talk." I put out an arm to indicate the way, and Jason brushes past me. The door's open, and he goes in without waiting.

"Have a seat." I indicate the kitchen table cum strategy center, thinking perhaps I should ask Sherilyn to install a drop-down whiteboard.

Jason pulls out his phone. "This is who's behind the kidnapping. His name is Yasam Jafari, age fifty-two. He's a former ISI operative who now leads an extremist group."

The headshot is of a lean man in a turban sporting a mustache and long beard, but I don't recognize him from past briefings or operations in Pakistan. "Did you learn anything else?"

"He's linked to assassinations of rivals and several bombings, including one on a train that killed fifty-three civilians. He was active in ISI when Markus Myles was a spy, so perhaps they crossed paths."

"Nothing definitive on their relationship?"

"No. We can speculate something happened back in the day, and the recent publicity brought Myles on his radar, or some issue came out of a Maxim Myles weapons deal."

"Anything about who's with him?"

"Nothing."

Warden was right to remind me of the difficulty of hostage rescues. With only Jafari's identity and no other information, saving Adair has a high chance of failure. His location, the number of foes, weapons, skill level, and motivation remains a mystery. Did they want to kill Markus? Where was our leverage?

"Ever been on a hostage rescue team?" I say.

"Long ago, at the start of my career."

Ignoring the set of his jaw, I say, "We need to share openly to save Adair."

Jason sits up straighter. "Contrary to the James Bond image, I'm used to working with a team and collaborating or persuading others to assist us."

"How accurate are you with a gun?"

"Very."

"Hand-to-hand combat?"

"I'm not on your level. That said, I won't be a liability."

Admitting he isn't my equal in anything makes his face turn sour.

"What about Adair? Does he have any training to protect himself?"

"Did he ever tell you about his childhood?"

"He told me some of it on his yacht."

Jason gives a bitter laugh. "He probably gave you the fairy tale version. Adair refused to train in anything, afraid he'd turn out like his abusive dad. I told him he was gormless because training teaches you not to use force unless needed, but he wouldn't."

"How traumatized was he after his dad died?"

"The big-hearted sod pretended to be okay, the new man of the house. He was only six or seven, a kid. What happened tore him apart, but he stuffed his trauma and put on a brave front."

I picture Adair as a little boy fighting to smile.

"Do you know how hard my father and I worked to keep the lad on the straight?" Jason continues. "As Adair got older, there was concern he would drink, do drugs, or anything else to numb his pain, but his mum, my dad, and I stayed on him like hawks. He's a combination of his attractive parents, not as big and husky as his dad, but still quite fanciable. Young ladies threw themselves at him early on, so we had another potential problem. We got him into therapy, but I think what pulled him forward was discovering his knack for finding patterns in the markets and making money. He wanted to care for his mum and sister and found a way."

Jason sits forward, gray eyes on mine. "Now, do you understand why I hate what you brought into his life? No matter how often I tried to dissuade him because I was concerned for his safety, all he talked about was how taken he was with you."

We stare at each other. My unresolved feelings for Adair led to where he predicted, and my gut twists.

"I can't change it," I say. "Right now, we need to be ready for when Yasim Jafari calls to demand a trade."

"Your man making off with Markus made this whole operation go pear-shaped," he accuses, but under his harsh tone is distress. Jason will do anything to bring Adair back, like me.

"I have an idea," I say.

Jason stops rubbing his forehead. "What?"

"Can you do an American accent?"

WHEN JASON LEAVES, I go to my closet to change into black combat pants, a black shirt, and boots. I pull out all necessary gear and first-aid equipment and pack the Rover. I'm in the kitchen gathering water bottles and food when a text comes through from Ava.

Where are you? Did you forget today's fashion show practice?

The rehearsal is nowhere in my mind.

I text back: *I can't make it.*

Ava: *Is everything okay?*

Me: *Yes, I have another commitment.*

Ava: *Lucky you.* (wink emoji)

I text back a smile emoji and return to the garage to lay in my supplies and continue my inventory of Kilburn's cache. I set aside the story of Adair's past, knowing this isn't the time for emotions and regrets.

I'm making a final audit when my phone vibrates.

Unknown Caller.

I answer. "This is Davia."

"Are you ready to turn over Markus Myles?" a now-familiar man's voice says.

"Yes. Do you like to be called Yasam or Mr. Jafari?"

"My identity doesn't matter."

"Let me speak to Adair."

Yasam says, "Your girl wants to talk to you."

"Davia?" Adair's voice is hoarse. Was it from screaming?

I push away my concern. "I'm coming for you, Adair."

"You can't. There are ten men here and—" A slap cuts off his words.

Yasam comes back on the line. "How cute, him trying to help you."

"We need to conclude this." I text Jason to be ready.

"If you don't comply, this man's face won't ever be fit to photograph."

"Tell me where you want to meet." I close the back of the Rover, get in, and start it up.

"I'm not giving you time to devise a rescue plan, so put the idea out of your mind," Yasim says.

Too late.

"My backup left today, so this will be a straight trade," I say.

"Only a fool would believe you, but it doesn't matter. You come in here with force, and your man dies."

"Are you done with your threats?"

Yasam provides an address, and the call disconnects.

I blaze to where Jason McCall waits.

25

Jason is on the passenger side, unrecognizable. He changed his hair color, posture, and mannerisms to become Markus Myles, the only ploy we have.

"This had better work," he says.

"Best we can do."

He studies a map on his phone. "The meeting place is a small building surrounded by fields in a rural area with only one dirt road for access."

"I guess he didn't want me to bring a platoon."

At the turnoff, Jason takes out high-def binoculars.

"One man guards the utility building, and two cars are parked nearby." He sketches the layout on a notepad.

"Anyone playing hide-and-seek?"

"Only if they're behind the structure. No one's lying in the fields or on the roof."

I head down the dirt track. "Here we go."

No plans survive first contact with the enemy. The military saying Kilburn mentioned is true, but my team made it irrelevant because we improvised and adapted on the go. What about now? Would my training be enough? One mistake, and Adair might die.

We bounce along the rutted road toward the location. Since Jason is as motivated as me, this won't end well for Yasam Jafari or his men.

I stop a distance from the building, and a man jumps up from a chair and pounds on the door. Two SUVs are parked facing the road, and I center my Rover so they can't drive past.

Yasam Jafari strolls out with another man. He's different than his picture because he's clean-shaven but holds his chin high and shoulders squared.

Why are terrorists always so cocky?

"Where do you think the others are?" I say.

"Not sure, but the only person I'm here for is Adair, and the rest be damned."

"Agreed."

After parking, I go to the passenger side and yank Jason out. He pretends to fight me, giving me a plausible excuse to pull my automatic. I shove it into his side. Jason's head and shoulders slump in mock defeat as I march him to the front of my car.

Two men I recognize as my Balboa Park followers flank Jafari.

"Here's Markus Myles. Show me Adair," I call across the fifteen-yard distance. Jafari turns to one of the minions beside him and relays an order. The man enters the building and returns with a prisoner, a dark pillowcase covering his head.

"That's not him," Jason whispers. The decoy doesn't possess Adair's breadth of shoulders and build.

"Take off the hood," I say.

"Want to check if he's still handsome? How cold," Jafari comments.

I don't answer. A slight movement at one side of the structure alerts me to the presence of another thug, bringing the total to five if I include the faux hostage.

There are ten men.

Where are the rest?

"I'm not here to play games," I say.

"Aren't you? American operatives are never on the level, right,

Markus?" He uses air quotes around the name. "Help me recall what name you used when we first met."

Jason repeats what Kilburn called Markus at his apartment, and I pray we have the correct identity.

Jafari tilts his head. "I thought you might have forgotten."

The irony is the name had also been a cover.

"How'd you find me?" Jason does a credible imitation of Markus Myles' thin, reedy voice, shrinking back to convey fear.

Jafari's face tightens. "Your company got some recent worldwide publicity. Did you think I would forget the face of the man who cost me most of my followers and almost my life?"

"Is that why you killed my family?" Jason says.

Jafari's head jerks up. "I thought you did that."

"Me? I never—"

The terrorist puts up a hand. "Please. You don't possess a conscience. I might be cold-blooded, but you've got me beat."

Have to love the false righteousness.

"Before you apply for sainthood, you or your men killed the Myles' gardener," I say.

Jafari shrugs off my words. "It was necessary. He was a witness to us scouting the property."

"Terrific reason to murder someone in their bed," I say.

"As if you've never killed anyone."

"Not like that." My thoughts flash on Kilburn and his breakdown. At least he has trouble living with what he's done.

Jafari stalks to within ten feet of where we stand, and his men drag the "hostage" forward, their guns out.

"Are you ready to trade?" Jafari's narrowed eyes are on Jason.

"I told you to take off the hood first," I remind him.

"Don't you trust me?"

"Do you need to ask? Where's the real hostage?"

The corner of Jafari's mouth lifts. "He's worth a lot of money, and I like to protect my assets. Several groups are working to outbid each other so he can star in a video. Many jihadists aren't keen on the British."

Death on camera, as Warden speculated.

"I love a double-cross." I tap Jason's arm with my finger in a pre-arranged signal to be ready.

"I think you mean a double-double cross. That's not Markus Myles," Jafari says.

Before his final word is out, I shoot the man to his left, and Jason draws a gun and drills the man in front of him. *Two down, eight to go.* I sprint toward Jafari, since my chance of finding Adair disappears if he does, but the man hiding near the outbuilding steps out to lay down fire with an assault rifle.

Jafari runs back toward the structure as the fake prisoner tears off his hood, pulls out a gun, and begins shooting. Bullets hit the ground near our feet and throw dust clouds as we retreat to where the Rover provides limited protection. Rounds thud into its side.

The damage will be fun to explain to a body shop.

Jason and I pause to reload as the terrorist leader makes it inside the building.

"Where's Adair?" I shove in a loaded magazine.

"No idea." Jason flinches away from a shot as it skitters across the hood.

I expect the missing men to pour out with weapons, but Jafari returns alone—carrying a rocket-propelled grenade launcher. He lifts the long tube over his shoulder and aims at us.

"Run!" I yell to Jason and race forward, firing at Jafari. One of my bullets hits him in the leg, causing his finger to jerk as he pulls the RPG's trigger. The grenade thunders past with a deafening roar and cuts a broad, deep opening across the Rover's front windshield.

The two remaining men hurry to their boss, put their arms under him, and pull him toward one of the SUVs. Despite the assault rifleman assisting Jafari, he holds us back with continual fire.

Seconds become hours as time slows, and everything presents itself in vivid detail. Bullets leave gun barrels and come at me. Blood pours down Jafari's leg, and he grips it, his face white. Hands reach for the doors of a waiting SUV. I aim at one of the car's front tires, shred an outside wall, and it deflates. The escaping men regroup, head for the other vehicle, open the back door, and help their boss inside.

Jason and I fire as we advance. The rifleman runs out of ammo at the same time I do. As he tries to reload, I close the distance and strike him with the butt of my gun. A bloody gash opens on his cheekbone. Jason reaches the other hostile, but I can't spare a moment to worry about him as my opponent pulls a handgun and aims it at me. I lock onto his wrist and redirect the shot away from my body.

Slamming him against the SUV, we fall over the hood, wrestling for control of the firearm. I elbow him in the throat, and he makes a choking sound, his hand going slack. The weapon tumbles to the ground, but he runs me backward into the disabled car with a roar. I crash into a side window and fall.

My rival rushes to retrieve his weapon, but I leap forward and tackle him around the waist. He wriggles free, and we trade punches, kicks, strikes, and blocks, each of us relentless. Every jarring blow that connects with my body makes me worry about my damaged leg. I need to finish the fight before anything happens to disable me.

In a quick move, I latch onto my adversary's right arm and trap his elbow.

Crack!

The man screams as the joint dislocates.

Catching hold of his shirt, I toss him against the sidelined SUV. He rebounds off its side and lands in a heap. I retrieve the dropped gun from where it lies near the front tire of Jafari's SUV and slap a tracking device in the wheel well. Returning to where my foe continues to writhe in agony, I knock him out.

And then there were seven.

The man Jason fought gets free, jumps in the driver's side of the SUV, and starts it up. Pedal to the floor, the car accelerates forward. Jason stands in front of the speeding vehicle, speed-firing to stop it, but is hit full force and thrown into the air. He lands at an odd angle and rolls across the ground. The SUV clips the front fender of my

Rover, moving it enough for the driver to go off-road and around. It zooms away, sending up a cloud of dust.

I run to Jason. "Are you all right?"

His face is a mask of pain. "My leg's broken."

"Can you move?"

He tries to stand and loses all color. "No."

"I'll get the Rover."

"Don't waste time on me. You can't let them get away."

"I stuck a tracking device on their car."

Jason falls back on his elbows. "How?"

"I'm excellent at multi-tasking."

"Go. You need to reach Adair before Jafari takes him and leaves the country."

I hustle to the Rover, retrieve a set of handcuffs, and return to secure the unconscious gunman.

"Here," I hand Jason the automatic from Kilburn's cache.

"Please save Adair." Jason's voice is thick with emotion.

"I will, I promise. Help will be here soon."

Ignoring the hole in the windscreen of the Rover, I start the engine. The tracking device blips a steady signal as I do a hard reverse and speed off, the sky casting sunset hues behind me.

I make a phone call.

"Agent Wills," says the gruff voice of my National Security handler, a distinguished man who resembles a younger Harrison Ford.

"One friendly is injured." I provide him with the address and details. "I'm headed to an unidentified location to rescue the hostage I briefed you on. Are you ready to come with support?"

"Yes."

Preparing a group of agents would require too much time, and a disorganized firefight might be fatal for Adair.

"I'll be in touch." I disconnect.

As I drive, I take stock of my condition. My back aches from the attacker throwing me into the SUV's window. I twist side-to-side in my seat, attempting to stave off stiffness. My arms, face, and legs throb from the repeated forceful blows landed by my opponent during our fight. I flex my fingers to ensure my bruised and scraped knuckles are ready to deploy a gun.

Popping open the center console, I pick up a bottle of aspirin and spill four pills into my hand. Twisting open a small energy drink, I wash them down. The mixture should dull my pain and provide me with needed endurance.

Seven men, plus Yasam Jafari, are left.

Is Adair's estimate correct, or will there be more?

Damn the odds.

26

The tracked vehicle turns into a deserted industrial complex with rows of decrepit warehouses. I stop and pull up an overview on an app to study the location and text the address to Agent Wills. I warn him to wait with backup until I contact him again.

What would I do if I were Yasam Jafari? He will likely prioritize getting treatment for his significant bleeding gunshot wound before taking Adair and leaving. My team carries emergency tourniquets and medicine on missions, but I doubt Jafari planned on an injury.

Burning a U, I head to an access road leading to a closed wrecking yard. My headlights illuminate its locked gate. I retrieve bolt cutters, cut the padlocked chain, and enter. Backing in, I go to the rear hatch to prepare.

The abandoned warehouse where Jafari and his men parked looms below, and I slink past stacks of flattened cars to peer through a slit in a wall of corrugated metal fencing. My night-vision binoculars are white phosphor, and their clarity provides an overview of the place.

The SUV the men arrived in is parked haphazardly near an entrance, the rear door still open. Two guards are engaged in animated conversation and not scrutinizing their surroundings. Are there more on the opposite side?

Every choice I make will determine if Adair lives or dies.

Hunkering down, I deploy my silent drone for the bird's eye, noting the entry points to the hulking building and the attack geography. After a thorough reconnaissance, I return the machine to my location. When it lands, I fold and stash it.

What next? Mourning the lack of supplies and the absence of my team's backup is unproductive. I only have one chance.

Time for some unconventional warfare.

Kyle once told me, "You can tear up the world with what's in a Home Depot."

What can the junkyard offer? A pile of parts leans against a building, and I sort through them. I select two lithium batteries, set them aside, and gather a small gas can, rags, string, and wire. As I assemble my improvised weapons, I plot my course of action and where to channel any tactical response. The icy composure of mission focus descends as I construct the final item.

Don't rush. Slow and steady.

Using the junkyard fence as cover, I ease through a side gate and set up my diversions on the far, unguarded side of the warehouse.

After finishing the setup, I check the back door. The knob turns, and I enter a dingy hall with peeling paint. The muted shine of a crescent moon gleams through a collapsed roof section, and a shallow layer of water on the floor reflects my wavering silhouette.

Where am I going? Did someone leave the door unlocked on purpose? Am I being led into a trap?

My finger stays close to the trigger of my compact, suppressed submachine gun. I smeared dark concealment paint on my face, and tucked my ponytail under my ball cap. Now, I work to blend with the shadows.

At the end of the corridor, I crouch behind a stack of dusty tires to assess the vast room ahead. Graffiti mars the walls, and a musty odor fills my nose. Rotten cement bags, piles of bricks, and discarded wood pallets litter one side of the room. On the opposite side, stacks of rusty pipes lie beneath a bank of small, broken windows. A metal staircase leads to a lighted office with closed blinds.

Is that where they're holding Adair? What happened to Jafari?

I take quick steps toward a steel pillar holding up the remnants of the roof. Checking my watch, I stay in position and wait.

Bam!

An explosion from a metal drum triggers outside. The shards hit the far side of the building with a massive concussion.

Bam!

Another explosion ignites, and the resounding noise is like someone banging a giant hammer against the structure at varying intervals.

The door to the office flies open, and a knot of men push through to the landing, necks craning.

A rending groan echoes, and the rotting metal staircase separates from the siding. The men cry out with alarm as they scramble back toward the office. Before they can reach safety, the apparatus collapses, dust shooting up in a cloud. When the haze clears, three men lie in a mangled, unmoving pile on the hard cement floor.

Four men plus Jafari are left, but if Adair's in the office, I can't reach him.

I move into the open as two armed men charge out of a corridor near the building's exit. I spin around and point my gun toward the interior, blending as one of their own. A roll-up door to my right opens, and the two guards from the outside rush in, flanking me.

"She's not one of us," one shouts in Urdu.

Before anyone can pull a trigger, I bolt toward the metal pillar. Steps from my goal, numbness shoots down my injured leg, and I crumple. Twisting as I fall, I fire quick bursts at the enemy and drag myself behind the narrow column. Bullets ping off its surface in a steady barrage.

I'm a literal sitting duck. What will I do?

Leaning out, I depress my trigger, conscious of expending ammo. My rounds zing past the group, and they run for cover. Two dive behind a pile of bricks while the others retreat toward the hall. The magazine clicks empty, and I drop and reload my final thirty rounds.

Emboldened by the pause, Jafari's men advance, laying down steady fire. A razor-sharp piece of shrapnel pierces my left arm, and another cuts a bloody path across my shoulder. Ignoring the burning hot pain, I drop a shooter.

Four additional men emerge from the hall, and my odds of survival hit a steep decline.

But there's good news mixed with the bad.

One of the men is Adair.

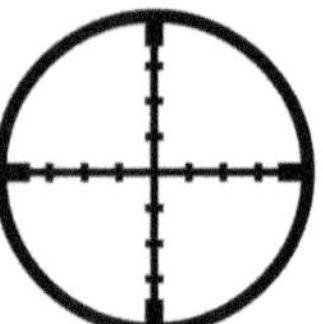

27

A house-sized ruffian guards Adair, whose face is a mass of bloody and swollen bruises. Nylon rope binds his hands in front, and his expensive suit is ripped and filthy.

Yasam Jafari follows with a lackey supporting him. Someone bandaged the terrorist's leg wound, but he walks with difficulty. A lethal man stalks beside him, his firearm pointed toward the ongoing battle. Jafari halts, anger clouding his face as he shouts orders to his men to wipe me from the planet.

You first.

"Adair!" I yell to alert him to my presence.

He stops, eyes closing as he shakes his head.

He must think he hears things.

The guard shoves him in the back, and Adair staggers forward, eyes fixed on the ground.

"Adair!" I punctuate his name with a burst of gunfire, taking down a bad guy who popped up from behind the pile of bricks.

Adair regards me without recognition.

Please see past the war paint and weapon.

"Adair, it's Davia." I blast more rounds.

Confusion floods his face before hope surfaces. His captor barks at Adair to move, but he becomes as stubborn as a toddler. He trips on purpose, dropping his body weight to the floor, and my heart clenches at his valiant effort.

I will get you out of here.

Another man rushes from the hall to support the giant's efforts, and they shove hands under Adair's arms to drag him forward. He fights, but it doesn't slow their progress. Fluorescent lights hang by chains from the roof above them, and I let off several controlled bursts. The fixture crashes to the floor, spraying shattered glass as the men jump back, but they regroup and pull Adair outside.

Jafari's gunman and I trade shots while Jafari limps out the door. I clip his thug in the arm, but he falls back to join his boss.

My magazine clicks empty.

Panic fills me. *I need to finish this fight before Adair disappears. Will my leg hold?*

Tossing the submachine gun aside, I pull my automatic. Cautious, I put some weight on my leg.

Extreme pain is exquisite.

Biting hard on my lower lip, I step into the room. A man jumps up from behind the bricks and runs for the exit, turning to shoot as he goes. I drop him. Maneuvering around his body, while ignoring the agony of each step, I go outside.

Adair's about twenty feet behind Jafari, still doing all he can to delay his progress toward a waiting car. He digs in his heels and throws his weight backward, but his efforts are nothing against the strength of his guards.

The goon I wounded opens the rear door of the SUV for Jafari as I shoot the man on Adair's right. He topples, and Adair stumbles from the sudden absence of support.

Jafari gets into the back seat, where one of his men is behind the wheel, ready to leave. His wounded guard makes it to the front passenger, and I aim for Jafari, but the car speeds off.

If he escapes, so be it. He's not my mission.

Adair's hulking escort shields himself with his prisoner, and Adair snaps his head back, hitting his guard in the face. Blood streams from the man's nose. I'm a few feet away and try for a shot, but he releases Adair and charges me. I hit his windpipe with my free hand, but his reaction's no more than if it were a mosquito sting. He grasps my pistol, and we wrestle for control. The weapon spins away and hits the ground.

"Watch out!" Adair yells.

One of the men from the stair collapse runs at me from behind with a raised pipe wrench. The tool narrowly misses my head. The arc of the blow connects with my injured shoulder, and near-incapacitating pain shoots through me, but I throw myself toward my fallen gun, scoop it up, and fire.

Another one bites the dust.

I turn to engage the behemoth at the same time he deploys a large-caliber handgun from his back waistband. He aims for my head, but Adair slams into the man and knocks him off balance.

We pull triggers.

Mine hit the giant's sternum as his two rounds punch me square in the chest. The force topples me over, and I crash to the ground.

"No!" Adair cries.

I gasp for air, lungs on fire and chest blazing with pain.

Will this be it for me?

Adair sidesteps his fallen captor, repeating my name as he rushes to where I lie. He drops to his knees beside me, and I think of Warden doing the same in Africa after Badger's man shot me. Both men share the same anguished expression.

"How bad is it, Davia?"

Did a round punch through my armor and leave a gaping wound?

With much effort, I pull myself onto an elbow, touch the entry point with a trembling hand and bring it to my face.

No blood.

I fall back with relief, grateful the ceramic plate did its job.

"I got the wind knocked out of me." I'm sure the force broke several ribs, but Adair doesn't need to know. Collecting myself, I strain to move into a seated position and then pull my knife from a holster on my right hip.

"Give me your hands." I cut the rope binding Adair, and he rubs his wrists. We get to our feet, both of us unsteady.

"Are the police coming?" he asks.

"No."

"No? Is Jason here?"

"No. We took on some members of this group earlier at a different location. He broke his leg, so I came alone."

"Just you and Jason? I don't understand—"

"We need to get out of here. Can you walk?"

"I think so."

"Let's go," I place an arm around him.

As we lean on each other and shuffle forward, I text Agent Wills. *Now.*

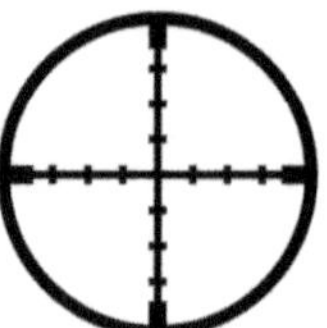

28

We limp back to my Rover, leaving the scene for Agent Wills and his men to secure. Adair surprises me when we reach my car by pulling me against him. We don't move for some time, not speaking. The relief he's alive mixes with other complex emotions brought on by being in his arms.

Adair looks into my eyes. "Thank you for saving me."

"The same to you."

Unspoken questions are plain on his damaged face, but he doesn't ask them.

Will the knowledge I'm an operative change our relationship?

"You promised me you wouldn't do anything dangerous again," he says.

"I shouldn't have." I step away to open the passenger door.

"I get that now. I imagine the whole 'I grew up shooting in the Midwest' line you told me last month isn't the full story." Adair props himself against the car, but his eyes fill with concern. "Your left arm and shoulder are bleeding."

I touch the injuries and come away with my fingers covered in blood. As I wipe them on my pants, I try for a teasing tone. "It's only a flesh wound."

"That's not funny, Davia. Why didn't you let the police handle my rescue?"

This is the beginning of the many questions he will have.

"Your captor told me if law enforcement showed up, he'd kill you, and he wasn't joking. Get in. We need to go."

Adair opens his mouth to protest but stops and pulls himself into the Rover with effort. I hobble to the back of the SUV to stow my gear and pour hemostatic powder on my bleeding wounds, cover them with gauze, and wipe the paint from my face. I leave the vest on as it will be painful to remove, and Adair doesn't need to know I'm hurt worse than he realizes.

How often had I been shot wearing body armor during missions, returning with deep bruises marking my body? My team kept a tally of who received the most black and blue badges and broken bones gifted by gunfire.

I send a text to Jason: *Adair is alive & with me.*

His reply is instant, with a hospital's name and address.

Unmarked cars and emergency vehicles speed past us when we reach the road, heading for the warehouse. Adair stares out the front windscreen, not questioning the significant damage nor seeming to care about the wind blasting through the opening. His aquiline nose isn't as straight as before, and his lips are bloodied and swollen. A hand with dirty and broken nails holds his ribs, and he winces each time I hit a bump.

"I'm taking you to a hospital where Jason is waiting." I hand him a canister containing water, and Adair sucks down the contents.

"When was the last time you ate or drank?"

"Don't know." He wipes his mouth with a hand. "How'd you find me?"

"I'll let Jason tell you. Do you want a protein bar?"

He nods, and I tell him one's in the glove box. As he retrieves it, I ask, "How did they kidnap you?"

"I left my meeting, went to my car in the underground parking, and was about to text you, but two guys rushed me." He tears the wrapper open. "I got thrown into an SUV, and they pulled a hood over my head. I somehow got my phone into a pocket. After being dragged out and tied to a chair, I blindly tried to ring Jason, but the call went through to you."

"Jason and I got to the location soon after, but you were gone." My tone is bleak.

"My days as a captive made me think I wouldn't survive. Thanks to you, I did."

As he wolfs down the bar, I say, "I have no right to be thanked for saving you. You got caught up in this because I went to the Myles' home the night of the murders. I work for the government in a capacity I can't disclose, and this is the second time you got hurt because of who I am."

Adair coughs and clutches his ribs tighter. "And because I didn't listen to you or Jason about bodyguards."

"The situation isn't that simple."

"Davia, the last time we saw each other, I told you I didn't want you to live in emotional lockdown. If you had told me why you're that way—"

"We can discuss this later, but I need to get you to the hospital."

We ride in silence from there, and Adair falls asleep. Despite his swollen and discolored face, he appears at peace, a lock of hair falling over a blackened eye. I fight the urge to push it back, hating Jafari, his crew, and myself.

Men clad in suits wait at the curb with Jason, whose leg is in a cast. He leans on crutches, giving orders. His assistants help Adair to the sidewalk, and Jason puts a hand on Adair's shoulder, his face filling with relief. When the passenger door closes, I force myself to drive away.

ONCE HOME, I place a hand on the wall for support as I lurch toward my bedroom, trying not to keel over before I get there. I strip off my jacket, the gauze on my injuries tears away, and blood drips down my arm. Dropping the garment, I stumble into the bathroom, where the mirror reflects my disheveled image. I touch a contusion on my left cheek.

I saved Adair, and I'm still standing, so today was a win.

Although my broken ribs make deep breathing painful, I suck in air, release the Velcro straps holding my vest, and lift it off. The two bullet holes punched in the front were deadly accurate, the center of a target bullseye.

My number wasn't up. I lived to fight another day.

I'm not ready to review the full extent of my actions, no matter how justified they were. Operatives can box things up and continue because we've done the right thing on missions. I just killed seven men to save one in an unofficial capacity. How will I deal with what happened without my team?

Taking scissors from a drawer, I cut away my shirt and sports bra. Between my breasts is a raised red area from the gunfire. The wound will become blue and purple in time, and I doubt the marks will be gone before the fashion show. Leaning my injured shoulder and arm toward the mirror, I can't tell if the wounds need stitches.

"Take a shower first," I say aloud.

Stripping off the rest of my clothes, I step into the steaming hot water. The spray stings my open injuries, and blood mixes with the flow into the drain at my feet. I prop my hands against the wall and fight the urge to sink to the floor.

When finished, I dry off, put antibiotic ointment on my shoulder and arm, then hold the deepest cut together and apply butterfly bandages. My bruised body looks like I went toe-to-toe with Mike Tyson, but my leg pain has settled to a manageable ache. As I pull a long t-shirt over my head, my phone vibrates on the counter.

"This is Agent Wills. We caught the target and his men when they fled the scene." He doesn't identify Yasam Jafari by name for security. "We also found two more men who were injured but alive in the warehouse."

"Great."

"Was your mission a success?"

"Yes."

"Given what we cleaned up at the scene, I doubt you got away unscathed. If you need a trip to Balboa Naval Hospital, I can send an agent to transport you."

"Not now. I don't want to go the opioid route, and I can handle the rest."

"If you change your mind, call." He disconnects.

I down more aspirin, sit in the chair facing my bedroom window, and call Kyle.

"Oh, thank god," he says when he answers.

I relay what I can on an unsecured line, and he doesn't interrupt.

"How bad off are you?"

"Took out seven, so you can imagine."

"Can you walk?"

"Yes, but I doubt I can do much for at least a week except whine about my broken ribs and aching body."

"Were you hit?"

"Caught some lead in the arm and shoulder, and then took two shots center mass."

Kyle lets out a long breath. "I'll come back."

"You don't have to. I can handle everything."

"Are you sure?"

"Yes."

"Keep me updated."

When we conclude our call, I text Warden.

Me: *Mission a success. I need to sleep.*

Warden: *R u ok?*

Me: *Yes, will call tomorrow.*

Warden responds with heart emojis.

A full moon illuminates the night sky, and I settle back into the chair.

My phone buzzes, and the caller is Adair.

"Davia, where are you?"

"I'm home. I guess Jason got you a new phone?"

Adair ignores this. "Why did you drop me and drive away? You should be at a hospital."

"I'm fine."

"That's rubbish."

"I took a shower, and I'm going to bed. You don't need to—"

"You can't be okay," he interrupts. "Is someone with you?"

"No, as I said, I'm—"

"You aren't fine. I'm at the hospital with an IV drip in my arm, but I'll pull it out and come over if you don't tell me the truth. You risked your life for me. What do you want me to do? Forget what happened? Forget the state you were in afterward? You hid how bad you were hurt to spare me, but I have eyes."

"I'm telling you the truth. If I need more care, I'll go in."

"You're telling me porkies. You shouldn't be alone."

I can't tell him this is nothing in the scheme of my life. But was it? I hadn't faced something like this without my team. I redirect the conversation. "How are you doing?"

"I'm a bit worked over, with my nose and ribs broken and a lot of bruises. No internal damage, though."

"I hope you'll get some rest."

"Davia, you're fearless, and I'm forever grateful you saved me, but you shouldn't bear this by yourself."

His concern is much different than the jokes and dark humor my team uses to cover the aftermath of our jobs.

"I appreciate your call, Adair, but I'm going to bed."

"I'm checking in with you again tomorrow, but if you need something before that, call me."

When I disconnect, I think of Warden's brief response by text. He accepted I was okay because he knew my capabilities and trusted me. Not telling him the whole of what occurred and my worries about dealing with any mental consequences alone is my fault.

Do Warden and I pretend we're fine when we're not? Do I want to continue to live this way, unable to admit dealing with my actions is difficult sometimes? I should forget Adair and eradicate my attraction to him, but why do I want him to hold me right now?

I put the phone down and do something I haven't done in years.

I begin to cry.

29

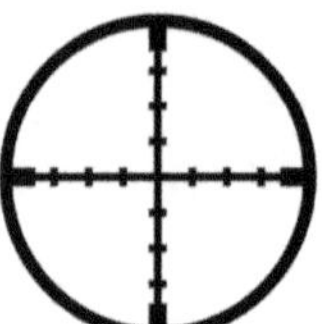

I lie on a recliner on Adair's yacht, bathed by warm sunshine. Adair relaxes in the hot tub wearing a thin, button-up white shirt and swim trunks. When he pulls himself out of the water and swings his leg over the edge, his sculpted pecs and six-pack abs mold to the fabric.

He picks up a towel and dries himself. "You were checking me out," he says.

"I wasn't." Heat rises in my cheeks.

What am I supposed to say? Every inch of you is temptation.

Adair comes close, places his hands on my bikini-clad hips, and bends to kiss me.

"You're getting me wet," I protest as water drips from his clothes.

"I hope so," he murmurs.

I slip my hand under his shirt and along his smooth skin.

Adair straightens, and the way he regards me makes it almost impossible to breathe. "I think we should go inside." He reaches for my hand.

The sharp crack of a rifle follows his words.

A stain of red appears on his shirt, right beside his heart.

Adair is uncomprehending, the light in his beautiful eyes fading. He falls as I search my surroundings for the gunman.

I don't have a weapon. What can I do?

Dread fills me as I turn Adair on his side and check for a pulse that isn't there.

"Adair! Please don't die," I plead, even though I know he's gone.

"Davia, Davia, wake up," a faraway voice says.

I kneel beside Adair's still form, my hand on his chest where blood seeps through my fingers.

"Wake up!" the voice repeats, louder this time as I surface from sleep.

I open my eyes, and Sherilyn sits on the edge of my bed, hands on my arms.

"What is going on?" she demands. "Why were you screaming Adair's name like something terrible happened?"

I scrub my eyes. "I had a nightmare, I guess."

Both men in my life died in my dreams, their blood on my hands. What did it mean?

"Adair called me early this morning and told me you had a rough time yesterday, and he's been trying to call you, but you turned off your phone," Sherilyn says. "Since he knows we're close friends, he told me to check on you, so I came over, and what did I find? A trail of clothes. I thought you two enjoyed one helluva night— and then I saw the blood. Blood on the carpet, blood tracked into the bathroom. If you're a sexual masochist into hard BDSM, I'm not judging, but—"

"Sherilyn," I sit up and cringe as a sharp pain from my cracked ribs hits. "I got in a car crash, and—"

"A car crash? Is Adair not here because he was also hurt?"

"Yes, but he's okay." I push the covers away, and Sherilyn stands to give me room.

"Did you go to the hospital? I told you to give me a copy of your medical insurance card because I knew something like this would happen."

"No, my injuries aren't serious." I set my feet on the carpet and attempt to stand. My legs won't hold my weight, and Sherilyn catches me before I hit the floor. She helps me sit on the mattress.

"I don't know your definition of serious, but I don't think it's the same as mine. What can I do?"

"Get me some aspirin?" I push away the vision of Adair lying dead, still unnerved by the dream.

Sherilyn is back in moments with water and several pills. After I take them, she plumps up my pillows and helps me get under the covers. When I'm settled, she says, "Davia, you did not get in a car crash."

"I did. I—"

"You're saying you and Adair went out last night and got in a traffic accident, right?"

"Yes."

"And you chose to wear black combat clothing to go on a date?"

"You know I have no fashion sense."

"True, but you paired that look with a bulletproof vest with two bullet holes in the center, and also wiped blood all over your clothes?"

Her voice grows harder with each question, and I realize my story won't hold up under scrutiny, but I'm so disoriented I can't think.

Sherilyn continues. "Last month, when some guy came here and attacked you, you said you had a connection in law enforcement. Are you working undercover or something? Is that how you met Detective Montoya? If James Warden is also in that line of work, that explains why you two have so many scars. I saw the jagged one on his side when we had the pool party, and—"

"I can't tell you anything," I interrupt. "I'm sorry."

"Whatever the rules are, Adair knows you got hurt, and he's freakin' losing his mind with worry. Does he work undercover, too? Who would suspect a hot billionaire? The ruse worked for Bruce Wayne."

"Batman is fiction, and Adair's a businessman, nothing more."

"Okay." She draws out the word. "I realize we haven't known each other long, but we're friends. You should tell me how you were injured so I don't waste my time coming up with ridiculous explanations."

What can I say? How much? Try for some truth.

"Adair doesn't have a house key but probably guessed you might. We spoke last night, and he knew I got hurt. I didn't put my phone on the charger, so it died."

"I see what you're doing, telling me stuff that might be true but is irrelevant to how you sustained these injuries. I'm not stupid, you know. My parents are both lawyers, and they taught me to listen to what people say. You left out why you look like a truck ran you over or why you have a vest with bullet holes in your bathroom."

"Uh, I was outnumbered."

"By how many?"

"Too many?"

Sherilyn sighs. "Fine. I accept you can't tell me what you do or details or anything, so I'll fix you something to eat while you call Adair. Where's your phone?"

I squeeze my eyes closed, thinking, then shake my head. "Last night was a blur."

Sherilyn returns to the bathroom, comes back out, and searches.

"Here it is." She picks up my phone from the chair I sat in last night after my shower. When did I get into bed? I can't remember. She returns to my bedside and plugs in the charger cord from my nightstand. "I'm going to make you some breakfast. Be back in a few."

When my phone powers on, I enter the code, and message and voicemail notifications flood the screen. All the calls and voicemails are from Adair. How many are there? Five? I think of Sherilyn's words. *He's freakin' losing his mind with worry.* Not ready to listen to his voice so soon after my dream, I scroll through the texts.

Warden: *Hope you got some rest. We're out.*

The team is gone again, giving me some respite. Warden will be furious if we video call. I won't be able to skate around his questions as I have with Sherilyn, and I need to come up with a reasonable explanation for my actions.

Next is a text from an unknown number: *Mum's the word from our little socio-spook. Too bad waterboarding's forbidden.*

Kilburn. He's sent me the promised update, although it gets me no answers. Detective Montoya will have to solve the case, since my involvement brought me and those around me nothing but problems.

I scan the other texts.

Kyle: *Check in with me when you're able.*

Mom: *I'm leaving for NYC next week. Thanks for sending me Mr. Morgenstern's information.*

Standing with caution, I manage to make a bathroom run. The bruise on my face is darker, and I don't want to inspect my chest or other aching areas, unwilling to deal with reality.

Sherilyn returns with a plate of food and a mug of tea after I get back in bed. The smell of eggs and toast makes me realize how hungry I am. When did I last eat? The lack of nutrition piled on top of my ordeal is a reason for my near-collapse.

"If I have to go back and forth from the kitchen carrying plates of hot food, you need serving trays. It never occurred to me to buy any. Who knew you'd be out of commission and in bed for an extended period? Did you call Adair?"

"Not yet, but I will when I finish eating."

"Ooh, I just had an idea about the trays. I can get some colorful ones that don't look like they belong in a hospital. They'll serve double duty if you want to fix Adair breakfast in bed some morning."

"We aren't sleeping together."

"You're not?" Sherilyn sets the plate on my lap with care.

"Adair's just a friend."

"Really, Davia? I don't mind you lying to me about your lifestyle of death and destruction since you're required to maintain secrecy, but your connection to Adair is another story. You told me you lost control and kissed him last week, which isn't something you do with friends."

I take a bite of the food to delay my answer. After swallowing, I say, "I'm not going to go out with him again."

Sherilyn makes a strangled sound, hands on her hips. "You think if you don't see him, that resolves the problem? Who are you kidding?"

Who was I kidding? Myself, as always.

When I don't answer, Sherilyn says, "You still need to call him."

"I will when I finish eating."

"Do you promise?"

I nod and take another bite of food, not registering its taste.

"Set your dishes on the nightstand and get some sleep after you call Adair. I'll be back later today, but I have to go to an appointment with a client right now. Text me if you need me to return sooner, and I will."

"Thank you."

Sherilyn bends down to hug me. "Friends support each other, even if one is a stubborn pain in the ass."

"Hello?" a man's quiet voice says when I ring Adair, and I realize Jason has answered.

"Jason, it's Davia. Adair called and..."

"Just a moment." His voice is a whisper. Footsteps sound and a door opens and closes. He speaks again at his normal volume. "He's asleep right now. What do you want?"

"How is he?"

"Yelling in terror in his sleep, soaking the sheets with sweat because of his ordeal, yet all that bloody idiot does is worry about you."

"I know you're angry."

"Angry?" A mocking laugh explodes through the phone. "Angry doesn't begin to describe it. I'm grateful you saved him, but you came into Adair's life and nearly got him killed—twice."

What can I say? Nothing.

"And you? How bad is your leg?"

"I'll live," he snarls.

"Tell Adair I called, I appreciate him sending Sherilyn over, and I'm okay."

The line disconnects.

I can't blame Jason for his abruptness. None of this would have happened if I hadn't involved myself in the Myles murder case. I wouldn't have helped Kilburn, Jafari's men wouldn't have kidnapped Adair, and my biggest concern would be getting healthy and waiting out my leave. Now I consider the mental and physical cost to myself and Adair.

Why did I cry last night? Were they tears of happiness at Adair coming out of this alive? Tears over the near-death experience of getting shot? Were the locked and chained mental compartments of my past cracking open and the horrors spilling out?

When I think of Adair battling night terrors, tears threaten again.

I'm sorry, Adair. You didn't deserve a taste of my world.

I lie back and stare at the ceiling. What should I do? I run options, coming up with no solution.

These are my last thoughts before I drift off to sleep.

30

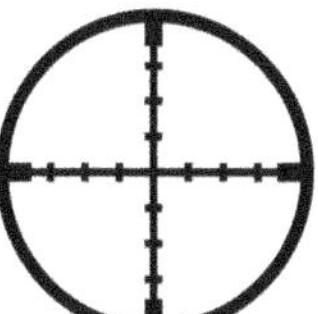

The Ladies League buzzes with activity. Models, hairstylists, makeup artists, and clothing racks surround me. Kincaid Foxx and Bronwyn give orders to minions who scurry to obey. A happy murmur of conversation accompanied by the clink of cutlery from a pre-fashion show luncheon in the gardens comes through an open door.

A loud crash from outside makes everyone pause.

"How dare the Ladies' League serve only your beverages," a man yells.

Roger O'Neill stumbles into view. He shouts at rival soda company owner Todd Hughes, who lies on the ground covered with dishes and food from a fallen server tray.

These two again.

Todd gets to his feet, grabs a soda can from a beverage-filled table before a bartender, and chucks it at Roger. A group of well-dressed women jump up, forced away from their lunches by the ensuing melee.

Some people will never grow up, but I'm leaving them to it today.

While the fight continues outside, people rush past me, engaged in varied tasks.

"Davia Glenn?" An assistant carries a clipboard, her frantic gaze bouncing between faces.

"Here." I raise a reluctant hand.

The young woman bustles over. "I'm Melody, and I'll be your coordinator today. First, you need your makeup done. Come with me."

She weaves through the tight, crowded space, and I follow her to a table covered with makeup equipment. Beside it, a thin man I recognize wears a harassed expression to accompany his glamorous eyeshadow.

"Hi, Christian," I greet. He did my makeup for the Ladies' League Gala.

"Adair Monroe's girl, sit." Christian pats the back of a chair as Melody's mouth falls open at his words. "I saw you two on the cover of a certain magazine, so I plan to make you even more spectacular today. I knew Adair was taken with you when he sent you the comb. You're one lucky girl."

What will happen if I protest? Nothing, because people will believe what they want, no matter the truth.

After I settle, Christian picks up a makeup sponge. "Girl, what happened to your face?"

Sherilyn brought me a tube of Arnica gel and hassled me daily about applying the ointment to my injuries, but the bruise on my cheek is noticeable.

"Car accident, nothing major," I say.

Christian studies the yellow spot and then turns to his supplies, picking up a small compact. "This concealer will make it disappear, so don't worry."

When Christian finishes his work, a bright royal blue shadow surrounds my eyes like a mask. My eyebrows are defined, my cheeks hollowed, and my lips pale with a heavy gloss.

"What do you think?" he says.

"Quite dramatic," I manage.

"The dress you'll wear is avant-garde, so the makeup adds to the presentation."

What was avant-garde? Did I want to know?

"Will Adair be here?" Christian says.

"I'm not sure. He's been out of the country on business."

In the week since my conversation with Jason, I didn't respond to any of Adair's texts or calls. I reasoned if I distanced myself from him, it might cause Adair to replace his concern for me with dislike so he'd be safe in the future. Or was I afraid of something for once in my life?

Thanking Christian for his work, I allow Melody to whisk me away to where Ramon, Bryce's partner, waits to style my hair. He's the size of a football lineman and Black. A broad smile gleams white as I approach.

"I need to make an appointment with you," I say as I sit.

"The state of your hair won't matter much today. Kincaid wants it straight and sleek, which doesn't take much."

While Ramon works, Sophie LaChance appears beside me.

"Davia, you didn't bother to come to the practice session. I doubt your ability to do anything today except fall on your face."

"Worse things have happened."

"At least no one will blame me when you crash and burn," she sniffs and departs.

Ramon bends down. "What a *B-i-tch*."

I grin at him with laughing eyes, and he says, "Put her out of your mind. Your instructor told me you'll do fine."

Ramon finishes, and Melody directs me to a corner of the room where Kincaid Foxx waits.

"I typically use one of my best models for the grand finale, but I saved the honor for you since your Adair Monroe's woman."

This again.

"You'll be the final model on the runway," he continues," and you won't be able to sit after you put on the dress. Promise me you won't."

"I promise." Not sitting in a dress is my most manageable recent challenge.

Around me, models pull on pieces from the collection. Beatrice proudly wears a long, black leather coat with crepe pants. She reminds me of Cruella de Ville, with her silver hair teased up and adorned with streaks of black spray. Brittany and Kennedy are indistinguishable from the professional models with their skinny bodies.

Where is Ava? Concern hits me. The show will begin soon, and Ava should be here by now. *Did someone hurt or kidnap her?*

Francis Downs enters from outside and comes to where I stand. "The guests are starting to take their seats. Are you ready?"

"As I'll ever be, have you seen Ava?"

Francis frowns. "No. How odd."

Her sentence is barely out when Ava enters with her brother, and I relax. She waves at Francis and me, and an attendant takes her to a makeup station. Alex wears a gray double-breasted suit, a cream shirt, leather tennis shoes, and a player's smirk. He catches my eye, and his hand goes to his mouth, a finger at his parted lips. I turn away.

"Alex Gordon is a cutie, and he appears to think the same about you," Francis says.

"He's not my type."

"I'm off to take tickets, but here's someone who is your type," Francis says, squeezes my arm, and departs.

Coming toward me is Adair.

DESPITE HIS FACE'S fading damage, he still looks like a god among mortals. Adair strides forward, gathers me in his arms, and kisses me on the forehead. My previous admonishments to keep my distance from him go out the window, and I breathe in his familiar scent.

"I didn't expect you." I listen to the steady beat of his heart to force away the lingering horror of my dream.

"I missed you." His words are husky, and he holds me like he never wants to let me go.

Why is he so caring? Shouldn't he hate me?

When I lift my head, Melody is next to us, frozen.

I make myself step back. "I thought you were still out of the country."

"Oh?" He winks, then introduces himself to my gaping assistant. "Got in a car smash while I was away."

"You look, well, you look—" she stammers.

"Smashing?"

"Excuse us, Melody." I take his arm, and we move to a secluded corner. "What are you doing here?"

"I said I wouldn't miss it. Besides, you aren't able to ignore me here."

"I owe you an apology. I acted like a juvenile when I didn't return your calls and texts, but being with me is dangerous."

"I'm pretty sure I got the memo." Adair gestures to his face.

"Why aren't you angry with me? I almost got you killed."

"Davia, I'm angrier about you ducking me than what happened. You couldn't have foreseen I would be kidnapped, and you risked your life to save me. I understand our situation is complex, but we need to have an open and honest conversation rather than not speaking to each other."

His request is beyond fair. "You're right."

"In the meantime, I hired a couple of bodyguards but told them not to be obtrusive." He nods toward two strapping men at the model tent entrance. "It calmed Jason down to a bearable degree."

"I'm glad. If anything happens to you again, I'll never forgive myself."

Adair's eyes soften. "I wish I could kiss you, but the makeup artist might get his knickers in a twist if I ruin your lipstick."

His proximity and the warmth of his words make everything around me melt away.

A man walks up behind us.

"Isn't this cozy?"

Warden.

BOTH MEN WEAR dark suits and might be rival CEOs. A light shadow accents Warden's sculpted jawline, and he exudes displeasure. When

Warden returned from his mission, I told him the truth about the Adair rescue and endured his ire. The conversation was rough, and the call concluded with neither of us happy. He hadn't mentioned a trip to California.

My heart pounds faster at seeing him, but before I can speak, Adair says, "We must stop meeting like this."

"I'd hit you, but it appears someone beat me to it," Warden drawls.

"I don't think Davia would like it if you decked a man she cares about," Adair says.

"And I don't think she cares about a man who had to be rescued."

"As if staying with you is any safer." Adair steps forward.

"Warden, what are you doing here?" I interrupt.

Warden doesn't answer. or take his focus off Adair.

Melody rushes up. "Excuse me, Ms. Glenn. Kincaid said you need to get dressed."

I put my hands on both men's forearms, squeezing until their dagger-locked eyes turn to me.

"You two need to behave." I direct my admonishment primarily at Warden.

He gives me a tight nod, and I hesitate, then follow Melody.

"Who's that man with Mr. Monroe?" Melody says as we step away.

Someone I hope won't get arrested for assault.

"James Warden."

"He showed up with four other gorgeous men, and they've caused quite the stir." She pulls aside a portion of the curtain screening our room from the audience.

My team wears suits. Ned's clean-shaven for the first time since I met him, but his wavy brown hair is still in a bun. He's chatting to four women who reach out to touch his muscular arms. Also surrounded by admirers, Hodge and K stand relaxed while Savant blows out his cheeks.

How are they here?

"Do you know them?" Melody says.

"Yes."

"They said they're in town to do a training presentation. I wish they'd train me," Melody gushes.

I glance back to where Adair and Warden continue to trade words. If they fight, what will I do? Adair's bodyguards draw close but regard Warden with trepidation. His size, coupled with his seething expression, would make anyone hesitate. It surprises me Adair hasn't backed away an inch.

Photographers roam the tent, snapping photos of the clothes and models. Ahead, Kincaid Foxx stands near a dress with a team of attendants steaming and fluffing areas of concern.

"There you are." He walks around me like I'm a prize horse up for auction.

"My people will help you dress, and you must remember to what?"

"Not sit down?"

"Correct. Now, strip."

"No." The Adair photo will be the last salacious shot taken of me.

"Did you just say no?"

"I did."

Kincaid rolls his eyes, claps his hands, and a sheet materializes, held by a squad of assistants. He raises an eyebrow at me, and I slip off my simple dress to reveal the nude undergarments Bryce advised me to wear.

Kincaid focuses on my bruises. "What happened to you?"

"Car accident, but nothing major."

Bandages cover my shoulder and arm wounds, more jagged lines added to my collection of scars, but a deep and sizable bruise from being shot still marks my sternum. I continue to ignore the discomfort of my broken ribs.

"Give me your hand." Kincaid helps me step over miles of royal blue fabric into the center of the garment. Once I'm inside, he says, "Drop the bra."

"You're kidding."

"Does it seem like I am?"

Inhaling, I do as instructed. Kincaid's helpers pull the dress up and on. The voluminous garment is the size of a float in a parade. The sides and back are reams of sheer, draped fabric, but the front shows my legs cut to the top of my thighs.

"Headpiece," Kincaid calls, and a towering creation made of flowers and crystals requires me to stoop. A jeweled band crosses my forehead, and assistants stick pins into my hair so hard they poke my scalp.

"Remember, no sitting," Kincaid admonishes.

"What about the shoes?" I ask, but he spies an issue with another model and leaves.

Melody says, "I'll help you with them later. I can't believe Mr. Foxx isn't making you wear them right now."

Perhaps being perceived as Adair's significant other has some unexpected benefits.

I check the corner, but Warden and Adair are gone. Are the pair now best buddies and sharing a drink, or did my team hog-tie Adair and his bodyguards and shove them into a closet?

"What do I do now besides not sit down?" I say to Melody.

"Would you like your phone to post to social media?"

"No."

"It vibrated a few times in your purse. Do you want to check?"

They might be texts from Warden explaining why he's here.

I take out the phone, not wanting Melody to note the revolver, and give the purse back to her.

The messages are from my mom, a series of photos she found at Aunt Lilah's penthouse.

Thought you might enjoy these. (Heart emoji) *Mom*

A photo shows Aunt Lilah hugging Uncle Edwin on their wedding day. They beam at the camera, and I'm surprised by my uncle's handsome appearance, as all my memories are of an older, stocky man. My aunt holds a cascading bouquet, and her hair is long, blonde, and flowing beneath her veil. She's so young, a recent high school graduate grabbing onto a new life.

The next, she's in a bright pink satin dress, bangles on her wrists, dancing with an eye-catching man. *Is that David Bowie?* I'm shocked to realize it is. Another photo is with a man in glasses, his hair wild, and is signed *Love, Andy Warhol.*

In photo after photo, Aunt Lilah poses in different fashionable outfits at society functions. She was always the center of attention. People put their arms around her, not the other way around. I scroll through the numerous images with speed until one makes me stop and return to it.

Zooming in, I stare at a face and over to where assistants help Ava into the outfit she's modeling. In this picture, Ava's younger, her hair lighter and longer, but it's her. Aunt Lilah and Ava's heads are close together, making silly faces at the camera.

Didn't she tell me she was on the fringes of my aunt's group? Was this a one-off done for forgotten reasons?

Moving through more photos, I pause and enlarge another image. Next to my aunt are three people.

Ava Gordon stands beside Markus and Stephanie Myles.

31

An announcement the fashion show is about to begin comes over the speakers as my thoughts spin. Ava said she didn't know the Myles family well on several occasions, so was this a brief encounter, or did she downplay their acquaintance? She stands across the room from me, talking to Brittany and Kennedy, all in fabulous creations and outré makeup. Her brother is nearby, flirting with some models.

A speaker beyond the curtain says, "Ladies and Gentlemen, I'm Rick Coleridge, anchor for Channel 10 News. Welcome to the premiere of Kincaid Foxx's Fall collection. Proceeds will benefit A Reading Life, a local non-profit supporting literacy. First, Ladies League board member Francis Downs will give you an official welcome."

After the applause dies, Francis says, "The Ladies League thanks you for making this a sold-out event to benefit a worthy cause. The show will be in two parts, with an intermission, and our community member models will appear in the second half. We've enlisted the assistance of some attractive male volunteers to entice you to buy some raffle tickets for fantastic prizes, so find one of them during our mid-show break. And now, I'm handing this back over to Rick Coleridge."

"Let's start the show," he says.

Models file past me toward a ramp leading to the catwalk, strutting in time to peppy music. After consideration, I select the two images and text them to Ava. Her phone is in her hand, and she checks when my texts chime their arrival, her slender fingers playing over the screen.

What will happen now? Will she find me and give a laughing explanation? Or will she be another person who only tells me lies?

Kyle to fourteen-year-old me, "Let's talk about how to spot a liar, which might come in handy when you start dating."

"I think I'll use the skill for more than that," I said.

Kyle smiled. "Today, I'll explain a few ways to catch liars. First, listen to their words. Sometimes when a person makes up a story, they use the wrong tense."

"What do you mean?"

"Let's say a man murdered his girlfriend. The police have him in for questioning, and he says, 'When I get home, she's on the floor with a stab wound.' Tell me what's wrong with that statement."

"He used present tense."

"Right. I would expect him to say, 'When I got home, she was on the floor with a stab wound' or 'Someone stabbed her.' Do you hear the difference?"

"Yes."

"He also didn't use her name, a possible signal he's trying to distance himself from the killing. Next, watch for confirmation glances."

"What do you mean?"

"Imagine you did something wrong and want to check if your parents believed what you told them."

"I've never done anything wrong," I protested.

"Oh? The quick peek you gave me just now to see if I bought your story was a confirmation glance."

Ava comes toward me, her expression curious, not concerned. "Where did you get these?"

"My mom sent them from Aunt Lilah's penthouse." I flip my phone to show her the photo with my aunt. "Tell me about this."

I use command language from my interrogation training, a start to what I hope won't be anything.

"About what?"

"What you guys were doing."

"I'm helping out at a fundraiser, and your aunt is too."

"Oh? Which one?"

"I don't remember. We were always at something. I told you how draining it was to be on the scene in New York."

I stay silent, letting Ava fill the space with her story.

Let the suspect do the talking. With sensitive subjects, ask fewer questions.

"I think this is a fundraiser for a charity I volunteer for, the one for foster children. Your aunt helps me serve the ice cream to the kids, and we're clowning around." Ava glances at me.

"I never saw my aunt goof around."

"Oh, she was quite the card. We had so much fun through the years."

"I thought you didn't move in her circle."

"I can't claim a close friendship with her."

"How about Markus Myles? Can you claim a close friendship with him?"

Ava's breathing shifts into her chest, causing the gold necklace she wears to rise and fall.

"No, I told you, I'm an investor, that's all."

"Are there any reasons you can think of that might prove otherwise?"

"Why are you asking me about this again?" The pitch of her voice is higher.

Is she trying to elicit information, or is this nothing?

"I spoke to him the other day."

Startled, she says, "Where?"

Time to tell a lie of my own. "He told me about the murders and your involvement."

Ava does what I don't expect.
She runs.

AVA SLIPS OUT A SIDE DOOR, the music cuts off, and the outer room erupts with applause. Rick Coleridge announces, "We'll take a fifteen-minute break, and our community members will finish the show. Be sure to find one of the men selling raffle tickets. You might win private cooking classes, a bottle of fine wine, a luxury vacation, or much more, so open those wallets for a great cause."

I lift the hem of my dress to pursue Ava. Did guilt or fear of false accusations cause her flight? Before I move, Sherilyn appears.

"Wow, Davia. This outfit is amazing! You'll never believe it, but Detective Montoya called and asked me to attend this—"

"Go find him. Tell him I have some information about the Myles murders, and please hold this for me." I press my phone into her hand, gather the copious amounts of billowing fabric around me, and head after Ava.

Melody is across the crowded space. "Ms. Glenn! Ms. Glenn! You need to stop."

"I need to use the restroom," I call to her and keep going. I can't waste time retrieving my gun, but Ava's high heels are her only weapon. Would she use them to attack me, or is this her having a panic attack due to her past?

I'm almost at the door Ava disappeared through when my forward progress halts. A ripping sound confirms someone stepped on the voluminous train. Dennis, a pudgy photographer I recognize from the Suprema Gazette, stumbles off the gown and pales at the damage.

"Kincaid's going to kill me," he says.

"If I don't beat him to it. I'm not happy you sold my photo with Adair to a magazine."

"I—I thought you wouldn't mind." Dennis backs further away.

"Fortunately for you, I need to go." I renew my trek, remembering to duck at the last second so the headpiece doesn't hit the doorframe, but the fabric catches on the door's edge. As I snatch it free, another rip resounds.

Who will notice? The train contains enough material to make forty gowns.

Navigating the narrow hall is like I'm a ship in a tight canal, the fabric making a swishing sound as it brushes against the walls. The right side of the dress tips a decorative table, and a vase of flowers falls to scatter blossoms all over the train and soak the hem.

Will the dress dry before the show begins?

I reach the end of the passage, which terminates in a t-intersection.

Where did Ava go?

The kitchen lies to the right, and servers and dishwashers fill it, so I go left. I'm only a few steps in when Ava hurtles out of a room, a pair of sharp pruning shears in her hand.

Why does the Ladies League offer floral arranging classes?

I jump back. The clippers plunge, shredding the fabric in a long line. As I retreat, the bunched-up material of my dress coils against the wall behind me and bounces me back in Ava's direction. She directs her improvised weapon toward my head, but I turn the blades away.

"You need to stop," I tell her, but she wrenches the shears from my grasp, her face incandescent with anger. Her socialite mask slips away, revealing a monster in a designer dress.

"I'm going to find Markus and kill him." She lunges for me again.

I dodge, but another slice tears through the translucent material. "That will be difficult."

"I know where he's staying," she says.

"He's not there."

"How do you know?"

We face each other, and she waits for another opportunity to strike.

"I bet you haven't been able to reach him for days now, right?"

Ava's eyes flicker. "You're bluffing."

"I'm not. He ran afoul of the feds and is in their custody." I don't specify the agency out of habit. "I helped the operative who took him back to Virginia."

"I don't believe you," she spits, but I catch a tinge of uncertainty.

"Markus said the murders weren't supposed to go down like that. Did you two plan them together?"

Ava gives a disbelieving shake of her head. "Is he pretending he gives a damn? He's a consummate actor."

I back away with my palms out and placating. "I believe you. Why don't you tell me what happened?"

"This is his stupid wife's fault. He told her she'd have as much money as she wanted, but she didn't listen. She made him leave New York after, um, after—" Her voice trails off.

"After you sent her threatening texts and trashed her makeup and clothes?"

"He told her not to mess with me or try to break us up, but she confronted me, so I had to make sure she got a clear message."

"And you met them in New York?"

"Yes, like I told you. I met Markus's wife volunteering, and she introduced me to him. After we met, Markus and I decided we were perfect for each other. We both knew how to make money, liked to travel, and loved an action-filled life."

Two little sociopaths sitting in a tree.

K-I-S-S-I-N-G.

"Why didn't she divorce him?"

Ava let out a bitter laugh. "Divorce? All she wanted was to be perceived as the perfect parent and spend Markus's money. She told him she didn't care what he did as long as he gave her whatever she wanted, and he did."

"She said she wanted another child with him, which doesn't sound like someone simply in it for the money."

"She knew the deal but pitched a fit when we went to Greece last month, and he refused to accompany her to the Ladies' League Gala. He told her he belonged to me, but she came up with this whole baby idea. She still didn't get the message, which is why I went to talk to her."

"With a suppressed gun?"

Ava's eyes are slits. "Yes. I'm an accurate shot if needs be."

I say nothing, waiting.

"I wasn't going to kill her. I wasn't. Markus left the front door open a crack for me and said he'd be in the office if anything went wrong. I mean, I knew their house like my own as he and I spent plenty of time together there when she was out of town with the kids for summer or spring break trips."

"If I woke to someone holding a gun in my bedroom at night, I wouldn't take it well."

"I went to the master—and her daughter was beside her in bed. I shook the wife to wake her up with a finger on her lips, hoping the kid stayed asleep. She got up, but the next thing I knew, her daughter was screaming. The bitch lunged for me, so I shot her. Her son, who was supposed to be out with a friend, came running into the room and only stopped when I told him his sister would die if he didn't behave. He put up his hands and went around to comfort her."

Was she explaining or bragging with this flow of villain vomit?

"The son got all brave and was about to try something heroic, so I aimed at his sister to make him stop."

"And you shot him."

"Yes, and a round hit his sister, too. Markus came into the room, telling me I needed to leave. He later said he picked up the casings as I ran out the front door and drove away."

"What did he do then?"

"He was going to call the cops and tell them a story. He's skilled at lying. But a car pulled in, and he panicked. He went out through the other side of the house and drove away. He parked out on the street in case something went wrong. Then he learned some Pakistani madman was after him, so he hid."

If something went wrong? The murders sound way more pre-meditated than Ava lets on.

"He didn't care his wife and her son was dead? His daughter was injured?"

Ava laughed. "Why would he? He never wanted a family. It was all *her* doing."

"He went to visit Tilly at the hospital, so I think he did care."

Or was I only hoping? He left his daughter gasping on the floor to save himself.

Running footsteps come toward us, and Detective Montoya appears.

"You need to put those down," he orders Ava.

"Ah, Detective. I'm surprised you're here. What are you going to do?" Ava sneers. "I'll drive these right through Davia's stomach if you make a move."

"You mean, you'll try," I say.

"Your aunt bragged about you, but I didn't believe her until Markus shot at me."

"Why did he do that?" Had their relationship taken a turn after the murders?

"He wanted to ensure police viewed me as a victim. How was I supposed to know what your aunt said about you was true? When you chased Markus, I thought you might catch him. The side benefit was I panicked, making Kyle believe the shooting shook me."

"And calling the police enhanced your victim story?" I say while Montoya listens.

"What a joke that was. I need my parties more than perception about some crime the police never tied me to," Ava scoffs. "I can't live without excitement."

"How about your brother?"

"What about him? Ever since I killed his pet puppy when he was a kid with a promise to do the same to anything else he loved, he does what I say."

"Did he know you killed the Myles?" I say.

"No. He has no idea about my relationship with Markus or anything else."

More footsteps come down the hall, and Ava clutches the shears with both hands, waving them side to side.

Warden comes into view. He takes in the situation, then says, "Sherilyn said you were back here, Davia. Want to buy some raffle tickets?"

32

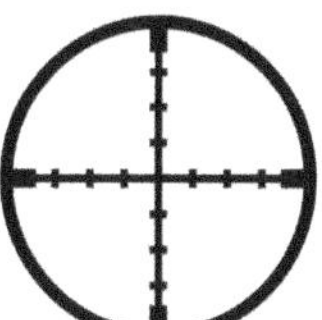

"Who are you?" Ava challenges, taking in the thick roll of red tickets he holds and his neutral expression.

"Just a guy who's selling tickets to benefit literacy. The prizes include a week in Barbados, and we offer a five-for-$20 special. Are you interested?"

He throws the roll straight at her head.

Ava ducks, and Detective Montoya and I spring forward to grab her arms. Montoya seizes the shears as my elaborate headpiece slips to the side.

"No!" Ava struggles against us, but we hold her tight.

Warden pulls zip ties from his jacket.

"I never come to one of these gatherings without them," he explains to the surprised detective as he secures Ava's arms behind her.

"That's not creepy or anything, Warden," I say.

Montoya looks between us. "Do you two know each other?"

Warden double-checks the bindings on a subdued Ava. "She's my girlfriend."

"Girlfriend? Adair Monroe and this guy?" Ava speaks like we're enjoying a casual conversation, all emotion gone. "Alex might not stand a chance."

"Picked up another suitor, Bombshell?" Warden says. "I can't leave you alone for a second, can I?"

Ignoring this, I say, "I'll buy all your raffle tickets if you help Detective Montoya with his prisoner."

Warden picks up the roll and hands them over. "Bribery works for me."

When I emerge into the model tent, Melody hurries over, holding a pair of heels.

"Where have you been? The second half is about to start." She bends to shove the shoes on my feet.

Kincaid Foxx is nearby, and his mouth drops open. "What did you do?"

"I didn't sit down."

He surveys the damage while I attempt to straighten the head-piece. "You ruined my dress."

Just then, a fashionable woman glides toward us.

"Kincaid," she purrs, stroking his arm. "This is genius. I picture a queen, the weight of her crown too much, so it droops to the side. She struggles to free herself from her enforced duties, rather like a Hew Locke *House of Windsor* creation come to life. And holding those raffle tickets like she's up for sale. Brilliant."

Kincaid's outrage disappears. "So clever of you to understand."

The pair wander away, speaking amicably.

"What just happened?" I ask Melody.

"That was a fashion editor for *Vogue*."

Was it acceptable to remain ignorant of fashion? Yes. Definitely yes.

Another assistant runs up. "Where's Ms. Gordon? I can't find her anywhere."

"What is it with the models disappearing?" Melody says.

"She's indisposed," I say. "She said to tell you she's gone home to lie down."

"But what about Mr. Foxx's garment?" the assistant says.

"I'm sure she'll get it back to him."

Rick Coleridge returns to the microphone. "All right, everyone. In a few minutes, we'll begin the show's second half. Please take your seats."

Order springs out of chaos, and assistants place the Rancho Suprema models in a line. I'm led to the back by Melody.

Kincaid returns to my side. "When you go on, I want you to appear bored and unimpressed."

"I can do that."

My trip down the catwalk is anti-climactic. I traverse the hazardous ramp without a problem while my team whoops, and Ned lets out a loud whistle. I expect the buttoned-up crowd to be scandalized, but they laugh and applaud.

Kincaid joins me to return to the stage for a final turn. "You somehow took my dress to another level. You have a real flair for fashion." He raises our hands at the ramp's top, and my team gives me a standing ovation. Warden is with them and puts his lips together to send me a pretend smooch.

At the end of the catwalk, I look down and right into Adair's face. He's on his feet, clapping, and no worse for wear. His expression contains admiration, promises, and tempting possibilities. The intensity of his gaze conveys his plan to make me forget anyone but him. With effort, I turn away.

"WILL YOU PLEASE REMOVE THIS MAKEUP?" I'm back in my clothes, relieved the show's over.

Christian says, "Doesn't Adair like it?"

"How'd you guess I only live to please him?"

"Sarcasm suits you, darling." Christian begins to wipe my face.

Bryce and Ramon appear. "You were *phénoménale*," Bryce exclaims.

"Thanks to you."

"Davia, did something happen before the show began?" Ramon

says. "I saw Kincaid put you in your dress, and it looked much different on stage."

"Uh, can we talk about this later?"

Sherilyn squeals my name and rushes over to throw her arms around me. "You were the star! What an exciting show. Imagine my surprise when I saw Warden was here, but I bet that made you so happy. And I finally had a date with Ric. He's leaving soon to deal with the murder case, but we got to talk over lunch before the show began."

"I'm sorry a case disrupted your date."

"I'll need to get used to him leaving since homicide cases take priority. Ric and I hit it off right away, though. He gave me his undivided attention, and his big brown eyes were *so sexy*. Oh, here's your phone."

She hands it to me, and I put it in my bag.

Bryce and Ramon stay to visit with Christian, but Sherilyn accompanies me toward the tent's exit. Attendees swarm around Kincaid Foxx, and assistants help take orders. Sherilyn decides to browse for clothes, but I keep going. Kincaid's collection sparked acquisition madness, and I intend to leave before I get infected.

A hand takes my arm, and I turn.

"Hello, Alex," I say.

He gives me a once-over and a cheeky grin. "Hey, little troublemaker."

"Did you need something?"

"Not really, just wanted to say hello. I'm glad we'll get to spend time together in the future."

"Why do you think that?"

"You don't know?" His eyes fill with mischief.

"No."

If he says something inappropriate, I will hurt him this time.

"I'm your financial advisor."

"You're what?" I exclaim before I can stop myself.

"I handled all your aunt's investments in New York, and she kept her business with me even after I moved to California. I didn't connect your name at first because we'd never met. Didn't Mr. Morgenstern give you my information?"

I think of the thick folder my aunt's lawyer provided at our first meeting about the will, which I only gave a cursory review. "More pressing concerns kept popping up."

He waves off my words like my inaction is no big deal. "You need to review your investments with me, but you'll be happy to hear I've been increasing your wealth by an above-average percentage despite the market fluctuations."

"Thank you." I hadn't recognized his name when Ava introduced him, but the transition to my life in Rancho Suprema made small details disappear.

"You're welcome. Say, have you seen my sister?"

What's the truth about his life with his psycho sibling? I hesitate to tell him what happened, but after considering, I step closer. "She got arrested for the Myles murders."

He takes an involuntary step back. "She what?"

"I'm sorry. The sheriff's department is transporting her right now."

Alex covers his mouth and loses color.

"Alex, I'm sorry," I repeat, but before I can say more, Beatrice marches toward me.

"Davia, where's Ava Gordon? I can't believe she didn't model. How embarrassing for our organization."

At her words, Alex wheels around and rushes out of the tent, looking ready to vomit. I want to go after him and ensure he's okay. Before I go, I say to Beatrice, "Why do you always think I know where people are?"

Sophie joins us before Beatrice can speak and says, "I'm shocked you did so well. Who was your coach?"

"I'm not saying, excuse me."

Outside, Alex is nowhere in sight.

Should I search for him? What would I say? Our acquaintance is too fresh to give me much insight. Was Ava being arrested a positive for him?

My team waits under the shaded porch, so I join them.

"You were purty as a peach." Hodge hugs me against him, eyes crinkling.

"I have to keep up with Ned." I run a hand down Ned's smooth face and squeeze his chin.

"You'll have to work harder," Ned replies.

"Why are you guys here?"

"We came out to teach a class to the Raiders at Pendleton." Warden refers to a special forces unit at a nearby Marine base. "We wanted to surprise you."

"Your timing was perfect. Again," I say to Warden.

Francis joins us. "Thank you, gentlemen, for your assistance with selling raffle tickets. You were so irresistible we set a record in sales. And you, Knowlton, you sold the most."

Knowlton? I never heard anyone use K's actual name.

"He only uses his golden voice for important occasions," I tell Francis.

Francis says to K, "You should be a voice actor and give James Earl Jones some competition."

Another Ladies League member informs Francis the head of catering needs to speak with her. When she leaves, Ned directs a question to Savant. "Did you sell one ticket?"

"I sold eighty-five," he retorts, flushing.

"Did you buy them all yourself?" Ned says.

"No. A woman in her mid-twenties with blonde hair, wearing a navy blue linen dress and a four-carat diamond ring on her left hand bought twenty, another woman in a red dress with brown hair going gray at the temples and a gold and diamond wedding band bought ten, and—"

"This isn't a debriefing," Ned interrupts and ruffles Savant's hair, laughing.

"How long are you guys staying?" I say.

Warden's lips twist. "We're running late. We're due to go back today."

"Really?" My face falls.

"If you miss us so much, keep your gun greased and come back to work," Hodge says.

"Unless you plan to burn daylight." Ned jabs an elbow into Hodge.

A group of women pauses on their way out of the building, checking out the men.

"Them gussied-up women might truss you like a chicken," I say to Hodge.

He raises his hands, laughing. "I give up."

The guys bid me farewell, leaving me alone with Warden. Before we speak, Detective Montoya approaches.

"I thought you left," I say.

"Patrol's transporting the suspect for me. I didn't plan on making an arrest today." He holds out the sides of his suit jacket. "Now, if I can find Markus Myles, I can close this case. I thought I should ask if you knew his whereabouts before I left."

"Uh, I think he's going to be unavailable for some time," I answer.

"Where is he, exactly?"

"Not sure."

"Generally?"

"Back east."

"He won't be going anywhere," Warden says.

"Why is it always a guessing game with people like you?" Montoya comments. "Davia, you'll have to come to my office for a statement this time. I heard the part about Ava Gordon playing as a victim, but not the rest."

"Was she on your radar?" I say.

"She hit all the right notes when I asked her about the person who shot up her party, but something was off. I planned to dig deeper into her connection to the Myles family."

"I'll make an appointment to come in on Monday. I need my .45 back anyway. What will happen to Tilly?"

"She's going to live with her mom's brother and his wife in Texas, and they've made arrangements for counseling. She still doesn't remember what happened."

"I'm glad she doesn't. Losing her mother and brother is enough." I think about the problematic future she will face and wish her strength to survive and thrive.

The detective departs, and Warden says, "Want to walk me out?"

We head toward the back parking lot.

"Thank you for the surprise support, both in the fashion show and taking down a murderer."

"I didn't expect to help arrest someone today. What happened?"

I show him the photos. "I thought these were chance meetings at society functions in New York since Ava claimed only to have a casual relationship with my aunt and Markus Myles. I texted the two photos to her and bluffed when she came to talk to me, saying I knew she was involved in the murders. I expected her to laugh, but she ran."

"She's the one who killed the Myles family?"

"Yes. I met her the morning after the murders, shopping at the local market. She acted like she didn't have a care in the world."

"I remember our team psychology instructor using an example about a sociopath walking toward an area with restaurants. He sees a car run over a pedestrian, killing them. The sociopath thinks, 'Should I have Chinese or Italian food?' and keeps going. They aren't like us."

"It makes me wonder about people."

Warden wraps one of my hands in his. "We would wonder anyway."

As we continue walking, I say, "I recall we also learned sociopaths like excitement, and Ava said she put on parties after moving here from New York because she needed them. She dressed to match me the next time we met, to make me like her more. If I'd stuck with my typical 'trust no one' rule, I would've caught on to her b.s. earlier."

"Don't be hard on yourself. Spotting an attractive, charming sociopath is difficult. Still, I worry more about you out here than with the team."

"I understand." I think again about how this split existence continues to make me vulnerable.

We stop as the isolated path nears the parking lot, and Warden kisses me with a hungry possessiveness, the stubble on his face scraping my skin. I put my arms around his neck, and he supports my waist with a strong arm, pulling me tight against him.

If only this were an everyday occurrence.

If only farewell kisses weren't the norm.

When he straightens, he says, "Even in the ridiculous get-up you had to wear on the runway, you looked beautiful."

"Most of life out here is ridiculous, but thank you."

Warden turns serious. "Davia, I know we exchanged some harsh words over your rescue mission, but you could have died."

"I'm sorry. I know you were worried, and what I did seemed reckless, but I'm still here." Not wanting to continue the subject, I put my hands on his coat's lapels. "And you in a suit brings back some nice memories of the last time you wore one, and I got to undress you."

At my words, Warden draws in a ragged breath and moves one of my hands to cover his heart. An expression of longing fills his face. "Remember, no matter the distance or circumstances, I'm yours."

The pain of another separation cuts me like a sword. I step closer, and Warden pulls me tight against him. His cheek and jaw are warm against my face as our bodies meld together, and I wish I could stop time.

After several minutes, Warden kisses me again, but this time he only brushes his lips across mine with tender care. Is it because he's leaving? Is this killing him inside, too? We release each other with regret, and Warden retakes my hand as I push down the hurt. We continue toward where the team waits beside a black SUV.

"By the way," Warden says, "that Brit told me he intends to give me a run for my money."

"What did you say?"

"Good luck."

EPILOGUE

The tow truck driver stares in disbelief at my Rover.

"Agent Wills told me to ask no questions, but I have questions," he says.

"An assault rifle, automatics, and an RPG." The information will go no further, or this guy from National Security will be out of work.

"Guess this isn't something you can use your AAA card for."

When he departs with the vehicle safely closeted in a trailer, I consider what to do. I want to go for a ride but decide I'm not up for the jostling despite my almost-healed injuries. Below me, José holds Ace's halter near the gate to the arena as the horse trots around, his sleek black mane and tail flying.

I run a hand down my leg, happy there hasn't been a flair-up since the Adair rescue. Ten more months should be enough time to heal and return to my team. As I move to go inside, my phone vibrates.

Adair: *Daily question: Do you prefer conversation or sex?*

A smile flickers on my lips. Should I respond? Before I decide, another text comes through.

Warden: *I love you.*

ACKNOWLEDGMENTS

First, thank you to all my readers who supported *Dior or Die*. I am humbled by the reviews, emails, and word-of-mouth recommendations from the many people who helped make my debut novel a success.

Next, thank you to my sweet and patient man, Russell Rice. I appreciate him dropping everything to read a rough draft chapter, giving me feedback, and for forgiving me when I forgot to thank him in the first book. (*Mea culpa*) I could never have made it this far without him.

Finally, thank you to Warren B., my inspiration for Kyle Kavanagh, Craig W. for Craig Kilburn, and John Sant, who gave me special insight into operatives. Thanks to my beta reader and ARC team members, with a special shout out to Patsy Robinson, Collings MacCrae, and Anne-Lucy Shanley for reading my rough drafts. A special acknowledgment to the talents of my cover artist, Cherie Foxley, and my audiobook narrator, Stacey Lind.

ABOUT THE AUTHOR

Laura E. Akers is a former prosecuting attorney who handled high-profile murder, rape, domestic violence, and gang trials.

She's a Distinguished Toastmaster, and enjoys speaking on self-confidence and teaching workshops on jury selection.

Suicide prevention is a cause close to her heart since losing a close attorney friend. She is an ambassador for Mission 22, an organization working to prevent veteran suicide.

Her interests include photography, Korean dramas, and spending time with her cats. If you'd like learn more, visit https://www.lauraakers.com

POSH AND PERILOUS

Read on for the riveting first chapter of
Book Three in the Davia Glenn Series.
Releasing soon on Amazon and through
other top booksellers worldwide.

CHAPTER 1

"What are you going to order, Davia?" Sherilyn asks.

"I've never heard of Branzino, so I'll be adventurous for a change and try some."

"That's an ironic statement coming from you," my friend and interior designer says. "Now that I know you're a deadly, top-secret, well, whatever you are, my curiosity is eating me alive. I know you can't tell me anything, but, like, why didn't I notice sooner? I thought you were a nerdy tomboy raised in a commune or something because you didn't know a thing about furniture, clothes, or how to act at a party."

"A commune?"

"Yes, you should see your face when I talk about buying furniture for your home that most people can't afford. I mention brands like Boca de Lobo, Delightfull, and Koket, and instead of sheer happiness, all I get is a blank stare. When I told you the modular sectional I ordered for the living room was $30,000, you didn't even blink. I swear you're not listening to me half the time."

"Wait. Thirty-thousand, *what*?"

"Don't worry; I didn't spend that much. I threw in a crazy high number just now to see if you pay attention to anything I say."

We sit in a booth upholstered with rich, dark leather at Château

Rouge, a five-star French restaurant in the exclusive community of Rancho Suprema, California. Around us, the jet-set crowd tucks into their meals. Patrons pretend not to notice each other, but hands with sparkling diamonds cover mouths to whisper gossip. Candlelight and relaxing music add to the atmosphere, perhaps to soothe customers before they receive bills totaling as much as a monthly car payment.

I set down the menu. "I'm glad you convinced me to come out. Since last week's fashion show, a sprinkler break in my yard's been the only excitement."

"You shouldn't complain, especially after—" Sherilyn begins, but an attractive raven-haired woman at a table next to us stands so fast her chair falls over.

"You're not going to divorce your wife?" she shouts. "Did you think telling me in a public setting would keep me quiet?"

"Erica, you need to sit down," her companion hisses. He's at least three decades older than his thirty-something mistress, and his face is a mask of pinched disapproval.

"Or what, Ray? I've had enough of your lies."

"My children—"

"Your 'children' are adults and have nothing to do with this."

"Erica, you're embarrassing me."

"You're embarrassed? *Embarrassed*?" With lightning speed, she pulls her knit top over her head and undoes the clasp of her black brassiere.

Two perfect breasts spring out.

The man's eyes widen as gasps and titters fill the restaurant.

"Take a good look, Ray, because this is the last time you'll see these." To punctuate her words, Erica picks up her glass of red wine and tosses the contents into his face.

The drops stain his white shirt like blood.

Ray sputters and grabs for a napkin while Erica gathers her garments and marches away, not bothering to cover herself, back straight and head high.

"Good for you," Sherilyn calls as she passes, and the woman's lips curve into a satisfied smile. Ray, red-faced from more than the wine, stumbles after her to a buzz of excited conversation and laughter.

"I don't know whether to be shocked or applaud," I say when they're gone.

Sherilyn laughs. "The story of their altercation will spread like wildfire. When we hear the tale again, they'll have removed all their clothes, smashed up the restaurant, or run away together."

"Ah, the wealthy and their problems."

We order, and it isn't long before the waiter arrives with our meals. Onions and cherry tomatoes smother my fish, and I'm pleased by the mild and sweet flavor. Sherilyn cuts her grilled salmon with the side of her fork.

"Now that it's May, summer fun's around the corner," she says. "Are you going to Virginia to visit Warden? Spending time with him naked would outweigh the heat and humidity."

A flash image of my operative team leader getting out of my bed makes me reach for my wine. I take a long drink.

Nothing is easy.

"Can we talk about something else? Missing Warden and trying to solve our long-distance relationship woes plague me enough."

We finish our meal, and a server presents us with dessert menus. I sit back, relaxed. "Are you full or going to order more?"

"Life's too short to be anything but happy, and dessert makes me happy. Tell me again, how much money did your aunt leave you?"

"Almost ninety million, but with conditions."

"Girl, even with conditions, you have way more reasons than the dessert menu to be happy."

Scanning the offerings, I ponder what a pear poached in red wine with a chamomile flower would taste like and the meaning of *Crèmeux.* My aunt didn't provide an instruction manual on the intricacies of life with the rich, so I order a lemon tart while Sherilyn settles on a deconstructed strawberry shortcake, another menu mystery.

When our hot tea and desserts arrive, Sherilyn's plate is an artful arrangement of cream-covered strawberries and small pieces of cake. She takes a mouthful and sighs with pleasure.

"This is yum! And speaking of yum, I want to know what you've decided to do about Adair."

"You're determined to stay on difficult subjects, aren't you? He's in Europe right now because a merger went sideways. He left after the fashion show."

"I bet you were relieved. Almost any woman on the planet would love to be kissed and courted by a hot British billionaire, but you? You don't have a problem taking on armed bad guys, but when the subject of Adair Monroe comes up, you look ready to bolt."

"You're not wrong."

Perhaps I won't have dreams about kissing him if he stays on another continent.

Determined to derail this topic, I ask, "What about Detective Montoya?"

Sherilyn squirms with excitement in her seat. "As long as Ric doesn't get a call about a homicide case, we have a date this weekend. We're going to Old Town for a Cinco de Mayo celebration. We'll drink margaritas, enjoy Mexican food, and become better acquainted. We haven't even kissed yet, but I almost melted into a puddle when we hugged, so I can't wait to see where this leads."

"You know San Diego Sherlock's my unofficial nickname for him, right?" I say after taking a bite of my tart.

"He is smart, isn't he? When we went on our date to the Ladies' League Fashion Show, he said, 'You have a cat,' and picked a small piece of cat hair from my hem. I hadn't noticed, but he was like a guided missile."

"Which is why he's so good at catching criminals."

"I hope he's as good at other things," Sherilyn says with a wink.

When we finish, we make our way to the front of the restaurant, where an auburn-haired hostess named Sarah is at her station. "Did you enjoy your meals?" she inquires.

"I didn't know you included theater with dinner," I joke.

"I've worked here for over twenty years, and tonight's drama was a minor event, believe me."

"Why doesn't that surprise me?" I say.

"I meant to ask when you came in, but are you two sisters?"

We both have fair complexions and blonde hair, but at 5'9", I tower over my petite friend.

Sherilyn loops her arm through mine. "We're not blood-related, but she's my soul sister."

"I thought for sure you were related," Sarah says. "Did you have umbrellas or coats? It just started raining."

We shake our heads.

"I can lend you some," she offers.

"I can survive some rain; how about you, Sherilyn?"

"I'm fine, thank you, though."

We step outside. Drops pelt a tiered fountain in the courtyard, and high winds cause the branches of a mature pepper tree to wave in an erratic dance. We huddle back into the entryway.

"Just our luck," I mutter, thankful I wore loafers and not heels with my slacks and long-sleeved blouse.

"Rain? Since when Southern California?" Sherilyn gripes. "The weather app's forty-percent-chance prediction seemed unlikely, so I didn't bring an umbrella. Now it's late, and I'll have to watch for drunk drivers *and* idiots who lose their minds when it rains. I mean, it's just water, people."

"You can stay with me if you want," I offer. "You know my home's less than a mile away."

"I'll be fine."

"Where'd you park?"

Sherilyn points. "On the side street."

"I'm the other way. Stay safe."

We exchange a quick hug, and Sherilyn runs into the storm. Placing my hands above my forehead to shield my face, I hurry across the Spanish-style courtyard and emerge onto the main street's sidewalk. It's nearing eleven p.m., so downtown is quiet, and most businesses are closed.

CRASH!

A block away, men in hoodies and black surgical masks swarm before a storefront. Several hold crowbars while others run back and forth carrying items to a waiting SUV.

Don't get involved, Wonder Woman.

Inaction is contra to my personality and training, but I remind myself of what occurred the last time I rushed headlong into a crime scene. I still bore injuries from the unforeseeable and near-tragic fallout.

Stepping under the roofline of a real estate office, I call 911.

"911. What's your emergency?"

"A group of four men is breaking into a business down the block from me in downtown Rancho Suprema." The heavy downpour kills visibility, and I can only provide a general description of their dark getaway vehicle.

"Do you know the name of the business?" the operator asks.

"I think it's Jenson's Jewelry, but I can't be sure from this angle."

By the time flashing lights come into view, the SUV is long gone, the whole break-in lasting no more than three minutes. A deputy pulls alongside me and rolls down her passenger-side window. Rain sprays through the opening, soaking the seat.

"Did you report this?"

"Yes, they went that way about five minutes ago." I gesture to the empty road.

She speeds off.

The turbulent wind whips my long hair, strands plaster my face and neck, and my soaked clothing clings to me. I check the street in both directions before running across and entering a trellised walkway leading to where I parked. The jasmine-vine cover does little to shelter me, the gale's force shaking the latticework so hard, I'm afraid it will break apart. I keep my head down as I rush along the path, which ends at Bryce's Boutique, a favorite upscale clothing store.

I stop.

The door to the business is open, and shattered glass lies on the ground. Ahead, a different knot of men carries bundles of clothing and accessories toward a cargo van, the back doors open and the interior already half-filled.

If this is a coordinated string of thefts, were they off schedule?

Did they wait for the sheriffs to chase the other vehicle so they would have more time?

What should I do?

Bryce is my friend, but the damp weather makes my still-healing broken ribs ache, reminding me this is not my fight. I back away, intent on returning to the main street and calling emergency services again.

Before I get more than a step away, a lookout catapults out of the shadows. He carries a heavy metal pipe, and I lash out with a kick. The blow connects with his knee, and he collapses, dropping his weapon.

The pipe hits the sidewalk with a loud clang.

The thieves freeze.

Mask-covered faces turn in my direction. Two thugs charge toward me. I go into a fighting stance and deliver a spinning roundhouse kick to the first man, but my back foot slips on the wet ground. My blow connects with his chin instead of the side of his head, but he staggers back. The second man is close enough now to punch in the throat, and he bends over, choking.

Stolen goods drop into the back of the van.

Three more men run straight at me, one carrying a crowbar. I reach for the firearm concealed in my crossbody bag.

Before I can raise my gun, the fallen lookout leaps up with his reacquired pipe.

I dodge, but a glancing blow connects with the back of my head, and the force slams me to the soaked sidewalk.

"You weren't supposed to hurt anyone," a man yells.

"She had a gun," my assailant says.

My surroundings grow hazy as his booted feet jump over me.

Everything goes dark.

www.ingramcontent.com/pod-product-compliance
Lightning Source LLC
Chambersburg PA
CBHW041047310726
48978CB00011BA/458